FEB 2016

A SKY OF SPELLS

(BOOK #9 IN THE SORCERER'S RING)

MORGAN RICE

Copyright © 2013 by Morgan Rice

All rights reserved. Except as permitted under the U.S. Copyright Act of 1976, no part of this publication may be reproduced, distributed or transmitted in any form or by any means, or stored in a database or retrieval system, without the prior permission of the author.

This ebook is licensed for your personal enjoyment only. This ebook may not be re-sold or given away to other people. If you would like to share this book with another person, please purchase an additional copy for each recipient. If you're reading this book and did not purchase it, or it was not purchased for your use only, then please return it and purchase your own copy. Thank you for respecting the hard work of this author.

This is a work of fiction. Names, characters, businesses, organizations, places, events, and incidents either are the product of the author's imagination or are used fictionally. Any resemblance to actual persons, living or dead, is entirely coincidental.

ISBN: 978-1-939416-64-3

DRIFTWOOD PUBLIC LIBRARY
801 SW HWY. 101
LINCOLN CITY, OREGON 97367

Books by Morgan Rice

THE SORCERER'S RING
A QUEST OF HEROES (BOOK #1)
A MARCH OF KINGS (BOOK #2)
A FEAST OF DRAGONS (BOOK #3)
A CLASH OF HONOR (BOOK #4)
A VOW OF GLORY (BOOK #5)
A CHARGE OF VALOR (BOOK #6)
A RITE OF SWORDS (BOOK #7)
A GRANT OF ARMS (BOOK #8)
A SKY OF SPELLS (BOOK #9)
A SEA OF SHIELDS (BOOK #10)
A REIGN OF STEEL (BOOK #11)

THE SURVIVAL TRILOGY
ARENA ONE (Book #1)
ARENA TWO (Book #2)

the Vampire Journals
turned (book #1)
loved (book #2)
betrayed (book #3)
destined (book #4)
desired (book #5)
betrothed (book #6)
vowed (book #7)
found (book #8)
resurrected (book #9)
craved (book #10)

"We few, we happy few, we band of brothers;
for he today that sheds his blood with me
shall be my brother."

--William Shakespeare
Henry V

CHAPTER ONE

Thor faced Gwendolyn, holding his sword at his side, his entire body trembling. He looked out and saw all the faces staring back at him in the stunned silence—Alistair, Erec, Kendrick, Steffen, and a host of his countrymen—people he had known and loved. *His* people. Yet here he was, facing them, sword at his side. He was on the wrong side of battle.

Finally, he realized.

Thor's veil had lifted as Alistair's words rang through him, filled him with clarity. He was Thorgrin. A member of the Legion. A member of the Western Kingdom of the Ring. He was not a solider for the Empire. He did not love his father. He loved all these people.

Most of all, he loved Gwendolyn.

Thor looked down and saw her face, staring up at him with such love, her eyes tearing. He was filled with shame and horror to realize he was facing her, holding this sword. His palms burned with humiliation and regret.

Thor dropped the sword, letting it fall from his hands. He took a step forward and embraced her.

Gwendolyn hugged him back tightly, and he heard her crying, felt her hot tears pouring down his neck. Thor was overwhelmed with remorse, and he could not conceive how it had all happened. It was a blur. All he knew was that he was happy to be back to himself, to have clarity, and to be back with his people.

"I love you," she whispered into his ear. "And I always will."

"I love you with everything that I am," Thor replied.

Krohn whined at his feet, limping over and licking Thor's palm; Thor leaned down and kissed his face.

"I'm sorry," Thor said to him, remembering hitting him as Krohn had defended Gwendolyn. "Please forgive me."

The earth, quaking violently but moments before, finally became still again.

"THORNICUS!" a shriek cut through the air.

Thor turned to see Andronicus. He stepped forward, into the clearing, scowling, his face red with rage. Both armies watched in stunned silence, as father and son faced each other.

"I *command* you!" Andronicus said. "Kill them! Kill them all! I am your father. You listen to me, and to me alone!"

But this time, as Thor stared back at Andronicus, something felt different. Something shifted inside. No longer did Thor view Andronicus as his father, as a family member, as someone he must answer to and give his life for; instead, he saw him as a foe. A monster. Thor no longer felt any obligation to give up his life for this man. On the contrary: he felt a burning rage against him. Here was the man who had ordered the attack on Gwendolyn; here was the man who had killed his fellow countrymen, who had invaded and ransacked his homeland; here was the man who had taken over his own mind, who had held him hostage with his dark sorcery.

This was not a man he loved. Rather, this was a man he wanted to kill more than anything on earth. Father or not.

Thor suddenly felt himself flood with rage. He reached down, picked up his sword, and charged full speed across the clearing, ready to kill his father.

Andronicus looked shocked as Thor charged, raised his sword high, and brought it down with both hands, with all his might, for his head.

Andronicus raised his huge battle axe at the last second, turning it sideways and blocking the blow with its metal shaft.

Thor did not relent: he swung his sword again and again, going for the kill, and each time Andronicus raised his axe and blocking it. The great clang of the two weapons meeting rang through the air as both armies watched in silence. Sparks flew with each blow.

Thor screamed and grunted, using every skill he had, hoping to kill his father on the spot. He had to do it, for himself, for Gwendolyn, for all those who had suffered by this monster's hand. With each blow, Thor wanted, more than anything, to wipe out his lineage, his own background, to start fresh again. To choose a different father.

Andronicus, on the defense, only blocked Thor's blows, and did not fight back. Clearly, he was refraining from attacking his son.

"Thornicus!" Andronicus said, between blows. "You are my son. I do not wish to harm you. I am your father. You have saved my life. I want you alive."

"And I want you dead!" Thor screamed back.

Thor swung down again and again, driving him back, across the clearing, despite Andronicus' great size and strength. Yet still,

Andronicus would not swing back at Thor. It was as if he was hoping that Thor would come back to him again.

But this time, Thor would not. Now, finally, Thor knew who he was. Finally, Andronicus' words were free from his head. Thor would rather be dead than at Andronicus's mercy again.

"Thorgrin, you must stop this!" Andronicus cried out. Sparks flew by his face as he blocked a particularly vicious slash with his axe head. "You will force me to kill you, and I do not wish to. You are my son. To kill you would be to kill myself."

"Then kill yourself!" Thor said. "Or if you do not wish to, then I shall do it for you!"

With a great cry Thor leapt up and kicked Andronicus with both feet in the chest, sending him stumbling and landing on his back.

Andronicus looked up, as if stunned that could have happened.

Thor stood over him and raised his sword high to finish him off.

"NO!" shrieked a voice. It was an awful voice, sounding like it erupted from the very depths of hell, and Thor glanced over to see a single man enter the clearing. He wore a long scarlet robe, his face hidden behind a hood, and an unearthly growl erupted from his throat.

Rafi.

Somehow, Rafi had made it back from his battle with Argon. He stood there now, holding both arms out wide at his sides. His sleeves fell as he rose his arms, revealing pale, blistery skin that looked as if it had never seen the sun. He emitted an awful sound from the back of his throat, like a snarl, and as he opened his mouth wide, it grew louder and louder until it filled the air, the low timbre vibrating and making Thor's ears hurt.

The earth began to quake. Thor was knocked off-balance as the entire ground shook. He followed Rafi's hands and saw before him a sight he would never forget.

The earth began to split in two, a great chasm opening, spreading wider and wider. As it did, soldiers from both sides fell, slipping down, screaming as they tumbled down into the ever-growing crevice.

An orange glow emitted from beneath the earth, and there came an awful hissing noise as steam and fog arose.

There appeared a single hand, emerging from the crevice, gripping the earth. The hand was black, lumpy, disfigured, and as it pulled itself up, Thor, to his horror, saw emerging from the earth an awful creature. It was in the shape of a human, but it was entirely black, with large glowing red eyes and long red fangs. A long, black tail dragged behind it. Its body was lumpy, and it looked like a corpse.

It leaned back its head and there came an awful roar, like Rafi's. It appeared to be some sort of undead creature, summoned from the depths of hell.

Behind this creature there suddenly emerged another. Then another.

Thousands more of these creatures surfaced, pulling themselves up from the bowels of hell, an army of undead. Rafi's army.

Slowly, they came to Rafi's side, facing Thorgrin and the others.

Thor stared back in shock at this army facing him; as he stood there, his sword still held high, Andronicus suddenly rolled out from under him and retreated back to his army, clearly not wanting to have to confront Thorgrin.

Suddenly, the thousands of creatures rushed towards Thor, flooding the clearing, coming to kill Thor and all of his people.

Thor snapped out of it and raised his sword high as the first creature leapt for him, snarling, claws extended. Thor sidestepped, swung his sword, and chopped off its head. It stumbled to the ground, unmoving, and Thor braced himself for the next one.

These creatures were strong and fast, but one on one, they were no match for Thor and the skilled warriors of the Ring. Thor fought them deftly, killing them left and right. Yet the question was, how many could he could fight at once? He was flooded by thousands of them, from all directions, as was everyone around him.

Thor fell in beside Erec, Kendrick, Srog and the others, each fighting beside each other, watching each other's backs as they swung left and right, taking out two and three creatures at a time. One of them slipped by, grabbed Thor's arm and scratched it, drawing blood, and Thor cried out in pain, swung around and stabbed in the heart, killing it. Thor was a superior fighter, but his arm already throbbed, and he didn't know how long it would be until these creatures took their toll.

First and foremost in his mind, though, was getting Gwendolyn to safety.

"Get her to the back!" Thor shrieked, grabbing Steffen, who was fighting with a monster, and shoving him toward Gwen. "NOW!"

Steffen grabbed Gwen and dragged her away, back through the army of soldiers, distancing her from the beasts.

"NO!" Gwen screamed, protesting. "I want to be here with you!"

But Steffen listened dutifully, dragging her back to the rear flank of the battle, protecting her behind the thousands of MacGils and Silver who valiantly stood there and fought back the creatures. Thor, seeing her safe, was relieved, and turned back and threw himself into the fight with the undead.

Thor tried to summon his Druid power, to fight with his spirit along with his sword; but for some reason, he could not. He was too exhausted from his experience with Andronicus, from Rafi's mind control, and his power needed more time to heal. He had to fight with conventional weapons.

Alistair stepped forward, by Thor's side, raised a palm, and directed it at the crowd of undead. A ball of light emanated from it, and she killed several creatures at once.

She raised both palms repeatedly, killing creatures all around her, and as she did, Thor felt inspired, his sister's energy infusing him. He tried once again to summon some other part of himself, to fight not only with his sword, but with his mind, his spirit. As the next creature approached he raised a palm and tried to summon the wind.

Thor felt the wind rush through his palm, and suddenly, a dozen creatures went flying through the air, the wind driving them, howling as they tumbled back into the crevice in the earth.

Kendrick, Erec and the others, beside Thor, fought valiantly, each killing dozens of creatures, as did all their men around them, letting out a battle cry, as they fought with all they had. The Empire army sat back and let Rafi's army of undead fight for them, let them weary Thor's men. It was working.

Soon, Thor's men, exhausted, were swinging more slowly. And yet the undead never stopped pouring out from the earth, a never-ending stream.

Thor found himself breathing hard, as were the others. The undead were starting to break through their ranks, and his men were beginning to fall. There were just too many. All around Thor there arose his men's screams as the undead pinned them down, sinking their fangs into the soldiers' throats and sucking out their blood. With each soldier a creature killed, the undead seemed to grow stronger.

Thor knew they had to do something fast. They needed to summon a tremendous power to counteract this, a power stronger than he or Alistair had.

"Argon!" Thor suddenly said to Alistair. "Where is he? We must find him!"

Thor looked over and saw Alistair getting tired, her strength waning; a beast slipped past her, backhanded her, and she fell, screaming. As the beast leapt on top of her, Thor stepped forward and thrust his sword through the creature's back, saving her at the last second.

Thor reached out a hand and yanked her quickly to her feet.

"Argon!" Thor screamed. "He's our only hope. You must find him. Now!"

Alistair gave him a knowing look, and raced into the crowd.

A creature slipped by, its claws plunging for Thor's throat, and Krohn rushed forward and leapt up on it, snarling, pinning it down to the earth. Another creature then leapt onto Krohn's back, and Thor slashed it, killing it.

Another creature jumped onto Erec's back, and Thor rushed forward, pried it off, grabbed it with both hands lifted it high overhead and hurled it into several other creatures, knocking them down. Another beast charged for Kendrick, who did not see it coming, and Thor took his dagger and stabbed it in the throat, right before it sank its fangs into Kendrick's shoulder. Thor felt that this was the least he could do to begin to make up for facing off against Erec and Kendrick and all the others. It felt good to be fighting on their side again, on the right side; it felt good to know who he was again, and to know who he was fighting for.

As Rafi stood there, arms out wide, chanting, thousands more of these beasts were spilling out from the bowels of the earth, and Thor knew that they would not be able to hold them back much longer. A swarm of black enveloped them, as more undead, elbow to elbow, rushed forward. Thor knew that soon, he and all of his people would be consumed.

At least, he thought, he would die on the right side of battle.

CHAPTER TWO

Luanda fought and thrashed as Romulus carried her in his arms, each step taking her farther from her homeland as they crossed the bridge. She screamed and flailed, dug her nails into his skin, did everything possible to free herself. But his arms were too muscular, like rocks, his shoulders too broad, and he wrapped her so tight, holding held her in his grips like a python, squeezing her to death. She could barely breathe, her ribs hurt so badly.

Despite all of that, it was not herself she worried for most. She looked up ahead and saw at the far end of the bridge a vast sea of Empire soldiers, standing there, weapons at the ready, waiting. They were all anxious for the Shield to lower so that they could race onto the bridge. Luanda looked over and saw the strange cloak that Romulus was wearing, vibrating and glowing as he carried her, and she sensed that somehow she was the key to his bringing down the Shield. It must have something to do with her. Why else would he kidnap her?

Luanda felt a fresh determination: she had to free herself—not just for herself, but for her kingdom, her people. When Romulus brought down the Shield, those thousands of men awaiting him would charge across, a vast horde of Empire soldiers, and like locusts, descend on the Ring. They would destroy what was left of her homeland for good, and she could not allow that to happen.

Luanda hated Romulus with everything she had; she hated all of these Empire, and Andronicus most of all. A gale swept through and she felt the cold wind grazing against her bald head, and she groaned as she remembered her shaved head, her humiliation at the hands of these beasts. She would kill each and every one of them if she could.

When Romulus had freed her from being tied up in Andronicus' camp, Luanda had at first thought that she was being spared from a horrible fate, spared from being paraded around like an animal in Andronicus' Empire. But Romulus had turned out to be even worse than Andronicus. She felt certain that as soon as they crossed the bridge, he would kill her—if not torture her first. She had to find some way to escape.

Romulus leaned over and spoke in her ear, a deep, throaty sound which set her hairs on edge.

"It won't be long now, my dear," he said.

She had to think quickly. Luanda was no slave; she was the firstborn daughter of a king. Royal blood ran in her, the blood of warriors, and she feared no one. She would do anything she had to in order to fight any adversary; even someone as grotesque and powerful as Romulus.

Luanda summoned all of her remaining strength and in one quick motion, she craned back her neck, leaned forward and sank her teeth into Romulus' throat. She bit down with all her might, squeezing harder and harder, until his blood squirted out all over her face and he shrieked, dropping her.

Luanda scurried to her knees, turned and took off, sprinting back across the bridge for her homeland.

She heard his footsteps bearing down on her. He was much faster than she'd imagined and as she glanced back, she saw him gaining on her with a look of pure rage.

She looked ahead and saw the mainland of the Ring before her, only twenty feet away, and she ran even harder.

Just steps away, Luanda suddenly felt an awful pain in her spine, as Romulus dove forward and dug his elbow down on her back. She felt as if he'd crushed her as she collapsed, face-first, onto the dirt.

A moment later, Romulus was on top of her. He spun her around and punched her in the face. He hit her so hard, her entire body flipped, and she landed back in the dirt. The pain resonated throughout her jaw, her entire face, as she lay there, barely conscious.

Luanda felt herself being hoisted high over Romulus' head, and she watched with terror as he charged for the edge of the bridge, preparing to cast her over. He screamed as he stood there, holding her high overhead, preparing to throw her.

Luanda looked over, down at the steep drop, and knew her life was about to end.

But Romulus held her there, frozen, at the precipice, arms shaking, and apparently, thought better of it. As her life hung in the balance, it seemed Romulus debated. Clearly, he wanted to throw her over the edge in his fit of rage—yet he could not. He needed her to fulfill his purpose.

Finally, he lowered her, and wrapped his arms around her even tighter, nearly squeezing the life out of her. He then hurried back across the Canyon, heading back towards his people.

This time, Luanda just hung there limply, reeling from the pain, nothing more she could do. She had tried—and she had failed. Now all she could do was watch her fate approach her, step-by-step, as she was carried across the Canyon, swirling mists rising up and enveloping her, then disappearing just as quickly. Luanda felt as if she were being taken to some other planet, to some place from which she would never return.

Finally, they reached the far side of the Canyon, and as Romulus took his final step, the cloak around his shoulders vibrated with a great noise, glowing a luminescent red. Romulus dropped Luanda on the ground, like an old potato, and she hit the ground hard, banging her head, and lay there.

Romulus's soldiers stood there, at the edge of the bridge, staring out, all of them clearly afraid to step forward and test whether the Shield was truly down.

Romulus, fed up, grabbed a soldier, hoisted him high overhead and threw him onto the bridge, right into the invisible wall that was once the Shield. The soldier raised his hands and screamed, bracing himself for a certain death as he expected to disintegrate.

But this time, something different happened. The soldier went flying through the air, landed on the bridge, and rolled and rolled. The crowd watched in silence as he rolled to a stop—alive.

The soldier turned and sat up and looked back at all of them, the most shocked of all. He had made it. Which could only mean one thing: the Shield was down.

Romulus' army let out a great roar, and as one they all charged. They swarmed onto it, racing for the Ring. Luanda cowered, trying to stay out of the way as they all stampeded past her, like a herd of elephants, heading for her homeland. She watched with dread.

Her country as she knew it was finished.

CHAPTER THREE

Reece stood at the edge of the lava pit, looking down in utter disbelief as the ground shook violently beneath him. He could hardly process what he had just done, his muscles still aching from releasing the boulder, from casting the Destiny Sword into the pit.

He had just destroyed the most powerful weapon in the Ring, the weapon of legend, the sword of his ancestors for generations, the weapon of the Chosen One, the only weapon holding up the Shield. He had hurled it down into a pit of molten fire and with his own eyes had watched it melt, flare up in a great ball of red, then disappear into nothingness.

Gone forever.

The ground had begun shaking since, and it had not stopped. Reece struggled to balance, as did the others, as he backed away from the edge. He felt as if the world were crumbling around him. What had he done? Had he destroyed the Shield? The Ring? Had he made the biggest mistake of his life?

Reece reassured himself by telling himself he had no choice. The boulder and the Sword were simply too heavy for them all to carry out of here—much less to climb the walls with—or to outrun these violent savages. He had been in a desperate situation, and it had called for desperate measures.

Their desperate situation had not changed yet. Reece heard a great screaming all around him, and a sound arose of a thousand of these creatures, chattering their teeth in an unnerving way and laughing and snarling at the same time. It sounded like an army of jackals. Clearly, Reece had angered them; he had taken away their precious object, and now they all seemed resigned to make him pay.

As bad as the situation had been moments before, now it was even worse. Reece spotted the others—Elden, Indra, O'Connor, Conven, Krog and Serna—all looking down in horror at the lava pit, then turning and looking around in desperation. Thousands of Faws were closing in from every direction. Reece had managed to spare the Sword, but he had not thought past that, had not thought through how to get himself and the others out of danger. They were still completely surrounded, with no way of getting out.

Reece was determined to find a way out, and with the burden of the Sword gone, at least now they could move quickly.

Reece drew his sword, and it cut through the air with a distinctive ring. Why sit back and wait for these creatures to attack? At least he would go down fighting.

"CHARGE!" Reece screamed to the others.

They all drew their weapons and rallied behind him, following as he sprinted away from the edge of the lava pit and right into the thick crowd of Faws, swinging his sword every which way, killing them left and right. Beside him, Elden raised his axe and chopped off two heads at a time, while O'Connor drew his bow and fired on the run, taking out all those in his path. Indra rushed forward and with her short sword, stabbed two in the heart, while Conven drew both of his swords and, screaming like a madman, charged forward, swinging wildly and killing Faws in every direction. Serna wielded his mace, and Krog his spear, protecting their rear flank.

They were a unified fighting machine, fighting as one, fighting for their lives, cutting their way through the thick crowd as they desperately tried to escape. Reece led them up a small hill, aiming for the high ground.

They slipped as they went, the ground still shaking, the slope steep and muddy. They lost some momentum, and several Faws jumped onto Reece, clawing and biting him. He spun and punched them; they were persistent and clung to him, but he managed to throw them off, kicking them back, then stabbing them before they could attack again. Cut and bruised, Reece kept fighting, as they all did, all fighting for their lives to climb the hill and escape from this place.

As they finally reached the high ground, Reece had a moment of reprieve. He stood there, gasping for air, and in the distance, caught a glimpse of the Canyon wall before it was covered by the thick mist. He knew it was out there, their lifeline back to the surface, and he knew they had to reach it.

Reece looked back over his shoulder and saw thousands of Faws racing uphill for them, buzzing, teeth chattering, making an awful noise, louder than ever, and he knew that they would not let them go.

"What about me?" a voice screamed out, cutting through the air.

Reece turned and saw Centra back there. He was still being held captive, beside the leader, and a Faw still held a knife to his throat.

"Don't leave me!" he screamed. "They'll kill me!"

Reece stood there, burning with frustration. Of course, Centra was right: they would kill him. Reece could not leave him there; it would go against Reece's code of honor. After all, Centra had helped them when they'd needed help.

Reece stood there, hesitating. He turned and saw, in the distance, the Canyon wall, the way out, tempting him.

"We can't go back for him!" Indra said, frantic. "They will kill us all."

She kicked a Faw that approached her and it fell backwards, sliding on its back down the slope.

"We'd be lucky to escape with our own lives as it is!" Serna called out.

"He's not one of us!" Krog said. "We can't endanger our group for him!"

Reece stood there, debating. The Faws were getting closer, and he knew he had to make his decision.

"You're right," Reece admitted. "He's not one of us. But he helped us. And he's a good man. I cannot leave him at the mercy of those things. *No man left behind!*" Reece said firmly.

Reece began to head down the slope, to go back for Centra—but before he could, Conven suddenly broke from the group and charged, racing down, leaping and sliding on the muddy slope, feet first, his sword out, sliding downward and slashing as he went, killing Faws left and right. He was hurling back to where they'd come from single-handedly, recklessly, throwing himself into the group of Faws and somehow cutting his way through them with sheer determination.

Reece jumped into action close behind.

"The rest of you stay here!" Reece shouted out. "Wait for our return!"

Reece followed in Conven's tracks, slashing the Faws left and right; he caught up with Conven and provided backup, the two of them fighting their way back down the mountain for Centra.

Conven charged forward, breaking through the crowd of Faws as Reece fought his way all the way to Centra, who stared back, wide-eyed in fear. A Faw raised his dagger to cut Centra's throat, but Reece did not give him the chance: he stepped forward, raised his sword, took aim and threw it with all his might.

The sword went flying through the air, tumbling end over end, and lodged itself through the throat of the Faw, a moment before it could kill Centra. Centra screamed as he looked over and saw the dead Faw, just inches away, their faces almost touching.

To Reece's surprise, Conven did not go for Centra; instead he kept running up the small hill, and Reece looked up, horrified to see what he was doing. Conven seemed suicidal. He cut his way through the group of Faws surrounding their leader, who sat high up on his platform, looking over the battle. Conven killed them left and right. They hadn't been expecting it, and it all happened too fast for any them to react. Reece realized that Conven was aiming for their leader.

Conven got closer, leapt into the air, raised his sword, and as the leader realized and tried to flee, Conven stabbed it through the heart. The leader shrieked—and suddenly, there came a chorus of ten thousand shrieks, all the Faws, as if they themselves had been stabbed. It was as if they all shared the same nervous system—and Conven had severed it.

"You shouldn't have done that," Reece said to Conven as he returned to his side. "Now you've started a war."

As Reece watched in horror, a small hill exploded, and out of it there streamed thousands and thousands of Faws, pouring out of it like a mound of ants. Reece realized that Conven had killed their queen bee, had incited the wrath of a nation of these things. The ground shook with their footsteps, as they all gnashed their teeth and charged right for Reece and Conven and Centra.

"MOVE!" Reece screamed.

Reece shoved Centra, who stood in shock, and they all turned and ran back for the others, fighting their way back up the muddy slope.

Reece felt a Faw jump on his back and knock him down. It dragged him by his ankles, back down the slope, and lowered its fangs for his neck.

An arrow sailed by Reece's head, and there came the noise of an arrow impacting flesh and Reece looked up to see O'Connor, atop the hill, holding a bow.

Reece regained his feet, Centra helping him up as Conven protected their rear, fighting back the Faws. Finally, they all raced up the remainder of the hill and reached the others.

"Good to have you back!" Elden called out, as he rushed forward and took out several Faws with his axe.

Reece paused at the top, peering out into the mist and wondering which way to go. The path forked two ways and he was about to go right.

But Centra suddenly raced past him, heading left.

"Follow me!" Centra called out as he ran. "It's the only way!"

As thousands of Faws began to ascend the slope, Reece and the others turned and ran, following Centra, slipping and sliding down the other side of the hill, as the ground continue to shake. They followed Centra's lead, and Reece was more grateful than ever that he'd saved his life.

"We need to make the Canyon!" Reece called out, not sure which way Centra was going.

They sprinted, weaving their way through the thick, gnarled trees, struggling to follow Centra as he deftly navigated through the mist on a rough dirt trail, covered in roots.

"There's only one way to lose those things!" Centra called back. "Stay on my trail!"

They followed Centra closely as he ran, tripping over roots, scratched by branches, Reece struggling to see through the thickening mist. He stumbled more than once on the uneven footing.

They ran until their lungs hurt, the awful screech of those things behind them, thousands of them, closing in. Elden and O'Connor's helping Krog was slowing them down. Reece hoped and prayed that Centra knew where he was going; he could not see the Canyon wall at all from here.

Suddenly, Centra stopped short, and reached out with his palm and slapped Reece's chest, stopping him in his tracks.

Reece looked down and saw at his feet a steep drop off, into a raging river below.

Reece turned to Centra, puzzled.

"Water," Centra explained, gasping for air. "They're afraid to cross water."

The others all stopped short beside them, staring down at the roaring rapids, as they all tried to catch their breath.

"It's your only chance," Centra added. "Cross this river and you can lose their trail for now, and gain time."

"But how?" Reece asked, staring down at the foaming green waters.

"That current would kill us!" Elden said.

Centra smirked.

"That's the least of your worries," he answered. "That water is filled with Fourens—the deadliest animal on the planet. Fall in, and they'll tear you to pieces."

Reece looked down at the water, wondering.

"Then we can't swim," O'Connor said. "And I don't see a boat."

Reece looked over his shoulder, the sound of the Faws getting closer.

"Your only chance is this," Centra said, reaching back and pulling a long vine attached to a tree, its branches hanging over the river. "We must swing our way across," he said. "Don't slip. And don't fall short of the shore. Send it back for us when you're done."

Reece looked down at the gurgling water, and as he did, he saw awful little glowing yellow creatures jumping out, like sunfish, all jaws, snapping and making strange noises. There were schools of them and they all looked as if they were awaiting their next meal.

Reece glanced back over his shoulder, and saw the army of Faws on the horizon, closing in. They had no choice.

"You can go first," Centra said to Reece.

Reece shook his head.

"I will go last," he answered. "In case we don't all make it in time. You go first. You brought us here."

Centra nodded.

"You don't have to ask me twice," he said with a smile, nervously watching the Faws closing in.

Centra grabbed hold of the vine and with a scream he leapt off, swinging quickly over the waters as he hung low on the vine, lifting his feet from the water and from the snapping creatures. Finally, he landed on the far shore, tumbling on the ground.

He made it.

Centra stood, smiling; he sent the vine back over the river.

Elden reached out and grabbed it, and held it out to Indra.

"Ladies first," he said.

She grimaced.

"I don't need pampering," she said. "You're big. You might break the vine. You go, and get it over with. Don't fall in—or else this woman will have to save you."

Elden grimaced, unamused, as he grabbed the vine.

"I was just trying to help," he said.

Elden jumped off with a shout, sailed through the air, and tumbled on the far shore beside Centra.

He sent the vine back, and O'Connor went, followed by Serna, then Indra, then Conven.

The last ones left were Reece and Krog.

"Well, I guess it's just the two of us," Krog said to Reece.

"Go. Save yourself," Krog said, glancing back over his shoulder nervously. "The Faws are too close There isn't time for both of us to make it."

Reece shook his head.

"No man left behind," he said. "If you won't go then I won't."

They both stood there, stubbornly, Krog looking increasingly nervous. Krog shook his head.

"You are a fool. Why do you care so much about me? I wouldn't care half as much for you."

"I am leader now, which makes you my responsibility," Reece replied. "I don't care for you. I care for honor. And my honor commands me to leave no one behind."

They both turned nervously as the first of the Faws reached them. Reece stepped forward, beside Krog, and they slashed with their swords, killing several.

"We go together!" Reece called out.

Without wasting another moment, Reece grabbed Krog, draped him over his shoulder, grabbed the vine, and the two of them screamed as they set off through the air, a moment before the Faws stormed the shore.

The two of them sailed through the air, swaying across for the other side.

"Help!" Krog screamed.

Krog was slipping off of Reece's shoulder, and he grabbed the vine; but it was now wet with the spray of the rapids, and Krog's hands slipped right through the vine as he plummeted down. Reece reached down to grab him, but it all happened too fast: Reece's heart plummeted as he was forced to watch Krog fall, just out of his grasp, down into the gushing waters.

Reece landed on the far shore and tumbled to the ground. He rolled to his feet, prepared to rush back to the water—but before he could react, Conven broke from the group, rushed forward and dove headfirst into the raging waters.

Reece and the others watched, breathless. Was Conven that brave, Reece wondered? Or that suicidal?

Conven swam fearlessly through the gushing current. He reached Krog, somehow not getting bitten by the creatures, and grabbed him as he flailed, draping an arm around his shoulder and treading water with him. Conven swam against the current, heading back to shore.

Suddenly, Krog shrieked.

"MY LEG!"

Krog writhed in pain as a Fouren lodged in his leg, biting him, its shiny yellow scales visible over the current. Conven swam and swam until finally he neared shore and Reece and the others reached down and dragged them out. As they did, a school of Fourens jumped into the air after them, and Reece and the others swatted them away.

Krog flailed and Reece looked down and saw the Fouren still in his leg; Indra pulled her dagger, bent over and dug it into Krog's thigh as he shrieked, prying the animal out. It flopped on shore, then back into the water.

"I hate you!" Krog seethed to her.

"Good," Indra replied, unfazed.

Reece looked at Conven, who stood there, dripping wet, and was in awe of his fearlessness. Conven stared back, expressionless, and Reece noticed with shock that a Fouren was lodged in his arm, flopping in the air. Reece couldn't believe how calm Conven was, as he reached over slowly, yanked it out and threw it back into the water.

"Didn't that hurt?" Reece asked, confused.

Conven shrugged.

Reece worried for Conven more than ever; while he admired his courage, he could not believe his recklessness. He had dived headfirst into a school of vicious creatures, and hadn't even thought twice about it.

On the far side of the river, hundreds of Faws stood there, staring out, infuriated, chattering their teeth.

"Finally," O'Connor said, "we're safe."

Centra shook his head.

"Only for now. Those Faws are smart. They know the river bends. They'll take the long way, run around it, find the crossing. Soon, they'll be on our side. Our time is limited. We must move."

They all followed Centra as he sprinted through mud fields, past exploding geysers, navigating his way through this exotic landscape.

They ran and ran, until finally the mist broke and Reece's heart was elated to see, before them, the Canyon wall, its ancient stone shining. He looked up, and its walls seemed impossibly high. He did not know how they would climb it.

Reece stood there with the others and stared up with dread. The wall seemed even more imposing now than it had on the way down. He looked over and saw their ragged state and wondered how they could possibly scale it. They were all exhausted, beaten and bruised, weary from battle. Their hands and feet were raw. How could they possibly climb straight up, when it had taken all they had just to descend?

"I can't go on," Krog said, wheezing, his voice cracking.

Reece was feeling the same way, though he did not say it.

They were backed into a corner. They had outrun the Faws, but not for long. Soon they would find them, and they would all be outnumbered and killed. All of this hard work, all of their efforts, all for nothing.

Reece did not want to die here. Not in this place. If he had to die, he wanted to die up there, on his own soil, on the mainland, and with Selese by his side. If only he could have one more chance to escape.

Reece heard a horrific noise, and he turned to see the Faws, perhaps a hundred yards away. There were thousands of them, and they had already skirted the river, and were closing in.

They all drew their weapons.

"There's nowhere left to run," Centra said.

"Then we'll fight to the death!" Reece called out.

"Reece!" came a voice.

Reece looked straight up the Canyon wall, and as the mist cleared, there appeared a face he at first thought was an apparition. He could not believe it. There, before him, was the woman he had just been thinking of.

Selese.

What was she doing here? How had she arrived here? And who was that other woman with her? It looked like the royal healer, Illepra.

The two of them hung there, on the side of the cliff, a long and thick rope coiled around their waists and hands. They were coming down quickly, on a long, thick rope, one easy to grasp. Selese reached back and threw the rest of it down, dropping a good fifty feet through the air and landing at Reece's feet.

It was the way out.

They did not hesitate. They all ran for it, and within moments were climbing up, as fast as they could. Reece let everyone else go first, and as he jumped up, the last man up, he climbed and pulled the rope with him as he went, so that the Faws could not get it.

As he cleared the ground, the Faws appeared, reaching up and jumping for his feet—and just missing as Reece climbed out of reach.

Reece stopped as he reached Selese, who waited for him on a ledge; he leaned over and they kissed.

"I love you," Reece said, his entire being filled with love for her.

"And I you," she replied.

The two of them turned and headed up the Canyon wall with the others. They climbed, higher and higher. Soon, they would be home. Reece could hardly believe it.

Home.

CHAPTER FOUR

Alistair sprinted her way through the chaotic battlefield, weaving in and out of the soldiers as they fought for their lives against the army of undead rising up all around them. Moans and shrieks filled the air as the soldiers killed the ghouls—and as the ghouls, in turn, killed the soldiers. The Silver and MacGils and Silesians fought boldly—but they were vastly outnumbered. For each undead they killed, three more appeared. It was only a matter of time, Alistair could see, until all of her people were wiped out.

Alistair doubled her speed, running with all she had, her lungs bursting, ducking as an undead swiped for her face and crying out as another scratched her arm, drawing blood. She did not stop to fight them. There was no time. She had to find Argon.

She ran in the direction she had seen him last, when he was fighting Rafi and had collapsed from the effort. She prayed it had not killed him, that she could rouse him, and that she could make it before she and all her people were killed.

An undead appeared before her, blocking her way, and she held out her palm; a white ball of light struck it in the chest, knocking it backwards.

Five more appeared, and she held out her palm—but this time, only one more ball of light emerged, and the other four closed in on her. Her powers, she was surprised to realize, were limited.

Alistair braced herself for attack as they closed in—when she heard a snarling noise and looked over to see Krohn, leaping beside her and sinking his fangs into their throats. The undead turned on him, and Alistair found her chance. She elbowed one in the throat, knocking it over, and ran.

Alistair pushed her way through the chaos, desperate, the ghouls increasing in number by the moment, her people beginning to be pushed back. As she ducked and weaved, she finally emerged into a small clearing, the place where she remembered seeing Argon.

Alistair scanned the ground, desperate, and finally, between all the corpses, she found him. He was lying there, slumped on the ground, curled up in a ball. He lay in a small clearing and clearly he had cast some sort of spell to keep others away from him. He was unconscious, and as Alistair rushed to his side, she hoped and prayed he was still alive.

As she came closer, Alistair felt enveloped, protected in his magic bubble. She took a knee beside him and took a deep breath, finally safe from the battle all around her, finding respite in the eye of the storm.

Yet Alistair was also struck with terror as she looked down at Argon: he lay there, eyes closed, not breathing. She was flooded with panic.

"Argon!" she cried out, shaking his shoulders with both hands, trembling. "Argon, it's me! Alistair! Wake up! You *have* to wake up!"

Argon lay still, unresponsive, while all around her, the battle was intensifying.

"Argon, please! We need you. We cannot combat Rafi's magic. We do not have the skills that you do. Please, come back to us. For the Ring. For Gwendolyn. For Thorgrin."

Alistair shook him, yet still he did not respond.

Desperate, an idea came to her. She lay both palms on his chest, closed her eyes and focused. She summoned all of her inner energy, whatever was left, and slowly felt her hands warm. As she opened her eyes, she saw a blue light emanating from her palms, spreading over Argon's chest and shoulders. Soon it enveloped his entire body. Alistair was using an ancient spell she had once learned, to revive the sick. It was draining her, and she felt all the energy leaving her body. Getting weak, she willed Argon to come back.

Alistair collapsed, exhausted from the effort, and lay at Argon's side, too weak to move.

She sensed movement, and looked over and to her amazement saw Argon begin to stir.

He sat up and turned to her, his eyes shining with an intensity that scared her. He stared at her, expressionless, then reached over, picked up his staff, and gained his feet. He reached out one hand, took hers, and effortlessly pulled her to her feet.

As he held her hand, she felt all of her own energy restored.

"Where is he?" Argon asked.

Argon did not wait for an answer; it was as if he knew exactly where he needed to go, as he turned, staff at his side, walked right into the thick of battle.

Alistair couldn't understand how Argon was not hesitant to stroll into the soldiers. Then she understood why: he was able to cast a magical bubble around him as he went, and as the undead charged him from all sides, none were able to penetrate it. Alistair stuck close to him as he marched fearlessly, harmlessly through the thick of the battle, as if strolling through a meadow on a sunny day.

The two of them made their way through the battlefield, and he kept silent, marching, dressed in his long white cloak and hood, walking so fast that Alistair could barely keep up.

He finally stopped at the center of the battle, in a clearing, opposite which stood Rafi. Rafi still stood there, holding both arms out at his sides, his eyes rolled back in his head as he summoned thousands of undead, pouring out of the crevice in the earth.

Argon raised a single palm high overhead, palm up, facing the sky, and opened his eyes wide.

"RAFI!" he screamed in challenge.

Despite all the noise, Argon's scream cut through the battle, resonating off the hills.

As Argon shrieked, suddenly the clouds parted high above. A white stream of light came beaming down from the sky, right to Argon's palm, as if connecting him to the very heavens. The stream of light grew wider and wider, like a tornado, enveloping the battlefield, enveloping everything around him.

There came a great wind and a great whoosh, and Alistair watched in disbelief as beneath her the ground began to shake even more violently, and the huge crevice in the earth began to move in the opposite direction, slowly sealing itself backup.

As it began to close on itself, dozens of undead shrieked, crushed as they tried to crawl out.

Within moments, hundreds of undead were slipping, sliding back down to the earth, as the crevice became more and more narrow.

The earth shook one last time, then grew quiet, as the crevice finally sealed itself, the ground whole again, as if no fissure had ever appeared. The awful shrieks of the undead filled the air, muted from beneath the earth.

There came a stunned silence, a momentary lull in battle, as everyone stood and watched.

Rafi shrieked and turned and set his sights on Argon.

"ARGON!" Rafi yelled.

The time had come for the final clash of these two great titans.

Rafi ran into the open clearing, holding his red staff high, and Argon did not hesitate, racing out to face Rafi.

The two met in the middle, each wielding their staffs high overhead. Rafi brought his staff down for Argon and Argon raised his and blocked it. A great white light arose, like sparks, as they met. Argon swung back, and Rafi blocked.

Back and forth they went, blow for blow, attacking, blocking, white light flying everywhere. The ground shook with each of their blows, and Alistair could feel a monumental energy in the air.

Finally, Argon found his opening, swinging his staff from underneath, upwards, and as he did, shattering Rafi's staff.

The ground shook violently.

Argon stepped forward, raised his staff high overhead with two hands, and plunged it straight down, right through Rafi's chest.

Rafi let out an awful shriek, thousands of small bats flying out of his mouth as his jaw remained wide open. The skies turned black for a moment, as thick black clouds gathered from the heavens, right over Rafi's head, and swirled down to earth. They swallowed him whole, and Rafi howled as he spun through the air, yanked upwards into the skies, heading up to some awful fate that Alistair did not want to imagine.

Argon stood there, breathing hard, as all finally fell silent, Rafi dead.

The army of undead shrieked, as one at a time, they all disintegrated before Argon's eyes, each falling into a mound of ashes. Soon the battlefield was littered with thousands of mounds, all that remained of Rafi's evil spells.

Alistair surveyed the battlefield and saw there was only one battle left to wage: across the clearing, her brother, Thorgrin, was already facing off with their father, Andronicus. She knew that in the battle to come, one of these determined men would lose their lives: her brother or her father. She prayed that it was her brother who came out alive.

CHAPTER FIVE

Luanda lay on the ground at Romulus' feet, watching in horror as thousands of Empire soldiers flooded the bridge, screaming with triumph as they crossed into the Ring. They were invading her homeland, and there was nothing she could do but sit there, helpless, and watch, and wonder if it was somehow all her fault. She could not help but feel as if she was somehow responsible for the Shield being lowered.

Luanda turned and looked out at the horizon, saw the endless Empire ships, and knew that soon it would be millions of Empire troops flooding in. Her people were finished; the Ring was finished. It was all over now.

Luanda closed her eyes and shook her head, again and again. There was a time when she had been so angry with Gwendolyn, with her father, and would have been glad to witness the destruction of the Ring. But her mind had changed, ever since Andronicus' betrayal and treatment of her, ever since his shaving her head, his beating her in front of his people. It made her realize how wrong, how naïve, she had been in her own quest for power. Now, she would give anything for her old life back. All she wanted now was a life of peace and contentment. She no longer craved ambition or power; now, she just wanted to survive, to make wrongs right.

But as she watched, Luanda realized it was too late. Now her beloved homeland was on its way to destruction, and there was nothing she could do.

Luanda heard an awful noise, laughter mixed with a snarl, and she looked up and saw Romulus standing there, hands on his hips, watching it all, a huge contended smile on his face, his long jagged teeth showing. He threw back his head and laughed and laughed, elated.

Luanda yearned to kill him; if she had a dagger in hand, she would run it through his heart. But knowing him, how thickly he was built, how impervious he was to everything, the dagger probably wouldn't even pierce it.

Romulus looked down at her, and his smile turned to a grimace.

"Now," he said, "it's time to kill you slowly."

Luanda heard a distinctive clang and watched Romulus draw a weapon from his waist. It looked like a short sword, except tapered to a long, narrow point. It was an evil weapon, one clearly designed for torture.

"You are going to suffer very, very much," he said.

As he lowered his weapon, Luanda raised her hands to her face, as if to block it all out. She closed her eyes and shrieked.

That was when the strangest thing happened: as Luanda shrieked, her shriek was echoed by an even greater shriek. It was the shriek of an animal. A monster. A primordial roar, one louder and more resonant than anything she'd ever heard in her life. It was like thunder, tearing the skies apart.

Luanda opened her eyes and looked up to the heavens, wondering if she had imagined it. It sounded as if it had been the shriek of God himself.

Romulus, also stunned, looked up to the skies, baffled. By his expression, Luanda could tell that it had really happened; she had not imagined it.

It came again, a second shriek, even worse than the first, with such ferocity, such power, Luanda realized it could only be one thing:

A dragon.

As the skies parted, Luanda was awestruck to see two immense dragons soar overhead, the largest and scariest creatures she had ever seen, blotting out the sun, turning day to night as they cast a shadow over all of them.

Romulus' weapon fell from his hands, his mouth open in shock. Clearly, he'd never witnessed anything quite like this, either, especially as the two dragons flew so low to the ground, barely twenty feet above them, nearly grazing their heads. Their great talons hung below them, and as they shrieked again, they arched their backs and spread open their wings.

At first, Luanda braced herself, as she assumed they were coming to kill her. But as she watched them fly, so fast overhead, as she felt the wind they left knock her over, she realized they were going elsewhere: over the Canyon. Into the Ring.

The dragons must have seen the soldiers crossing into the Ring and realized the Shield was down. They must have realized that this was their chance to enter the Ring, too.

Luanda watched, riveted, as one dragon suddenly opened its mouth, swooped down, and breathed a stream of fire onto the men on the bridge.

Screams of thousands of Empire soldiers arose, shrieking to the heavens as a great wall of fire engulfed them.

The dragons continued flying, breathing fire as they crossed the bridge, burning all of Romulus' men. Then they continued to fly, into the Ring itself, continuing to breathe fire and to destroy every Empire man who'd entered, sending wave after wave of destruction.

Within moments, there were no Empire men left on the bridge, or on the mainland of the Ring.

The Empire men who were heading for the bridge, who were about to cross, stopped in their tracks. They dared not enter. Instead, they turned and fled, running back to the ships.

Romulus turned to watch his men leave, irate.

Luanda sat there, stunned, and realized this was her chance. Romulus was distracted, as he turned and chased after his men and tried to get them to head for the bridge. This was her moment.

Luanda jumped to her feet, her heart pounding, and turned and raced back for the bridge. She knew she had only a few precious moments; if she were lucky, maybe, just *maybe*, she could run long enough, before Romulus noticed, and make the other side. And if she could make the other side, maybe her reaching the mainland would help restore the Shield.

She had to try, and she knew it was now or never.

Luanda ran and ran, breathing so hard she could hardly think, her legs shaking. She stumbled on her feet, her legs heavy, her throat dry, flailing her arms as she went, the cold wind grazing her bald head.

She ran faster and faster, her heart pounding in her ears, the sound of her own breathing filling her world, as all became a narrow blur. She made it a good fifty yards across the bridge before she heard the first scream.

Romulus. Clearly, he had spotted her.

Behind her there suddenly came the sound of men charging on horseback, crossing the bridge, coming after her.

Luanda sprinted, increasing her pace, as she felt the men bearing down her. She ran past all the corpses of the Empire men, burnt by the dragons, some still flaming, doing her best to avoid them. Behind her, the horses grew even louder. She glanced back over her shoulder, saw their spears raised high and knew that this time Romulus aimed to have her killed. She knew that, in just moments, those spears would be thrust into her back.

Luanda looked forward and saw the Ring, the mainland, just feet in front of her. If only she could make it. Just ten more feet. If she could just cross the border, maybe, just maybe, the Shield would go back up and save her.

The men bore down on her as she took her final steps. The sound of horses was deafening in her ears, and she smelled the sweat of horses and of men. She braced herself, expecting a spear point to puncture her back at any moment. They were just feet away. But so was she.

In one final act of desperation, Luanda dove, just as she saw a soldier raise his hand with a spear behind her. She hit the ground with a tumble. Out of the corner of her eye she saw the spear sailing through the air, heading right for her.

Yet as soon as Luanda crossed the line, landed on the mainland of the Ring, suddenly, behind her, the Shield was activated again. The spear, inches behind her, disintegrated in mid-air. And behind it, all the soldiers on the bridge shrieked, raising their hands to their faces, as they all went up in flames, disintegrating.

In moments, they were all just piles of ashes.

On the far side of the bridge Romulus stood, watching it all. He shrieked and beat his chest. It was a cry of agony. A cry of someone who had been defeated. Outwitted.

Luanda lay there, breathing hard, in shock. She leaned down and kissed the soil. Then she threw her head back and laughed in delight.

She had made it. She was safe.

CHAPTER SIX

Thorgrin stood in the open clearing, facing Andronicus, surrounded by both armies. They stood at a standstill, watching as father and son faced off once again. Andronicus stood there in all his glory, towering over Thor, wielding a huge axe in one hand and a sword in the other. As Thor faced him, he forced himself to breathe slowly and deeply, to control his emotions. Thor had to remain clear-minded, to focus as he fought this man, the same way he would any other enemy. He had to tell himself that he was not facing his father, but his worst foe. The man who had hurt Gwendolyn; the man who had hurt all of his countrymen; the man who had manipulated him. The man who deserved to die.

With Rafi dead, Argon back in control, and all the undead creatures back beneath the earth, there was no more delaying this final confrontation, Andronicus' facing off with Thorgrin. It was the battle that must determine the fate of the war. Thor would not let him get away, not this time, and Andronicus, cornered in, finally seemed willing to face off with his son.

"Thornicus, you are my son," Andronicus said, his low voice reverberating. "I do not wish to harm you."

"But I wish to harm you," Thor replied, refusing to give in to Andronicus' mind games.

"Thornicus, my son," Andronicus repeated, as Thor took a wary step closer, "I do not wish to kill you. Lay down your weapons and join me. Join me as you had before. You are my son. You are not *their* son. You carry my bloodline; you do not carry theirs. My homeland is your homeland; the Ring is but an adopted place for you. You are *my* people. These people mean nothing to you. Come home. Come back to the Empire. Allow me to be the father you always wanted. And become the son I always wanted you to be.

"I will not fight you," Andronicus said finally, as he lowered his axe.

Thor had heard enough. He had to make a move now, before he allowed his mind to be swayed by this monster.

Thor let out a battle cry, raised sword high and charged forward, bringing it down with both hands for Andronicus' head.

Andronicus stared back in surprise, then at the last second, he reached down, grabbed his axe from the ground, raised it and blocked Thor's blow.

Sparks flew off of Thor's sword as the two of them locked weapons, inches away, each groaning, as Andronicus held back Thor's blow.

"Thornicus," Andronicus grunted, "your strength is great. But it is *my* strength. I gave you this. My blood runs in your veins. Stop this madness, and join me!"

Andronicus pushed Thor back, and Thor stumbled backwards.

"Never!" Thor screamed, defiant. "I will never return to you. You are no father to me. You are a stranger. You don't deserve to be my father!"

Thor charged again, screaming, and brought his sword down. Andronicus blocked it; Thor, expecting it, quickly spun around with his sword and slashed Andronicus' arm.

Andronicus cried out as blood squirted from his wound. He stumbled back and looked Thor over with disbelief, reaching over and touching his wound, then examining the blood on his hand.

"You mean to kill me," Andronicus said, as if realizing for the first time. "After all I've done for you."

"I most certainly do," Thorgrin said.

Andronicus studied him, as if studying a new person, and soon his look changed from one of wonder and disappointment to one of anger.

"Then you are no son of mine!" he screamed. "The Great Andronicus does not ask twice!"

Andronicus threw down his sword, raised his battle axe with both hands, let out a great cry and charged for Thor. Finally, the battle had begun.

Thor raised his sword to block the blow, but it came down with such force that, to Thor's shock, it shattered Thor's sword, breaking it in two.

Thor quickly improvised, dodging out of the way as the blow continued to come down; it just grazed him, missing by an inch, so close he could feel the wind brush his shoulder. His father had tremendous strength, greater than any warrior he'd ever faced, and Thor knew this would not be easy. His father was fast, too—a deadly combination. And now Thor had no weapon.

Andronicus swung the axe around again without hesitating, swinging sideways, aiming to chop Thor in half.

Thor leapt into the air, high over Andronicus' head, doing a somersault, using his inner powers to propel him, and landed behind Andronicus. He landed on his feet, reached down and grabbed his father's sword from the ground, spun around and charged, swinging for Andronicus' back.

But to Thor's surprise, Andronicus was so fast, he was prepared. He spun around and blocked the blow. Thor felt the impact of metal hitting metal reverberate throughout his body. Andronicus' sword, at least, held; it was stronger than his. It was strange, to hold his father's sword—especially when facing his father.

Thor swung around, and came down sideways for Andronicus' shoulder. Andronicus blocked, and came down for Thor's.

Back and forth they went, attacking and blocking, Thor driving Andronicus back, and Andronicus, in turn, pushing Thor back. Sparks flew, the weapons moving so fast, gleaming in the light, their great clangs riveting the battlefield, the two armies watching, transfixed. The two great warriors pushed each other back and forth across the open clearing, neither gaining an inch.

Thor raised his sword to strike again, but this time Andronicus surprised him by stepping forward and kicking him in the chest. Thor went flying backward, landing on his back.

Andronicus rushed forward and brought down his axe. Thor rolled out of the way, but not quickly enough: it sliced Thor's bicep, just enough to draw blood. Thor cried out, but nonetheless, swung around, and swung his sword and sliced Andronicus' calf.

Andronicus stumbled and cried out, and Thor rolled back to his feet, as the two faced each other, each wounded.

"I'm stronger than you, son," Andronicus said. "And more experienced in battle. Give in now. Your Druid powers will not work against me. It is just me against you, man to man, axe to sword. And as a warrior, I am better. You know this. Yield to me, and I shall not kill you."

Thor scowled.

"I yield to no one! Least of all you!"

Thor forced himself to think of Gwendolyn, of what Andronicus had done to her, and his rage intensified. Now was the time. Thor was determined to finish Andronicus off, once and for all, to send this awful creature back to hell.

Thor charged with a final burst of strength, giving it all he had, letting out a great cry. He brought his sword down left and right, swinging so fast he could barely contain it, Andronicus blocking each one, even as he was pushed back, step by step. The fighting went on and on, and Andronicus seemed surprised that his son could exhibit such strength, and for so long.

Thor found his moment of opportunity when, for a moment, Andronicus' arms grew tired. Thor swung for his axe head and connected, and managed to knock the blade from Andronicus' hands. Andronicus watched it fly through the air, shocked, and Thor then kicked his father in the chest, knocking him down, flat on his back.

Before he could rise, Thor stepped forward and placed a foot on his throat. Thor had him pinned, and he stood there, looking down at him.

The entire battlefield was riveted as Thor stood over him, holding the tip of his sword to his father's throat.

Andronicus, blood seeping from his mouth, smiled between his fangs.

"You cannot do it, son," he said. "That is your great weakness. Your love for me. Just like my weakness for you. I could never bring myself to kill you. Not now, not your entire life. This entire battle is futility. You will let me go. Because you and I are one."

Thor stood over him, hands shaking as he held the sword tip at his father's throat. Slowly, he raised it. A part of him felt his father's words to be true. How could he bring himself to kill his father?

But as he stared down, he considered all the pain, all the damage, his father had inflicted on everyone around him. He considered the price of letting him live. The price of compassion. It was too great a price to pay, not just for Thorgrin, but for everyone he loved and cared about. Thor glanced behind him and saw the tens of thousands of Empire soldiers whom had invaded his homeland, standing there, ready to attack his people. And this man was their leader. Thor owed it to his homeland. To Gwendolyn. And most of all, to himself. This man might be his father by blood, but that was all. He was not his father in any other sense of the word. And blood alone did not make a father.

Thor raised his sword high, and with a great cry, he swung it down.

Thor closed his eyes, and opened them to see the sword, embedded in the soil, right beside Andronicus' head. Thor left it there and stepped back.

His father had been right: he had been unable to do it. Despite everything, he just could not bring himself to kill a defenseless man.

Thor turned his back on his father, facing his own people, facing Gwendolyn. Clearly he had won the battle; he had made his point. Now, Andronicus, if he had any honor, would have no choice but to return home.

"THORGRIN!" Gwendolyn screamed.

Thor turned to see, with shock, Andronicus's axe swinging at him, coming right for his head. Thor ducked at the last second, and the axe flew by.

Andronicus was fast, though, and in the same motion he swung back around with his gauntlet and backhanded Thor across the jaw, knocking him down to his hands and knees.

Thor felt an awful cracking in his ribs, as Andronicus' boot kicked him in the stomach, sending him rolling, gasping for air.

Thor lay on his hands and knees, breathing hard, blood dripping from his mouth, his ribs killing him, trying to muster the strength to get up. Out of the corner of his eye he watched Andronicus step forward, smile wide, and raise his axe high with both hands. He was aiming, Thor could see, to chop off Thor's head. Thor could see it in his bloodshot eyes that Andronicus would have no mercy, as Thor had had.

"This is what I should have done years ago," Andronicus said.

Andronicus let out a great scream, as he brought his axe down for Thor's exposed neck.

Thor, though, was not done fighting; he managed one last burst of energy, and despite all his pain, he scrambled to his feet and charged his father, tackling him around the ribs, driving him backward, onto the ground, on his back.

Thor lay on top of him, wrestling him down, preparing to fight him with his bare hands. It had become a wrestling match. Andronicus reached up and grabbed Thor's throat, and Thor was surprised by his strength; he felt himself losing air quickly as he was choked.

Thor grasped at his waist, desperate, searching for his dagger. The royal dagger, the one King MacGil had given him before he died. Thor was losing air fast, and he knew if he didn't find it soon, he'd be dead.

Thor found it with his last breath. He raised it high, and plunged it down with both hands, into Andronicus' chest.

Andronicus shot up, gasping for air, eyes bulging in a death stare, as he sat up and continued to choke his son.

Thor, out of breath, was seeing stars, going limp.

Finally, slowly, Andronicus' grip released, as his arms fell to his side. His eyes rolled sideways, and he stopped moving.

He lay there frozen. Dead.

Thor gasped as he pried his father's limp hand from his throat, heaving and coughing, rolling off his father's dead body.

His entire body was shaking. He had just killed his father. He had not thought it was possible.

Thor glanced around and saw all the warriors, both armies, staring at him in shock. Thor felt a tremendous heat course through his body, as if some profound shift had just occurred within him, as if he had wiped some evil part of himself. He felt changed, lighter.

Thor heard a great noise in the sky, like thunder, and he looked up and saw a small black cloud appear over Andronicus' corpse, and a funnel of small black shadows, like demons, whirl down to the ground. They swirled around his father, encompassing him, howling, then lifted his body high into the air, higher and higher, until it disappeared into the cloud. Thor watched, in shock, and wondered to what hell his father's soul would be dragged.

Thor looked up, and saw the Empire army facing him, tens and tens of thousands of men, vengeance in their eyes. The Great Andronicus was dead. Yet still, his men remained. Thor and the men of the Ring were still outnumbered a hundred to one. They had won the battle, but they were about to lose the war.

Erec and Kendrick and Srog and Bronson walked to Thor's side, swords drawn, as they all faced the Empire together. Horns sounded up and down the Empire line, and Thor prepared to face battle one last time. He knew they could not win. But at least they would all go down together, in one great clash of glory.

CHAPTER SEVEN

Reece marched beside Selese, Illepra, Elden, Indra, O'Connor, Conven, Krog and Serna, the nine of them marching west, as they had been for hours, ever since emerging from the Canyon. Somewhere, Reece knew, his people were on the horizon, and, dead or alive, he was determined to find them.

Reece had been shocked as they had passed through a landscape of destruction, endless fields of corpses, littered by feasting birds, charred from the breath of dragons. Thousands of Empire corpses lined the horizon, some of them still smoking. The smoke from their bodies filled the air, the unbearable stench of burning flesh permeating a land destroyed. Whomever had not been killed by the dragon's breath had been marred in the conventional battle against the Empire, MacGils and McClouds lying dead, too, entire towns destroyed, piles of rubble everywhere. Reece shook his head: this land, that had once been so abundant, was now ravaged by war.

Ever since arising from the Canyon, Reece and the others had been determined to make it home, to get back to the MacGil side of the Ring. Unable to find horses, they had marched all the way through the McCloud side, up over the Highlands, down the other side, and now, finally, they marched through MacGil territory, passing nothing but ruin and devastation. From the looks of the land, the dragons had helped destroy the Empire troops, and for that, Reece was grateful. But Reece still did not know what state he might find his own people in. Was everyone dead in the Ring? Thus far, it seemed so. Reece was aching to find out if everyone was okay.

Each time they reached a battlefield of dead and injured that was not seared by the dragons' flames, Illepra and Selese went from corpse to corpse, turning them over, checking. Not only were they driven by their professions but Illepra also had another goal in mind: to find Reece's brother. Godfrey. It was a goal Reece shared.

"He's not here," Illepra announced yet again, as she finally stood, having turned over the last corpse of this field, disappointment etched across her face.

Reece could tell how much Illepra cared for his brother, and he was touched. Reece, too, hoped that he was okay and among the living—but from the looks of these thousands of corpses, he had a sinking feeling he was not.

They moved on, marched over yet another rolling field, another series of hills, and as they did, they spotted another battlefield on the horizon, thousands more corpses laid out. They headed for it.

As they walked, Illepra cried quietly. Selese laid a hand on her wrist.

"He's alive," Selese reassured. "Do not worry."

Reece stepped up and placed a reassuring hand on her shoulder, feeling compassion for her.

"If it's one thing I know about my brother," Reece said, "he's a survivor. He finds a way out of everything. Even death. I promise you. Godfrey is likely already in a tavern somewhere, getting drunk."

Illepra laughed through her tears, and wiped them away.

"I hope so," she said. "For the first time, I really hope so."

They continued their somber march, silently through the wasteland, each lost in their own thoughts. Images of the Canyon flashed through Reece's mind; he could not suppress them. He thought back to how desperate their situation had been, and was filled with gratitude to Selese; if she hadn't appeared when he had, they would still be down there, surely all dead.

Reece reached over and took Selese's hand and smiled as the two held hands as they walked. Reece was touched by her love and devotion for him, by her willingness to cross the entire countryside just to save him. He felt an overwhelming rush of love for her, and he could not wait until they had a moment alone so he could express it to her. He had already decided he wanted to be with her forever. He felt a loyalty to her unlike he had ever felt to anyone else, and as soon as they had a moment, he vowed to propose to her. He would give her his mother's ring, the one his mother had given to him to give to the love of his life, when he found her.

"I can't believe you crossed the Ring just for me," Reece said to her.

She smiled.

"It wasn't that far," she said.

"Not far?" he asked. "You put your life in danger to cross a war-ravaged country. I owe you. Beyond what I could say."

"You owe me nothing. I am just glad you're alive."

"We *all* owe you," Elden chimed in. "You saved all of us. We would all be stuck down there in the bowels of the Canyon, forever."

"Speaking of debts, I have one to discuss with you," Krog said to Reece, coming up beside him with a limp. Since Illepra had splinted his leg at the top of the Canyon, Krog had at least been able to walk on his own, if stiffly.

"You saved me down there, and more than once," Krog continued. "It was pretty stupid of you, if you ask me. But you did it anyway. Don't think I owe you, though."

Reece shook his head, caught off guard by Krog's gruffness and his awkward attempt to thank him.

"I don't know if you are trying to insult me, or trying to thank me," Reece said.

"I have my own way," Krog said. "I am going to watch your back from now on. Not because I like you, but because that's what I feel called to do."

Reece shook his head, baffled as always by Krog.

"Don't worry," Reece said. "I don't like you either."

They all continued their march, all of them relaxed, happy to be alive, to be above ground, to be back on this side of the Ring—all except Conven, who walked quietly, apart from the others, withdrawn into himself as he had been ever since the death of his twin in the Empire. Nothing, not even an escape from death, seemed to shake him from it.

Reece thought back and recalled how, down there, Conven had thrown himself recklessly into danger, time and again, nearly killing himself to save the others. Reece could not help but wonder if it came more from a desire to kill himself than to help the others. He worried about him. Reece did not like to see him so alienated, so lost in depression.

Reece walked up beside him.

"You fought brilliantly back there," Reece said to him.

Conven just shrugged and looked down to the ground.

Reece wracked his brain for something to say, as they marched on in silence.

"Are you happy to be home?" Reece asked. "To be free?"

Conven turned and stared at him blankly.

"I'm not home. And I'm not free. My brother is dead. And I have no right to live without him."

Reece felt a chill run through him at his words. Clearly, Conven was still overwhelmed with grief; he wore it like a badge of honor. Conven was more like the walking dead, his eyes blank. Reece recalled them once filled with joy. Reece could see that his mourning was deep, and he had the sinking feeling that it might not ever lift from him. Reece wondered what would become of Conven. For the first time, he did not think anything good.

They marched and marched, and hours passed, and they reached yet another battlefield, shoulder to shoulder with corpses. Illepra and Selese and the others fanned out, going corpse to corpse, turning them over, looking for any sign of Godfrey.

"I see a lot more MacGils on this field," Illepra said hopefully, "and no dragon's breath. Maybe Godfrey is here."

Reece looked up and saw the thousands of corpses and wondered, even if he was here, whether they could ever find him.

Reece spread out and went corpse to corpse, as did the others, turning each over. He saw all the faces of his people, face to face, some he recognized and some he didn't, people he had known and fought with, people who had fought for his father. Reece marveled at the devastation that had descended on his homeland, like a plague, and he earnestly hoped that it was all finally passed. He'd seen his fill of battles and wars and corpses to last a lifetime. He was ready to settle down into a life of peace, to heal, to rebuild again.

"HERE!" shouted Indra, her voice filled with excitement. She stood over a body and stared down.

Illepra turned and came running over, and all of them gathered around. She knelt beside the body, and tears flooded her face. Reece knelt down beside her and gasped to see his brother.

Godfrey.

His big belly sticking out, unshaven, his eyes closed, too pale, his hands blue with cold, he looked dead.

Illepra leaned over and shook him, again and again; he did not respond.

"Godfrey! Please! Wake up! It's me! Illepra! GODFREY!"

She shook him again and again, but he did not rouse. Finally, frantically, she turned to the others, scanning their belts.

"Your wineskin!" she demanded to O'Connor.

O'Connor fumbled at his waist, hastily removed it and handed it to Illepra.

She took it and held it over Godfrey's face and squirted wine on his lips. She lifted his head, opened his mouth, and squirted some on his tongue.

There came a sudden response, as Godfrey licked his lips, and swallowed.

He coughed, then sat up, grabbed the wineskin, eyes still closed, and squirted it, drinking more and more, until he sat all the way up. He slowly opened his eyes and wiped his mouth with the back of his hand. He looked around, confused and disoriented, and belched.

Illepra cried out with joy, leaning over and giving him a big hug.

"You survived!" she exclaimed.

Reece sighed with relief as his brother looked around, confused, but very much alive.

Elden and Serna each grabbed Godfrey under the shoulder and hoisted him to his feet. Godfrey stood there, wobbly at first, took another long drink and wiped his mouth with the back of his hand.

Godfrey looked around, bleary-eyed.

"Where am I?" he asked. He reached up and rubbed his head, which had a large welt, and his eyes squinted in pain.

Illepra studied the wound expertly, running her hand along it, and the dried blood in his hair.

"You've received a wound," she said. "But you can be proud: you're alive. You're safe."

Godfrey wobbled, and the others caught him.

"It is not serious," she said, examining it, "but you will need to rest."

She removed a bandage from her waist and began to wrap it around his head, again and again. Godfrey winced, and looked over at her. Then he looked about and surveyed all the corpses, eyes opening wide.

"I'm alive," he said. "I can't believe it."

"You made it," Reece said, clasping his older brother's shoulder happily. "I knew you would."

Illepra embraced him, hugging him, and slowly, he hugged her back.

"So this is what it feels like to be a hero," Godfrey observed, and the others laughed. "Give me more drink like this," he added, "and maybe I'll do it more often."

Godfrey took another long swig, and finally he began to walk with them, leaning on Illepra, one shoulder around her, as she helped him balance.

"Where are the others?" Godfrey asked as they went.

"We don't know," Reece said. "Somewhere west, I hope. That's where we're heading. We march for King's Court. To see who lives."

Reece gulped as he uttered the words. He looked off into the horizon, and prayed that his countrymen had met a similar fate to

Godfrey. He thought of Thor, of his sister Gwendolyn, of his brother Kendrick, of so many others that he loved. But he knew that the bulk of the Empire army still lay ahead, and judging from the number of dead and wounded he'd already seen, he had a sinking feeling that the worst was still to come.

CHAPTER EIGHT

Thorgrin, Kendrick, Erec, Srog and Bronson stood as a unified wall against the Empire army, their people behind them, weapons drawn, preparing to face the onslaught of Empire troops. Thor knew this would be his death charge, his final battle in life, yet he had no regrets. He would die here, facing the enemy, on his feet, sword in hand, his brothers-in-arms at his side, defending his homeland. He would be given a chance to make up for what he had done, for facing his own people in battle. There was nothing more he could ask for in life.

Thor thought of Gwendolyn, and he only wished that he had more time for her sake. He prayed that Steffen had taken her safely out and that she was safe back there, behind the lines. He felt determined to fight with all he had, to kill as many Empire as he could, just to prevent them from harming her.

As Thor stood there he could feel his brothers' solidarity, all of them unafraid, standing there valiantly, holding their ground. These were the finest men of the kingdom, the finest knights of the Silver, MacGils, Silesians—all of them unified, none of them backing away in fear, despite the odds. All of them were prepared to give up their lives to defend their homeland. They all valued honor and freedom more than life.

Thor heard Empire horns, up and down the lines, watched their divisions of countless men line up in precise units. These were disciplined soldiers he was facing, soldiers with merciless commanders, who had fought their whole lives. It was a machine, trained to carry on in the face of their leader's death. A new nameless Empire commander stepped up to lead the troops. Their numbers were vast, endless, and Thor knew there was no way they could defeat them with so few men. But that mattered not anymore. It did not matter if they died. All that mattered was *how* they died. They would die on their feet, as men, in a final clash of valor.

"Shall we wait for them to come to us?" Erec asked aloud. "Or shall we offer them the greeting of the MacGils?"

Thor smiled, along with the others. There was nothing like a smaller army charging a larger one. It was reckless, yet it was also the height of courage.

As one, Thor and his men all suddenly let out a battle cry, and they all charged. They raced on foot, hurrying to bridge the gap between the two armies, their battle cries filling the air, their men following close on their heels. Thor held his sword high, running beside his brothers, his heart thumping, a cold gust of wind brushing his face. This was what battle felt like. It reminded him what it felt like to be alive.

The two armies charged, racing as fast as they could to kill each other. In moments they met in the middle, in a tremendous clang of weapons.

Thor slashed every which way, hurling himself into the front row of Empire soldiers, who wielded long spears, pikes, lances. Thor slashed the first pike he encountered in half, then stabbed the soldier through the gut.

Thor ducked and weaved as multiple lances came his way; he swung his sword, whirling in every direction, slicing all the weapons in half with a splintering noise and kicking and elbowing each soldier out of his way. He backhanded several more with his gauntlet, kicked another in the groin, elbowed one in the jaw, head-butted another, stabbed another, and spun and slashed another. The quarters were close, and it was hand to hand, and Thor was a one-man machine, cutting his way through the vastly superior force.

All around him, his brothers were doing the same, fighting with incredible speed and power and strength and spirit, even though they were outnumbered, throwing themselves into the much larger army and cutting through the rows of Empire men which seemed to have no end. None hesitated, and none retreated.

All around Thor, thousands of men met thousands of others, men screaming and grunting as they fought hand-to-hand in the huge vicious battle, the determining battle for the fate of the Ring. And despite the vastly superior forces, the men of the Ring were gaining momentum, holding the Empire at bay and even pushing them back.

Thor snatched a flail from an Empire soldier's hands, kicked him back, then swung it around and smashed him in the side of the helmet. Thor then swung it high overhead in a broad circle and knocked down several more. He threw it into the crowd and took down even more.

Thor then raised his sword and went back to hand-to-hand fighting, slashing every which way until his arms and shoulders grew tired. At one point he was a touch too slow, and a soldier came down at him with a raised sword; Thor turned to face him, too late, and braced himself for the blow and injury to come.

Thor heard a snarling noise, and Krohn whizzed by, leaping into the air and locking his jaws on the soldier's throat, driving him down, saving Thor.

Hours of close fighting passed. While Thor was at first encouraged by all their gains, it soon became apparent that this battle was an act of futility, prolonging the inevitable. No matter how many of them they killed, the horizon continued to be filled with an endless array of men. And while Thor and the others were growing weary, the Empire men were fresh, more and more pouring in.

Thor, losing momentum, not defending as quickly as he had been, suddenly received a sword slash on the shoulder; he cried out in pain as blood gushed from his arm. Thor then received an elbow in the ribs, and a battle axe descended for him, which he just barely blocked with his shield. He had nearly raised the shield a second too late.

Thor was losing ground, and as he glanced around, he saw that the others around him were, too. The tide was beginning to turn yet again; Thor's ears were filled with the death cries of too many of his men, beginning to fall. After hours of fighting, they were losing. Soon, they would all be finished. He thought of Gwendolyn, and he refused to accept it.

Thor threw his head back to the heavens, desperately trying to summon whatever powers he had left. But his Druid power was not responding. Too much of it, he sensed, had been drained from his time with Andronicus, and he needed time to heal. He noticed Argon on the battlefield, not as powerful as he had been either, his powers, too, drained fighting Rafi. And Alistair was weakened, too, her powers drained from reviving Argon. They had no other backup. Just their strength of arms.

Thor threw his head back to the heavens and let out a great battle cry of desperation, willing for something to be different, for something to change.

Please God, he prayed. *I beg of you. Save us all on this day. I turn to you. Not to man, not to my powers, but to you. Give me a sign of your power.*

Suddenly, to Thor's shock, the air was filled with the noise of a great roar, one so loud it seemed to split the very heavens.

Thor's heart quickened as he immediately recognized the sound. He looked at the horizon and saw bursting out of the clouds his old friend, Mycoples. Thor was shocked, elated to see that she was alive, that she was free, and that she was back here, in the Ring, flying towards him. It was like a part of himself had been restored.

Even more surprising, beside her saw Thor a second dragon. A male dragon, with ancient, faded red scales, and huge, glowing green eyes, fiercer-looking even than Mycoples. Thor watched the two of them soaring through the air, weaving in and out, and then plunging down, right for Thor. He realized then that his prayers had been answered.

Mycoples raised her wings, arched back her neck and shrieked, as did the dragon beside her, and the two of them breathed a wall of fire down onto the Empire army, lighting up the sky. The cold day was suddenly warm, then hot, as walls of flames rolled and rolled towards them. Thor raised his arms to his face.

The dragons attacked from the back, so the flames did not quite reach Thor. Still, the wall of fire was close enough that Thor felt its heat, the hairs on his forearm singed.

The shouts of thousands of men rose up into the air as the Empire army, division by division, was set on fire, tens of thousands of soldiers screaming for their lives. They ran every which way—but there was nowhere to flee. The dragons were merciless. They were on a rampage, and they were filled with fury, ready to wreak vengeance on the Empire.

One division of Empire after the next stumbled to the ground, dead.

The remaining soldiers facing Thor turned in a panic and fled, trying to get away from the dragons crisscrossing the sky, breathing flame everywhere. But they only ran to their own deaths, as the dragons zeroed in on them, and finished them off one at a time.

Soon, Thor found himself facing nothing but an empty field, black clouds of smoke, the smell of burning flesh filling the air, of dragon's breath, of sulfur. As the clouds lifted, they revealed a charred wasteland before him, not a single man left alive, all the grass and trees withered down to nothingness but black and ash. The Empire army, so indomitable just minutes ago, was now completely gone.

Thor stood there in shock, elated. He would live. They would all live. The Ring was free. Finally, they were free.

Mycoples dove down and sat before Thor, lowering her head and snorting.

Thor stepped forward, smiling as he went to his old friend, and Mycoples lowered her head all the way to the ground, purring. Thor stroked the scales on her face, and she leaned in and rubbed her nose up and down his chest, stroking her face against his body. She purred contentedly, and it was clear she was ecstatic to see Thor again, as ecstatic as he was to see her.

Thor mounted her, and turned, atop Mycoples, and faced his army, thousands of men staring back in wonder and joy, as he raised his sword.

The men raised their swords and cheered back to him. Finally, the skies were filled with the sound of victory.

CHAPTER NINE

Gwendolyn stood there, looking up at Thorgrin, atop Mycoples, and her heart soared with relief and pride. She had made her way through the thick crowd of soldiers, back to the front lines, throwing off the protection of Steffen and the others. She had pushed her way all the way into the clearing, and she stood before Thor. She burst into tears of joy, as she looked out and saw the Empire defeated, all threats finally gone, as she saw Thor, her love, alive, safe. She felt triumphant. She felt as if all the darkness and grief of the last several months had finally lifted, felt that the Ring was finally safe once again. She felt overwhelmed with joy and gratitude as Thor spotted her and looked down at her with such love, his eyes shining.

Gwen prepared to go forth and greet him, when suddenly a noise cut through the air that made her turn.

"BRONSON!" came the shriek.

Gwen and the others turned, and her heart sank with dread to see a man emerge from the ashes of the Empire side. The man had been lying face-down on the ground, covered with the bodies of Empire soldiers, and he stood and knocked them off as he rose to his full height.

McCloud.

Gwen felt a shudder. McCloud had somehow survived, having been a coward, taking refuge under the bodies of others, somehow surviving the wall of flames. He stood there with his disfigured body, his face branded, missing an eye, and now, half-burnt from flames, his clothes still smoldering. Yet he was alive, sword in hand, glaring right at his son, Bronson.

Gwen felt a supreme distaste rise up within her. There was a man she loathed with every fiber of her being, the man of her nightmares, the ones she relived every night, the man who had attacked her. There was nothing more she had wished for all these days than to see him dead.

There he stood, at his full height and breadth, which was considerable, a nightmare come to life, the sole survivor of the entire conflagration.

"BRONSON!" McCloud shrieked again, stepping forward into the clearing.

Bronson answered the call: he stepped forward from the MacGil side, his own sword in hand, prepared to greet his father in one last battle.

Mycoples snarled, arched her neck, and prepared to breathe fire on McCloud.

But Thor placed a hand on her, stopping her, as he dismounted and clutched his sword, stepping forward, towards McCloud, to finish him off.

Bronson stepped forward, to Thor's side, and laid a hand on Thor's shoulder.

"It is my battle," Bronson said.

"He attacked my wife," Thor said. "I crave vengeance."

"But he is my father," Bronson replied. "Surely you understand. I crave it more."

Thor stared back at Bronson, long and hard, then finally, understanding, he stepped aside.

"Both of you attack!" McCloud shouted, his voice raspy, "I shall kill you both easily!"

Bronson turned and faced him, and he rushed forward with a great cry, raising his sword high, as McCloud charged back.

Father and son met in the middle of the open field, and Bronson brought his sword down with all his might. McCloud raised his and blocked it with a clang. Sparks flew, and the fight had begun.

Bronson, in a rage, swung his sword around, slashing again and again and again, driving his father back, who nonetheless blocked every blow, and parried back with several of his own. The two of them drove each other back and forth, sparks flying in every direction as the epic fight went on and on, neither gaining an inch, both out for blood. Clearly, the enmity between them ran deep.

Finally, in one quick move, Bronson got the better of his father, knocking the sword from his grasp and stepping forward and butting him in the nose with the hilt of his sword, breaking it.

McCloud reached up and grabbed his nose, gushing blood, screaming, and Bronson kicked him back, knocking him down to the ground.

Bronson stepped forward and McCloud suddenly swept around with the back of his heel, kicking Bronson hard in the back of the knee, making him drop to the ground. McCloud then sat up, swung around, and smashed Bronson in the back of the head with his gauntlet, sending his son face-first in the dirt.

McCloud snatched the sword from Bronson's hand, raised it and prepared to bring it down on Bronson's exposed neck and sever his head.

Gwendolyn, horrified, stepped forward and screamed: "NO!" She could not stand to see Bronson lying there, prone, about to die, this man she had come to love and respect, who had fought so intensely for her cause.

McCloud lowered his sword and a horrific shriek cut through the air, and Gwendolyn flinched, sure it was Bronson's death cry.

But as she opened her eyes, she was shocked to see it was not Bronson who shrieked, but McCloud. He stood there, missing an arm. Thor stood over him, sword out, having just chopped off his arm, right before he could bring down his sword on Bronson.

"That's for Gwendolyn," Thor said to McCloud.

As McCloud sank to his knees, grasping his arm stump, shrieking, Bronson rose and faced him, beside Thor, the two of them staring him down.

"Justice is served, father," Bronson said. "You took my hand. Now yours is taken."

"I would've taken both of your hands if I could," McCloud snarled.

Bronson shook his head, leaned back, and kicked his father in the face, and he went flying back, his head slamming on the ground.

"You won't be taking anyone's hand anymore," Bronson replied.

His father lay there, groaning, and Bronson reached down and retrieved his sword from the dirt.

"He's mine to kill," Bronson said to Thor.

Thor nodded in respect and stepped aside, as Bronson stood over his father, preparing to kill him.

Gwen stepped forward, past all the men, past the stares of all the soldiers, and came up beside Bronson and laid a hand on his wrist.

Bronson turned to her.

"Ask not for compassion for him, my lady," Bronson said.

"I do not," Gwendolyn said. "I've come for vengeance."

Bronson looked back at her, surprised.

"It was my honor that he took," Gwendolyn continued, "and I must set wrongs right. Justice must be done by my hand. Not by yours."

Bronson looked at her long and hard, then finally understood. He nodded and stepped aside.

"Kill the man who haunts your dreams," Bronson said. "Just as he haunted mine my entire life. Once he is dead, may both our nightmares vanish."

Gwendolyn took the sword with both hands, gripping the hilt, squeezing tight. Slowly, she raised it high overhead. Never before had she killed a man, up close, who had lay there, prone. Her hands trembled, even though she knew justice demanded it.

She felt the blood coursing through her veins. The blood of the MacGils; of seven generations of kings; the blood of a ruler of a great people; the blood of someone charged to set wrongs right. She felt an overriding need to rid the world of an evil that never should have existed in the first place.

"You won't do it," McCloud snarled up at her. "You're just like my boy. You don't have the nerve."

Gwendolyn breathed deep and thrust the sword down, straight down, into McCloud's heart, piercing it. The sword continued, through his body, into the frozen ground.

McCloud's eyes bulged open with a look of shock, as he stared up at her in agony and surprise. He remained that way for several seconds, frozen.

Then finally he fell backwards, limp. Dead.

Gwendolyn extracted the bloody sword and held it out before her, as she turned and faced her people. She raised it high.

As one, her entire army, all of her people, knelt before her, and shouted:

"GWENDOLYN!"

CHAPTER TEN

Thor rode on the back of Mycoples, Gwen behind him, clutching his waist. The two of them soared high above the Ring, circling through all the territories, taking it all in from above. They cut through the cool winter air, through parting clouds, but Thor did not feel the cold. All he felt was Gwen, her hands clutching him from behind, holding him tight, and moment by moment, he felt himself restored. For the first time in as long as he could remember, he felt at peace again. He felt that all was right in the world, and he never wanted this moment to end. Gwendolyn behind him, riding Mycoples, Andronicus dead, Thor felt a sense of completeness that he had always hoped for.

They dove down low, nearly skimming the tops of the trees, taking in all the devastation of the Ring, entire lands covered with the charred corpses of Empire. Thor could see how hard at work Mycoples and Ralibar had been, unleashing a wave of destruction unlike any the Ring had ever known.

They flew over ravaged towns and cities, torn apart from the Empire's invasion, fields of MacGil corpses, those brave souls who had lost their lives trying to fend off the invasion. Thor felt overwhelmed with guilt that he had fought on the wrong side for a time. He wished he could make it better, could go back, could make things play out differently. He thought back to the day when he had flown to accept Andronicus' surrender; he had felt in his stomach that something was wrong. He remembered Mycoples' foreboding, her reluctance to land, all the signs that pointed to danger. He realized now that he should have listened. He wished that he never had been caught, his mind never been manipulated, that none of his men had suffered and died as a result.

But it was meant to be. He realized that now. No matter how much he may want things to be different, the world had its own destiny. That was the cruelty of the world. Yet it could also, sometimes, be the kindness of the world, too.

Thor flashed back to the moment before they had flown off, when he and Gwendolyn had embraced all of their people. Many tears of joy had been shed, as Thor, wracked with guilt, had begged their forgiveness. They had been all too happy to grant it: after all, he had not killed any of them, and he had, in fact, done more to kill the Empire than any of them. But he still felt he needed Gwen's forgiveness most of all: he still could not believe he had raised a sword to her. Just the thought of it made him want to kill himself.

Gwendolyn had been gracious. She had not been hurt by him, nor had anyone else, and she was willing to forgive him. She even understood, and recognized that he had been under a spell, one not of his control. Thor had apologized to Krohn, too, who had been all too quick to accept his apology, licking him and jumping into his arms as Thor hugged him back. Thor apologized to Erec, too, for facing off with him, and to Kendrick, and to all the men he'd known and fought with, asking for forgiveness. They had all been quick to oblige, knowing he had been under a spell. Their kindness made Thor feel even more guilty.

Thor had mounted Mycoples, eager to fly her again; the men had agreed they would all rendezvous at King's Court. It had been their original capitol, and now, with the Empire gone, they all concurred there was no more fitting place for them to return to.

Thor had mounted Mycoples, Gwen behind him, and had flown off. Ralibar had taken a liking to Gwen, and for a moment, it seemed that he might even let her ride him; but then he'd suddenly, unpredictably, leapt into the air and taken off, heading in his own direction. Gwen was happy he had: she wanted to ride with Thor, to be close again.

The two of them had been flying now for what felt like hours, taking stock of all the landscapes of the Ring, realizing the immensity of the work that lay ahead of them, of all the rebuilding that needed to be done. Finally, down below, through the clouds, there appeared the vestige of King's Court, and Thor directed Mycoples to dive down low.

Mycoples obliged, breaking through the clouds, flying so low to King's Court that Thor and Gwen could nearly touch its remaining parapets. Thor saw the outlines of the vast complex, of King's Castle, of the Legion training grounds, the halls of the Silver, the Hall of Arms, dozens of buildings, the moats and ramparts and endless dwellings of the extended city—and it broke his heart. Here was a place that had once been so dear to him, so resplendent, the very backbone of the kingdom, the bastion of strength, of everything that Thor knew to be power. Here was the place he had always aspired to, the place he had first met and trained with the Legion. It was the place that had once loomed so indomitable in his mind.

And now here it lay: in ruin, a fragment of what it once was. Thor could hardly conceive that anything so powerful could be reduced to this. The foundations remained, the remnants of stone walls, the outline of the greater city; there was certainly a foundation left to build on. But most of its great, ancient stones and statues were toppled in heaps of rubble. Only half of King's Castle stood.

"Seven generations of MacGils," Gwendolyn said, shaking her head, "all wiped out because the Shield had been lowered, because the Sword had been stolen. It all started with her brother, Gareth. And now there lies my father's kingdom. Gareth always wanted to destroy our father: and now, somehow, he has."

Thor could feel her tears down the back of his neck.

"We will rebuild it," Thor said.

"Yes, we will," she replied confidently.

As they dove down lower, circling again and again, this place brought back so many memories for Thor. Here was a place he had been afraid and intimidated to enter as a boy, its gates and powerful sentries looming larger than life. And yet now here he was, no longer a boy, but a man, riding on the back of a dragon, the head of the Legion and already one of the Kingdom's famed warriors. It was hard for Thor to process all that had happened in his life, and so quickly: it was surreal. Was anything in life, he wondered, stable? Was everything always changing, shifting? Was there ever anything that one could really hold onto?

The sight below brought Thor great sadness—yet it also brought him great hope. Here was a place they could build again, a place they could make even more resplendent. With the Empire finally gone, the Ring finally secure, Thor felt every cause for hope. They were all alive and safe, and that was all that mattered. The stones, they could all go back to the way they had been. And with Gwendolyn at his side, Thor felt that anything was possible.

Thor felt his mother's ring, bulging inside his pocket, and he knew the time had come to propose. The time had come for them to be together, forever. He did not want to wait another moment. He opened his mouth to speak.

"Set down there," Gwendolyn suddenly called aloud to Mycoples. "I see the knights approaching."

Thor looked down and saw the men traveling down the road, beginning to filter in through the gates of King's Court. Mycoples dove down, as Gwen had requested.

They landed right before the incoming army, Mycoples setting down in the center of the courtyard, the men rushing out to greet them. Thor knew that his moment to propose was gone. But it would come again. He'd be sure of it. Before the day had passed, he would find a way to make Gwendolyn his wife.

CHAPTER ELEVEN

Luanda marched and marched, exhausted, weak from hunger, freezing, feeling as if her trek would never end. She couldn't allow herself to stop. She had to make it back, to her homeland, to Bronson. She was still reeling as she thought how lucky she had been to escape, what a close call it had been. She had been looking over her shoulder the entire march back, still fearing that somehow, maybe, Romulus would find a way to take down the Shield, to follow her, to grab her and bring her back.

But he was never there. He was gone now, the Shield was truly up, and Luanda had been safe marching, all this way, through the wasteland of the Ring, determined to make it home. She was relieved, yet she also felt a sense of dread. Would her people take her back in, after all she had done? Would they want to kill her? She could hardly blame them. She was embarrassed by her own actions.

Yet she had nowhere else to go. This was the only home she knew. And she loved Bronson, and ached to see him again, to apologize in person.

Luanda was remorseful for what she had done, and she wished it could have been otherwise. She wished she could take it all back, could do it all differently. Looking back on it now, she didn't understand what had come over her, how she had allowed her ambition to overcome her. She had wanted it all. And she had failed.

This time, she had learned her lesson; she was humbled. She did not yearn for power now. Now, she just wanted peace. She just wanted to be back with her people, in a place to call home. She saw firsthand how bad life could be with the Empire, and she wanted to get as far away from ambition as possible.

Luanda thought of Bronson, of how much he had cared for her, and she hated herself for letting him down. She felt that if there was anyone left that might forgive her, might take her back in again, it was he. She was determined to find him, not matter how far she had to march. She only prayed he was still alive.

Luanda came upon the rear camp of the MacGils, all of them marching towards King's Court on the wide road leading West, thousands of men, exhausted but jubilant, fresh off their victory. She was thrilled to catch up with them, to see that they had won, and she weaved her way through, asking each if they knew where Bronson was. She asked them all the same thing: if they had seen him, if he was alive.

Most had ignored her with a grunt, turning away from her, shrugging, ignorant. And those that recognized her, sent her away with disparaging remarks.

"Aren't you the MacGil girl? The one who sold us all out?" asked a soldier, elbowing his friends, who all turned and examined her with scorn.

I am a member of the MacGil royal family, the firstborn daughter of King MacGil. You are a commoner. You remember that and keep your place, she wanted to say. The old Luanda would have.

But now, humbled and ashamed, she merely lowered her head. She was no longer the woman she once was.

"Yes, that is I," she answered. "I am sorry."

Luanda turned and disappeared back into the camp, weaving her way in and out, until finally she tapped yet another soldier on the shoulder, and as he turned, she prepared to ask him if he knew were Bronson was.

But as he turned she stopped cold.

So did he.

All around him the men kept marching, yet the two of them stood there, frozen, staring at each other.

She could hardly breathe. There, facing her, was her love.

Bronson.

Bronson stared back at Luanda in shock. She stood there and, for several seconds, she did not know if he would hate her, send her away, or embrace her.

But suddenly his eyes welled with tears and she could see relief flood his face, and he rushed forward and embraced her. He held her tight, and she embraced him back. It felt so good to be in his arms again, and she clung to him as she began sobbing, her body wracked with tears, not realizing how much she'd held in, how upset she was. She let it all out, crying, ashamed.

"Luanda," he said, holding her. "I love you. I'm so glad you're alive."

"I love you too," she said through her tears, unable to let go, to back away.

She pulled back and, unable to look into his eyes, lowered her head, tears rolling down her cheeks.

"Forgive me," she said softly, unable to meet his gaze. "Please. Forgive me."

He embraced her again, holding her tight.

"I forgive you for everything," he said. "I know it wasn't the real you."

She looked up and met his eyes, and she saw that they did not look at her with scorn. She could see that he still loved her as much as the day she had met him.

"I knew that you were just caught up in the grips of something," he continued. "Ambition. It overwhelmed you. But it wasn't you. It wasn't the Luanda I know."

"Thank you," she said. "You're right. It wasn't me."

She smiled, breathing deep, collecting herself as she wiped away her tears.

"And what of the others?" she asked nervously. "Thorgrin? My sister? Are they alive?"

She knew that if the answer was no, she would face an angry mob who would blame it on her and want her dead.

Bronson smiled and nodded back, and as she saw his face, she was overwhelmed with joy and relief.

"They are indeed," he replied. "They have all gone to King's Court, which is where we head now. I am sure they will accept you back."

He took her hand, but she stopped and pulled it away, shaking her head.

"I am not so sure," she said. "How can they ever trust me again?"

"That's her," came a dark voice.

Luanda turned to see several soldiers approaching, one pointing at her.

"There's the MacGil girl," he added. "The one who betrayed Thor."

A group of soldiers marched forward and grabbed Luanda from behind, quickly, before she could react, and began to bind her wrists with rope.

"What you doing?" Bronson called out, indignant, approaching them. "That is my wife!"

"She is also a traitor," the soldier replied firmly. "The one who sold out our army. She is under arrest. It is for the queen to decide her fate—not us. And not you."

"Where are you taking her?" Bronson pressed, blocking their way. "I demand for her to have an audience with the Queen!"

"An audience she will indeed have," they replied. "But as a prisoner."

"No!"

Bronson lunged forward to free her, but a group of soldiers blocked his way and drew their swords.

"Bronson, please!" Luanda cried out. "Let it go. They are right to take me. Please don't fight them. They've done nothing wrong."

Bronson slowly lowered his sword, realizing they were right. In a just society, justice needed to be served. There was nothing he could do about it. He loved Luanda; but he also served the queen.

"Luanda, I will talk to her for you," Bronson said. "Do not worry."

She opened her mouth to speak, but the soldiers were already taking her away, to the distant horizon, to King's Court. It was a city that Luanda had once entered as royalty—and now, ironically, she would enter as a prisoner. She did not need honors anymore; she only prayed her sister would allow her to keep her life.

CHAPTER TWELVE

Gwendolyn walked through the remains of King's Court, accompanied by Thor, her brothers Kendrick, Reece and Godfrey, and flanked by Erec, Steffen, Bronson, Srog, Aberthol and several new advisors, the large group taking stock, surveying the damage that had been done to this once-great city. Gwendolyn's heart broke as she walked through this city she had been raised in, this city that embodied her childhood. Every corner was haunted with memories, time she had spent here with her father, her brothers, the places she had learned to ride a horse, to wield a sword, to read the lost language. It was the place where she had learned to leave childhood behind.

It was all changed now, a place she barely knew. The bones of it were there, remnants of stone walls, charred by dragon's breath, crumbling buildings, traces of ramparts. The ground was still littered with corpses, and she held back tears as she walked between them, all the brave Silver and MacGils and Silesians who had died for their country, making a heroic stand against the Empire. She was in awe at their bravery, at what they had sacrificed.

"They all put up a stand knowing it would mean their lives," Gwen said aloud as she walked, the others listening. "Yet they made a stand anyway. This is the very height of courage. These are the great heroes of the Ring. The unknown and unnamed fallen warriors all around us. It is to them that we owe our greatest debt."

There came a grunt of affirmation from among the warriors as they walked with her. Gwen was overcome by the honor and courage that ran in her people's veins, and she felt a huge responsibility to live up to it, to be as honorable and fearless a leader as her people deserved. She hoped she could.

"Our first task must be to honor our dead," Gwendolyn said, turning to her entourage. "Summon all of our people to collect all of these bodies, and to prepare them for a great funeral pyre, which we shall have tonight. The corpses of the Empire can be discarded in the fields, beyond the walls of the outer ring of our city, where they can be eaten by the dogs."

"Yes my lady," one of her generals said, turning and hurrying back to the crowd, dispatching officers immediately to do her will. All around them soldiers broke into action, as they began to collect the dead. Gwendolyn could not look at their faces anymore; she needed the city cleared of them to not be haunted.

They finished circling the perimeter of the inner courtyard, past the toppled statue of her father, past the fountain which no longer bubbled, and Gwen paused beside it. She looked down at the huge stone figure of her father, now lying in several pieces, and was inflamed with rage at Andronicus and the Empire.

"I want my father's statue rebuilt," she commanded. "I want the fountains around him bubbling again, and I want this walkway lined with flowers."

"Yes, my lady," said another of her men, hurrying off to do her bidding.

"But my lady," one of her new advisors said, "would it not be more appropriate for there to be a statue of you up here now? After all, this is the center of King's Court, and this is where the ruler's statue stands, and you are our ruler. Your father is no longer with us."

Gwen shook her head.

"My father will always be with us," she corrected, "and I do not need a statue to honor myself. I would rather remember those whose shoulders we stand on."

"Yes my lady," he said.

Gwendolyn turned and saw the approving eyes of all of her men, and her eyes rested on Thor's. More than anything, she just wanted time to walk with him alone. The two of them never seemed to have enough time alone together, and there was something she needed to say to him. She was burning to tell him about her pregnancy. About *his* baby. She felt the baby flip in her stomach even as she thought of it.

Soon, she told herself. When all of this was done, all these affairs of state, all settled down, she would tell him. Perhaps even tonight. She felt a rush of excitement just thinking about it.

They continued circling the courtyard, until finally they reached the doors to King's Castle. Gwendolyn looked up, and felt a pain in her stomach at the sight. It had once been the finest castle in both kingdoms, sung of, praised by poets, even outside the Ring. It had been the seat of MacGil Kings for seven generations, the seat of her own father.

Now there it stood, half destroyed, half its walls standing, the other half open to the sky. She could hardly fathom it, how something of this height and breadth could be damaged. It had always seemed so impervious to her. It felt like a metaphor for the Ring: half of it destroyed, and half of it still standing, a foundation on which to rebuild. A daunting task lay ahead of her, not just here but everywhere, in every town throughout the Ring.

Gwen breathed deep as she surveyed it, and she felt inspired by the challenge.

"Let us go inside," Gwen said to the others.

Her entourage looked at her with a flash of concern.

"My lady, I do not know how stable it is," Kendrick said. "Those walls, they could collapse."

Gwen slowly shook her head.

"It was our father's castle, and his father's before him. It has lasted for centuries. It will hold us."

Gwen boldly stepped forward, and the others followed close behind. They walked through the massive stone and iron gates, one of them intact, the other hanging crooked on its hinges. The portcullis lay burnt and twisted on its side, now but a relic.

The wind whistled through as they walked, no sound heard but that of their footsteps crunching on gravel. They passed beneath a tall stone archway and Gwen expected to find the ancient oak, carved doors that had marked the entrance to the castle. But they were gone, torn off their hinges, stolen. It pained Gwen to see. They were doors Gwen had walked through nearly every day of her life.

They all entered the main chamber, and Gwen felt a draft, and looked up at the gaping holes in the high, tapered ceilings, letting in winter sunlight and gusts of cold. Their boots echoed in this empty hall, piles of rubble everywhere. But beneath the dirt and rubble, Gwen could still spot the original marble floors. She also saw that many of the frescoes still remained on the walls, covered by dirt.

They crossed the chamber, a trapped bird fluttering on the ceiling, and Gwen walked up a series of stone steps, wide enough to hold them all side-by-side, its railings gone. The steps felt sure, and she ascended, unafraid.

They continued down corridor after corridor, holes in the walls letting in sunlight and cold. The walls caved in in places, but the structure seemed intact. As they went, they passed scattered corpses of soldiers, men who had fought bravely, hand-to-hand, giving their lives to defend this place.

"Make sure these men are collected, too," Gwendolyn commanded.

"Yes, my lady," said one of her attendants, hurrying off to do her will.

One corpse hung over the stone railing, eyes wide open, staring up into the sky. Gwen reached over and gently closed his eyes. She had seen so much death these last few days; she did not know if these images would ever leave her mind.

They continued down several more corridors until finally they reached the main doors to the Great Hall, the hall her father had used, had spent the greater part of his day, surrounded by counselors and generals, making decisions and passing judgments, running the daily business of the Western Kingdom. The grand council table had been destroyed, lying in rubble in the center of the room. But Gwen took heart as she saw the ancient golden doors that had heralded this room were still there. She stepped up, feeling their hinges, running her hand along the ancient carvings on the door, made centuries ago, the handiwork of the first architect of the Ring, one of the greatest treasures of this castle. Gwen felt a burst of hope. She turned and faced her men.

"We shall build a new council chamber around these doors. And around that chamber, a new castle to hold it—and around that castle, a new King's Court!"

The men cheered in approval.

"We shall find a new craftsman," she added. "As fine as the man who carved these doors. And he shall adorn every inch of King's Court. No expense shall be spared. These doors will be a shining symbol for all who come here that the Ring is strong. That it will always be strong. That it can be rebuilt."

The men cheered, all looking to her with hope, and she could see she inspired confidence. Gwen could feel that they needed a leader at this time, and she was determined to give these great people whatever it was they needed. These people were all like family to her. Maybe her father had been right after all: maybe she had been meant to lead.

They all passed through the doors and entered what remained of the castle chamber, walking amidst piles of rubble, looking up at the broken stained-glass that lined the walls. Some of the windows were intact, Gwen noticed; others were gone forever.

Gwen walked down the center of the hall, right up to the great throne, where her father had sat countless times, and examined it. It was still intact, she was relieved to see, its seven ivory and gold steps still leading up, its wide arms still lined with gold. It was all covered in layers of dirt, yet still it was recognizable.

Steffen hurried forward and wiped the dirt off the seat, off its arms, until the gold shone through once again.

"Please sit, my lady," he said, stepping aside.

Gwen hesitated, unsure.

"It was my father's throne," she replied.

"It is your throne now," Kendrick said, stepping forward. "The people need a leader. The people need you. Please, sit. Father would want you to."

Gwendolyn looked to Thor, who nodded back at her.

"Sit, my love," he said reassuringly. "Sit for all of us."

Gwendolyn took strength in Thor's presence, and in the presence of all the others. She realized they were right. It was no longer about her: it was now about something bigger than her.

Gwen slowly ascended the ivory and gold steps, her boots clicking in the empty hall as she went, until finally she reached her father's throne. She turned and sat on it.

From up here she looked down at all these great men who had accompanied her, and as one, they all knelt before her.

"My Queen," they all said as one.

"Rise," Gwendolyn said.

Slowly, they stood.

"I may be a Queen, but I am merely my father's daughter. You need not kneel for me. This was my father's seat: I sit on it only out of duty to him."

"Yes, my lady," they said.

"Excuse me, my lady," Aberthol said, stepping up, "but there are many urgent matters of state that must be attended to. What better time and place than here and now to address them, while we are here in the council chamber?"

"My father never delayed any matter, and I shall not either."

Aberthol nodded, pleased.

"My lady, first and foremost, you will need to name a new council of advisors. Remember your father's old council? Most left when your brother Gareth took the throne. Now is a chance for you to start again."

Gwendolyn nodded, thinking it through.

"I shall honor those who honored my father. Any of his old advisors may join. In addition, Aberthol, you shall be on it; so shall my brothers, Kendrick, Godfrey, and Reece; Thorgrin, you will be on it; and so will you, Erec, Srog, Bronson, and Steffen."

Steffen opened his eyes wide in shock.

"*Me*, my lady?" he asked. "I am but a humble servant. I am a simple man, not an important ruler of the Ring. It is not an honor befitting me to sit on the Queen's Royal Council."

"How wrong you are," she said. "It befits you like few others. You shall sit on my Council and advise me on all matters. There are few men I trust more. Do you accept this honor?"

Steffen lowered his head.

"My lady, it shall be the greatest honor."

Gwendolyn nodded, pleased. It was past due that Steffen had a station befitting his special place in her heart, that his selfless loyalty was rewarded. Given his humility, if anyone deserved to be elevated, it was he.

"Very good, my lady," Aberthol said, "a most excellent choice of council indeed. Now, the most pressing matter of business is the McClouds. With the Empire gone, the McCloud cities sacked, and the McCloud ruler dead, you are ruler now of all that remains of the Ring, of both kingdoms, of both sides of the Highlands. Surely, the McClouds will look to us to lead, to unify. Never before in the history of the MacGils has there been such an opportunity for unification. No MacGil before you has had the power you now have."

"They are disorganized now," Srog chimed in. "Weak. Now might be an opportunity. Now might be the time to attack them, to crush them once and for all and occupy their side."

Kendrick shook his head.

"We must try to unify the kingdoms peacefully. The Ring has seen enough war. Win their hearts at this difficult time, and you will win their loyalty."

"The McClouds are a savage people," Erec said. "No diplomacy, no gestures, will win them. They are who they are, and their nature will not change. They are not us. Pacify them, and they will turn on you. Now is the time to wipe them out. It is the only way to assure true peace in the Ring."

"The McClouds fought for us when we needed it," Bronson reminded.

"Yes, but they only did so because they were also under attack," Erec said.

"Gestures of peace and kindness can be interpreted by some as acts of weakness," Srog said. "Our kindness to them might embolden them to attack us."

The men broke out in disagreement, arguing amongst themselves, and Gwen thought it all over quietly as they did. She wondered what her father would have done if faced with this situation. Then she shook her head and realized that did not matter. She was ruler now. She had to trust herself.

Gwen finally cleared her throat, and the room fell silent.

"There is greater might in love than fear," she said.

The men turned and looked to her, quiet, hanging on her every word. She could see the love and respect in their eyes.

"We must try to make the McClouds love us," she continued. "We must try to unify the two Rings. If we attack , we may occupy them for a while; but not for the long run. Force is short-lived; the greater strength lies in harmony. Which of you would want to make peace with a kingdom that has slaughtered your wives and children?"

All the men looked down, humbled, silent, realizing she had a point.

"Peace may be the harder course," Gwen continued, "but it is the course we must embark on. The McClouds may look upon as an enemy still; but they may also be looking to us for leadership. We must assume the best in them until they give us reason otherwise."

"Yes, my lady," Aberthol said.

"Bronson!" Gwen called out.

Bronson stepped forward, kneeling.

"You have served our kingdom bravely in our fight with the Empire. I owe you an apology. You should have not been mistrusted due to the deeds of my sister."

Bronson bowed.

"Thank you, my lady. All is forgiven. I am grateful to you for taking me in and giving me a second chance."

"To reward your loyalty," Gwen said, "I will give you leadership of the Eastern Kingdom of the Ring. You will rule the McClouds, and you will rule with my name."

"My lady," he gasped, shocked. "Are you certain? I am but a simple warrior."

Gwen shook her head.

"You are far more," she said. "You are the son of a king. And you are a McCloud. The McClouds know and respect you. You know them. Who better to lead them? Embark and cross the highlands and act as my emissary. Show them love and peace, and help them rebuild. Unify our armies."

Bronson nodded quickly.

"As you say, my lady."

"A most wise and tempered decision, my lady," Aberthol said. "Your father would be proud."

He cleared his throat and pulled out another scroll, squinting as he read.

"While we're on the topic of the McClouds, there is another, more unpleasant, matter that needs to be dealt with. Your sister. Luanda. She has been caught."

Gwen gasped. So, her sister, who had betrayed them, had survived after all.

"What shall be her fate?" Aberthol asked.

The men broke into an agitated murmur.

"She must be hanged for her crimes," Srog said.

"She betrayed all of our people," Erec said.

"She betrayed Thorgrin most of all," Kendrick said.

Gwen burned as she thought of it. She turned and looked at Thor.

"My lady," Thor said. "I hold no grudge against her. She is your sister, after all."

Gwendolyn thought it all through, debating. Luanda had been a thorn in her side her entire life. Her ambition was limitless, she had a streak of ruthlessness in her, and Gwen knew that would never change.

"My lady, if I may," Bronson said, clearing his throat, stepping forward. "Forgive me, I do not mean to intrude on affairs not my own. But Luanda is more than your sister—she is also my wife. I do not dispute her faults, or her wrongdoing. And yet, I ask you a favor. I ask for your forgiveness, your mercy, on her behalf. If I have done any good to merit it, please forgive her. It is greater for a leader to show mercy when underserved than to punish when it is."

Gwen paused, debating, seething with conflicting emotions.

"Where is she?" Gwen asked Aberthol.

"She waits outside, my lady."

Gwen thought long and hard, debating. Finally, she nodded.

"Bring her in."

Aberthol whispered to an attendant, who ran from the room. Shortly, he returned, accompanying Luanda, hands bound behind her back with ropes.

The men parted for her as she walked down the center and was placed before her sister. Luanda hung her head low, not even meeting her eyes.

Gwen was shocked at her appearance. She looked much aged. She looked broken. Her head was shaved, her face covered in bruises and scratches. She looked as if she had been through hell and back.

Luanda also wore a look that Gwen had never seen: humility. She continued to look down to the floor, her lips bruised and chapped, her cheeks swollen. Despite everything, she could not help but feel some pity for her.

"Forgive me, my sister," Luanda said, and she dropped to her knees and burst out sobbing. She wept, and as Gwen watched, her heart went to her. She'd always had a rivalry with Luanda—one of Luanda's own making—yet despite that, she had never wished her harm.

"I am ashamed of what I have done," Luanda said. "Not just to you, and Thor, but to the entire Ring. To our family. I do not know what overcame me. If I could take it all back, I would. It is your prerogative to have me killed. But I beg your forgiveness. I do not wish to die."

Gwen watched her sobbing, the room quiet. Gwen sighed, realizing all eyes were on her.

She thought long and hard and realized there was much truth in what Bronson had said: there was more power in mercy than justice. She knew that any good ruler must exhibit both, and weigh both carefully.

"I will pardon you," Gwendolyn said.

Luanda looked up with shock, and hope.

"But your face is not welcome here anymore. I have dispatched your husband to the Eastern Kingdom, and it is with him that you shall go, not to cross to this side of the Highlands ever again, on pain of execution. Not because of what you did to me, but because of what you did to Thorgrin."

Gwen thought Luanda would be relieved to have averted a death sentence; yet to her surprise, she seemed dismayed.

Luanda wept again.

"You are my *sister*," she said. "This is my home. You cannot banish me. I love you."

"No you don't," Gwen said. "It's taken me my whole life to realize that. You love ambition. Not your family."

Gwen nodded, and two of her attendants stepped forward and took Luanda's arms, and led her away.

Bronson bowed.

"Thank you, my lady, for granting her mercy. I shall never forget this kindness."

Gwen nodded back.

"Accompany your wife to the Eastern Kingdom," she said. "Represent me. Our people are counting on you. I am counting on you. A Ring divided will always be weak."

Bronson bowed, turned, and hurried from the room, and a long silence followed.

As Luanda was being dragged from the room, she resisted, bucking.

"No!" she cried. "Don't do this! This is my home, too!"

The men continued to drag her away. Before she reached the door, she turned and yelled out to Gwendolyn one last time.

"You are my younger sister! When we were young, you would do anything for me. What has happened to you?"

Gwen stared back at her, watching her sister's face for the last time, feeling much aged herself, feeling, oddly, as if she were *her* older sister.

"I grew up," Gwen replied.

The doors slammed behind her, and they all stood there in the long, reverberating silence. Gwen saw the glances of the men, and saw that they looked upon her with a new respect. She had made a hard choice.

Gwen was already feeling tired, older, weighed down by her rule; she heard the distant cheer of revelers, and she wanted to be outside, to be anywhere but here. She could feel the baby turning inside her, and she just wanted to be somewhere alone with Thor.

"Is there anything else that is pressing?" she asked Aberthol, hoping the answer would be no. "I would like to go back out and join our people."

"Just one more pressing matter, my lady," he answered. "The fate of Tirus."

Tirus. It all came rushing back to Gwen—his betrayal. She had been foolish to trust him, and because of her trust, many of her men, good men, had died. She felt ashamed—and determined to set wrongs right.

"He was captured, along with his sons. All of them alive," Aberthol said.

"He must be executed, my lady," Kendrick said. "Tirus is a traitor of a different sort than your sister. His treachery is far more insidious."

"You set an example for all traitors, my lady," Erec added.

"Consider it all carefully, my lady, before you perform any hasty actions," Aberthol said. "The Ring will never be truly stable until you put an end to the scheming nature of the men of the Upper Isles."

"As much as we may detest them, we need the other MacGils. Your father knew that—which was why he tolerated them. This might be your chance, my lady, to make history. To unite the two warring MacGil factions, as they once were," Srog said.

"We do not need them," Kendrick said. "They need us."

Aberthol shrugged.

"That was what your father believed," he said. "He chose to deal with them by ignoring them. Yet as you can see, that only left time and room for Tirus to revolt."

Gwendolyn sat there, thinking.

"Where is Tirus now?" she asked.

"He awaits judgment outside this hall," Aberthol said. "This matter of the Upper Isles, of Tirus, cannot wait. It must be resolved now. For the stability of the Ring."

Gwendolyn nodded, sighing.

"Bring him in," she said.

Aberthol sent an attendant, who rushed out the room and returned shortly, several soldiers leading Tirus and his three sons. They were all brought before her.

Tirus was defiant even in captivity, even in his haggard state. He sneered up at her.

"You inhabit my brother's seat," he said scornfully to her. "Yet you are but a young girl."

Gwen was filled with distaste at the sight of her uncle; she always had been.

"I inhabit this seat because I am Queen," she corrected in a confident voice. "The *lawfully* appointed Queen. Because my father, your brother, the lawfully appointed king, placed me here. You, on the other hand, stand before me today because you tried to usurp what was not yours. It is not *I* on trial here, but *you.*"

Tirus' three sons looked to the ground, clearly humbled, yet Tirus, still defiant, turned and looked to Kendrick.

"You are the eldest," Tirus pleaded to Kendrick. "The firstborn of MacGil, and a man, bastard or not. It is you who should rule, if not I. Do something here. Tell Gwendolyn to know her place and get down from that throne."

Kendrick shook his head, staring back at Tirus coldly and gripping the hilt on his sword.

"Watch your tongue around my sister," he said. "She is our Queen, make no mistake about it, and she carries the full authority of our kingdom. Insult her again and you will face my wrath."

Tirus turned reluctantly back to Gwen.

"If it is an apology you want," he said, "you will not get one out of me. The throne you sit on is rightfully mine. It always has been. I was passed over for your father, who was a lesser man than myself."

Gwendolyn felt her cheeks redden at his words, but she breathed deep, remembering her father's advice: never let people know what you're thinking. And never let emotions sway your decisions. There were so many traps to avoid as ruler.

"You are nothing but an ambitious traitor," Gwendolyn said, "a disgrace to the MacGil bloodline. By all rights of our kingdom I should have you executed."

Gwen paused, debating, letting her words resonate in the thick and heavy silence.

"But I shall not. Instead, you shall be banished to live out your days back on the Upper Isles, never to set foot on the mainland of the Ring again. Furthermore, you shall be imprisoned there, under guard of my own watch. You shall live out the remainder of your days in a dungeon cell."

Tirus stared back defiantly.

"Then I should rather you would execute me. I choose that over life in prison."

Gwen smirked.

"You've lost the privilege to choose. The choices are mine now. Justice is done, for the Ring, for my family, and for my dead father. Enjoy your time underground."

Gwen turned to her attendants.

"Get him out of my sight," she commanded.

They rushed to do her bidding, dragging him away, and Tirus screamed and resisted, forcing them to drag him.

"You shall never get away with this!" he screamed, while being led away. "My people are a proud people! They will never allow this indignity! They will never allow their king to be imprisoned!"

Gwen stared him down coldly.

"Whoever said you were King?"

They dragged him outside, screaming, and finally slammed the door behind them.

The room was thick with a heavy silence, and Gwen could feel the fear and respect for her in the room. She also was beginning to feel tougher, stronger, than she ever had. Finally, wrongs were being set right, and it no longer intimidated her to do it.

Gwendolyn turned and looked over at Tirus' three sons, all standing there, staring back, clearly afraid. Two of them looked like the father, and appeared equally defiant. The third, though, with long, curly hair and hazel eyes, seemed different than the others.

"He spoke the truth," one of the sons said. "Our people are as hard as the rocks our island was formed on. They will never abide his imprisonment."

"If your people take affront at the imprisonment of a traitor, then they are not a people who are welcome in the Ring," Gwen replied coldly.

"My lady," Aberthol said, clearing his throat, "I suggest you imprison Tirus' sons as well. They are clearly loyal to their father, and nothing good can come from allowing them to roam free."

"My lady," Kendrick interrupted, "please do not jail the youngest of the sons, Matus. He was instrumental in helping our cause during the war, in freeing all of us and sparing our lives from death."

Gwendolyn studied Matus, who looked different than the other two: he did not have the dark eyes and features of his brothers, and he had more of a proud, noble spirit to him. He did not look like an Upper Islander; he appeared to look more like one of her own people. He even looked as if he could belong to her own family. She remembered all of these boys from her childhood, these distant cousins they would visit once a year, when their father visited the Upper Isles. She remembered Matus' always being apart from the others, kinder; and she recalled the other three as mean-spirited and cold. Like their father.

"Release his binds," she commanded, and an attendant rushed forward and severed the ropes binding Matus' wrists.

"The MacGil blood flows strongly in you," she said approvingly to Matus, "I thank you. Clearly, we owe you a great debt. Ask anything of us."

Matus stepped forward and lowered his head humbly.

"It was an honor, my lady," he said. "You owe me nothing. But if you ask me, then I shall ask you to release my brothers. They were swept up in my father's cause, and they did you no harm."

Gwen nodded approvingly.

"A noble request," she said. "You ask not for yourself but for others."

Gwen turned to her attendants: "Release them," she commanded.

As attendants rushed forward and released them, the two other sons watched with surprise and relief.

Aberthol stepped forward in outrage.

"You make a mistake, my lady!" he insisted.

"Then it is mine to make," she replied. "I shall not punish sons for the sins of the fathers."

She turned to them.

"You may return to the Upper Isles. But do not follow in your father's footsteps, or I will not be so kind the next time, cousins or not."

The three brothers turned and walked quickly from the hall. As they were leaving, Gwen called out: "Matus!"

Matus stopped at the doorway, with the others.

"Stay behind."

The other brothers looked at him, then frowned and walked out without him, closing the doors.

"I need people I can trust. My new kingdom is fragile, and has many positions to fill. Name yours."

Matus shook his head.

"You do me too great an honor, my lady," he said. "Whatever actions I took were out of love—not out of a desire for position. I did what I did because it was the right thing to do, and because what my father did, I am ashamed to say, was wrong."

"Noble blood runs in your veins," she said. "The Upper Isles will need a new lord now that your father is imprisoned. I would like you to take his place and be my regent."

"*Me*, my lady?" Matus asked, voice rising in shock. "Lord of the Upper Isles? I could not. I am but a boy."

"You are a man, who was fought and killed and saved other men. And you have shown more honor and integrity than men twice your age."

Matus shook his head.

"I could not take the position my father held—especially before my older brothers."

"But I ask you to," she said.

He shook his head firmly.

"It would sully the honor of what I did. I did not do what I did to gain position or power. Only because it was the right thing to do. I am indebted to you and humbled for the offer. But it is an offer I cannot accept."

She nodded, studying him.

"I understand," she said. "You are a true warrior and you do the MacGils much honor. I hope that you will at least stay close to court."

Matus smiled.

"I thank you, my lady, but I must return to the Upper Isles. I may not agree with all the people there, but nonetheless it is my home. I feel it is where I am needed, especially in these tumultuous times."

Matus bowed, turned, and walked out the council doors, an attendant closing them gently behind him. As Gwen watched him go, she had a feeling they would meet again; he almost felt like another brother to her.

"Srog, step forward," Gwen said.

Srog stood before her.

"The Upper Isles still need a lord. If you are willing, there are few men I trust more. I need someone who can tame these Upper Islanders. You have ruled a great city in Silesia, and I have no doubt you can keep them in order."

Srog bowed.

"My lady, truth be told, after all these wars, I dearly miss Silesia. I ache to return, to rebuild. But for you, I would do anything. If the Upper Isles is where I am needed, then it is to the Upper Isles that I shall go. I shall rule in your name."

Gwen nodded back, satisfied.

"Excellent. I know you shall do a fine job of it. Keep Tirus imprisoned. Keep an eye on the sons. And get these stubborn people to like us, will you?"

Everyone in the room laughed.

Gwen sighed, exhausted. Matters of court never seemed to end.

"Well, if that is all, then I would like to go and participate—"

Before she could finish the words, the doors to the hall opened yet again, and Gwen was shocked to see two young girls enter, perhaps twelve and ten, followed by Steffen, who nodded to them with encouragement. They were beautiful, simple, proud, and they walked right into the hall of men and stood before Gwen.

"My lady," Steffen said. "Our men were approached by these two young women, who insist they have an urgent message for you."

Gwen was impatient, baffled, feeling pain in her stomach and wanting to leave this throne.

"We haven't time for young girls' games," she said, exasperated.

Steffen nodded.

"I understand, my lady," he said. "Yet they seem very serious. They claim it is a matter of the utmost urgency, and that the entire kingdom is at stake."

Gwendolyn raised one eyebrow, wondering what it could be. The expressions on their faces did indeed seem earnest.

She sighed.

"I do not know what matter could be of such vital importance, that it cannot wait, coming from the mouths of two young girls. But they have survived this war, and that says something. I am sure they know the consequences of wasting the Queen's time. If they remain determined, let them come forth."

The girls turned and looked to Steffen, afraid, and he nodded back with encouragement. They turned back to Gwen and stepped forward.

They looked exhausted from the war, wearing soiled clothing, emaciated, clearly starved from rationing. Gwen could see from the looks on their faces that they were serious girls and bore serious news. As they came close, she also took an immediate liking to them. They reminded her of herself as a young girl.

"My lady," the eldest said respectfully, curtsying and prodding the other to curtsy with her. "Forgive us, but we bear news which cannot wait."

"Well, out with it then," Gwen said, impatient, exhausted, sounding more curt than she'd wanted.

"I am Sarka and my sister is Larka. We live in a small cottage outside the city, with our mother. Some time ago, a man crashed into our home and held us hostage, until we captured him and my father brought him to the authorities. The Empire killed my father, though, and took the prisoner."

The girl took a deep breath, clearly nervous, as if reliving the trauma.

"Some time later, while playing in the fields, I spotted this same man. I would recognize him from anywhere. I am sure it was your brother, my lady. Gareth."

Gwendolyn's heart stopped at the word, and her eyebrows arched in surprise.

"Gareth?" she repeated.

"Yes, my lady."

"My brother? Gareth? The former King?" she asked, in shock, trying to process it all. She had not expected this. Gareth's name had been so far form her consciousness, with everything else going on, that she had nearly forgotten about him. If she had thought of him, she merely assumed he'd been killed in the war.

"We know where he is," Sarka said.

Gwendolyn stood, her body electrified.

Gareth. Her father's assassin. The man who had tried to kill her; who had thrown her brother Kendrick in jail. The man who had escaped justice for far too long, who her father's spirit cried out for vengeance. The man who had stolen the Sword, lowered the Shield, who had set the entire Ring in a tailspin. The man to whom they owed all this calamity.

It was time for vengeance.

"Show me."

CHAPTER THIRTEEN

Romulus stood at the helm of the ship, looking out into the foaming waves of the open sea before him, grabbing onto the wooden rail and squeezing so hard that he snapped it in half. Splinters flew all around him and he grimaced at the open sea, cursing the gods of the land, of the wind, of the sea—and most of all, of war. Cursing his bad fate. Cursing his defeat, the first defeat of in his life.

Romulus replayed in his head, again and again, what had happened, how everything had gone so wrong. He could hardly fathom it. It felt like just moments ago when he'd had that girl, the MacGil girl, in his arms, was across the bridge, had succeeded in lowering the Shield, had watched his men stampede into the Ring. The Ring had been his.

Then it had all gone so wrong, so quickly. Those two dragons had appeared, like a vision from hell, and he'd had to watch all his men set to flame, all his carefully laid plans brought to ruin. Worst of all, that sneaky girl had escaped from his grasp, had crossed the bridge and had reached the other side just a moment before his men could catch her. As she'd landed he'd watched with horror as the Shield came back up, and as all his dreams fell apart.

He had lost. He had to admit it. He'd been forced to retreat, to regroup for another day. He still had the cloak, but with those dragons inside the Ring, with the Empire crushed, and with Luanda on alert, he could not risk going back in to hunt for her. As a good commander, he knew when to attack and when to retreat.

As Romulus sailed, heading back for the Empire, he thought and thought. He needed a new strategy. He needed to gather his men, to solidify his position back home, in the Empire. He had been gone too long, and he could not allow himself to be left vulnerable, as Andronicus had.

There was no room for mistakes now. Romulus had to take control of what he could. He had to forget the Ring. He could not allow it to become an obsession and to become his ruin, as Andronicus had. He needed to learn from Androncius' mistakes.

The Ring was miniscule in relation to the Empire: after all, the Empire still dominated ninety nine percent of the world. And once he solidified his position at home, he could always find a way back in, on another day, to crush the Ring.

As Romulus sailed, huge rolling waves sending the bow up and down, foam spraying all around him, he pondered what sort of traps might be awaiting back home, in the Empire. It would be a tricky path to maneuver, the path to solidify a nervous Empire, to take over Andronicus' spot, to unify all the various armies and worlds, to fill that power vacuum. Others, surely, would be vying for it. But none as ruthless as Romulus. Anyone who stood in his way, he would crush quickly and definitively.

As he stood there pondering, Romulus was momentarily confused; he thought he spotted movement out of the corner of his eye, and at the last second he turned and spotted several soldiers coming up behind them. One held a wire in both hands, and before Romulus could react, the soldier leaned forward, looped it around Romulus' throat, and yanked with all his might.

Romulus gasped for air, eyes bulging from his head, his breathing stopped. The wire was wrapped around twice, and the soldier behind him yanked with all he had. Romulus realized he was being choked to death, by his own people.

Romulus saw his entire ship, dozens of officers, rushing forward. But not to save him, as he thought; rather, to help kill him. It was a mutiny.

Romulus' life flashed before his eyes, flailing, gasping as the soldier squeezed tighter and tighter. He felt that in another moment, he would be dead. He saw his whole life flashing before his eyes, all his victories, and now his defeat. He saw all his conquests, and all the conquests yet to come, and one overriding thought coursed through his mind: he was not ready to die.

Romulus summoned some deep part of himself, and somehow mustered one last burst of strength. He leaned forward then threw his head back, impacting his assailant with the back of his skull, on the bridge of his nose, breaking it.

The soldier dropped to his knees, and Romulus quickly unraveled the wire from his throat, blood dripping as it left a deep wound, his throat bleeding. Because of all of his muscle, the wire had not yet gone deep enough to sever his arteries. Romulus had always been told he had the widest and thickest neck in the Empire—and this proved it.

Romulus did not hesitate: he reached down, grabbed a flail from his waist, spun it high overhead and smashed the soldier in the face before him. He then continued to swing it, the spiked metal ball soaring through the air, and connected with a half-dozen soldiers in a broad circle, knocking them all to the ground as they neared. The others, charging for him, stopped in their tracks.

But he would not let them go. Now Romulus was in a rage, and he charged *them.* He swung the flail over his head, again and again, taking out soldier after soldier, and within moments, took down a dozen more. Many tried to turn and run, but he hunted these down, and they had nowhere to go, smashing them in the backs, their cries filling the air.

A horn was sounded, and hundreds of men came rushing up from below deck. Romulus was relieved; finally, his loyal soldiers would rush to his aide and help put down the mutiny.

But as he saw them all charging right for him, wild-eyed, wielding swords and spears and axes, as he saw the look in their eyes, he realized they were not coming to protect him: they, too, were coming to kill him. This was a well-planned mutiny. Every single man on his ship had turned against him.

Romulus was in a panic. He turned and looked out at the sea, at his vast flotilla of ships filling the horizon, and looked to see if any of the other ships were watching, waiting, were part of the mutiny. He was relieved to see they were not. They were unaware. This was an isolated mutiny, on his ship alone, not spread throughout his fleet.

Romulus thought quickly, as the men bore down on him. He could not kill all of these men alone. He would have to do something else. Something drastic.

Romulus heard the crash of the waves against stone as they passed a lone group of rocks jutting out in the midst of the ocean, and an idea came to him.

There were no men between he and the helm, and Romulus sprinted for it, a lead of a good twenty yards on the others. He grabbed hold of it and spun it frantically, again and again, clockwise—right for the rocks.

The ship lurched, turning hard right, and all the men went flying across the deck, smashing into the side rail. Romulus grabbed on tight to prevent himself from falling, and finally, as the ship was on course for the most jagged rocks, he straightened it out. The men were thrown the other way.

Romulus looked out and saw he had achieved what he had wanted: the ship was now on course for the rocks, only feet away. Too close to change course.

As the hundreds of soldiers regained their footing and began charging him again, Romulus turned, ran for the side rail, jumped up on it and dove headfirst for the water. He soared through the air and landed headfirst in the icy cold waters, plunging deep. He used his momentum to continue swimming underwater, as far as he could, to get away from the spears being hurled after him.

Romulus held his breath a good sixty seconds, as he swam farther and farther away from the ship. He forced himself to stay down below even longer, pushing himself until his lungs were at the point of bursting, until finally the spears stopped and in their stead he heard a faint, distant rumble, the sound of wood smashing against rock.

Romulus finally surfaced, gasping for air, far from the ship, and turned and watched. His former ship was destroyed, impaled by the rocks, waves crashing all around it, smashing it into them again and again. The ship soon took on water and within moments sank vertically; his men shrieked and flailed as they sank into the water, to a cold and frigid death, the waves smashing them against the rocks.

Romulus turned and looked to the horizon. His other, loyal, ships were but a few hundred yards away, and he already set off swimming.

It would take more than a mutiny to kill him.

CHAPTER FOURTEEN

Gwendolyn marched with her entourage of advisors, all of them following the two girls as they led them twisting and turning through the burnt-out back streets of King's Court and finally through the rear gates of the city.

They continued along a narrow path, leading them just outside the city walls, and Gwen was beginning to wonder where they were going, if this were all just a fantasy. Suddenly, they stopped before a structure which Gwen recognized: the crypt of the MacGils.

Ironically, of all the things that were destroyed, this ancient and beautiful crypt, carved of marble, dating back seven centuries, still stood perfectly intact. Somehow, it had escaped the ravages of war. It sat there, built into the hill, half-submerged beneath the earth, its roof covered in grass, rising up in a semi-circular shape. Her father's body had been transferred here after the funeral, and he lay inside, with all of his ancestors.

But why had the girls led them here?

The eldest girl, Sarka, stopped and pointed.

"He's in there, my lady. I saw him enter. And he never came out."

Gwendolyn peered at the entrance of the crypt, disappearing in blackness, baffled.

"Are you sure you are not mistaken?" she asked, doubtful.

"Yes," Sarka answered.

"That is a crypt, young girl," Aberthol said. "That is where bodies are brought to be buried. Why would Gareth come here?"

Sarka shrugged, and began to look nervous as she turned to Gwen.

"I do not know, my lady. But I am certain of what I saw. He went in there and he never came out."

Gwendolyn turned and looked at Thor and Kendrick and Erec and all her other advisors, who stared back at her doubtfully.

"This girl has a fanciful imagination," Kendrick said. "I doubt that our brother, of all places, would choose to take refuge beside our father's corpse."

"Stranger things have happened," Erec said.

"We are wasting time here," Srog said. "Let us move on and get on with affairs of state."

"No," Gwen said. "I want to know. We shall see for ourselves."

Gwendolyn turned and nodded to Kendrick.

"Would you like to see if our brother lies inside?"

Kendrick hurried for the crypt, ducking his head and descending the steps to the blackness.

Aberthol turned to the girls, who seemed increasingly nervous.

"Do you know the punishment for misleading the queen?"

"I know what I saw!" Sarka insisted, "he went—"

They were interrupted by a sudden shout from inside the crypt, followed by the sound of a scuffle down below.

Gwendolyn's men burst into action: Thor, Erec and the others all rushed down the steps, to Kendrick's aid. Gwendolyn peered into the blackness in surprise, wondering what on earth could have happened down there, especially if the crypt were empty. Had he encountered an animal?

Kendrick emerged moments later, with the others, and Gwen was in absolute shock to see him dragging Gareth. It was like a dream.

Gareth emerged into the day like a rat from a hole, looking more pale and sickly than she'd ever seen, looking more dead than alive. Gareth. The former king. Her father's usurper. Alive. Somehow, he had survived.

It all came rushing back to Gwen: Gareth's repeated attempts to have her killed, and her body flushed with a hot rage. Vengeance was long overdue. She studied him, and she saw that her former older brother was gone. He had been replaced by this wasted piece of decaying flesh, nearly unrecognizable from the boy he once was.

Gareth squinted into the sunlight as he looked back at her, arms and body trembling.

Gwen took a step forward and examined him, as the others held his arms.

"So, you live after all," she said with contempt. "What a shame."

Gwen's eyes slowly opened as he scowled back at her, eyes darting, taking in all the men around him with fear. Yet still, somehow, he managed to exude arrogance.

"Guards, arrest her!" Gareth screamed to the soldiers. "I am still lawful King! She has no claim! My lordship was ratified by the council! You break the law to lay a hand upon me!"

The soldiers looked at each other in confusion, yet none made a move towards Gwen. They were all obedient to her.

Gwen shook her head slowly.

"Pathetic to the end," she said to him. "No one here is loyal to you. No one ever has been. You are not a King—you never were. You are merely the assassin of our father. And your day of judgment has come."

Aberthol cleared his throat.

"My lady, if I may," he chimed in. "Technically, Gareth is correct. He was ratified, and the strength of our Ring lies in our upholding our law. Even if we do not reinstate his kingship, we cannot execute him without witnesses to his crime. If we are to follow the strict letter of the law, you have no legal right to kill Gareth."

Gwen studied Gareth, feeling all the eyes of the men on her. It was one of those moments in her reign, she could feel it, all men looking to her to see what she would do. Would she follow the strict letter of the law? It was a moment like this that would let all of her subjects know what sort of leader she would be.

"You are right," she finally replied. "It is against the law. And as such, I shall not have any of my men kill Gareth."

Gareth slumped in relief.

Gwen leaned over, drew the shining sword from Thor' scabbard, a clang ringing through the air, then stepped forward, pulled back her hand, and stabbed her brother through the heart.

All the men gasped, as Gareth collapsed silently to his knees, the sword up to the hilt in his chest.

He fell to his face, his head turned sideways, eyes wide open.

Dead.

Gwen looked up and slowly studied all the faces looking back at her. She could see a fresh look of respect on them.

"There is a time to follow laws," she said. "And a time to write them."

CHAPTER FIFTEEN

Thorgrin walked through the jubilant crowd in the center of King's Court, winding his way through the festivities, thousands of soldiers celebrating in a great throng. The city was in ruin, but one could not tell from the high spirits of these revelers. It warmed Thor's heart to see King's Court alive again with the spirit of his countrymen, all celebrating, all elated to be alive, to be liberated from the Empire.

Having just left Gwendolyn, Thor's mind was consumed by thoughts of her. He had been so impressed by how she had stepped into the role of Queen, handling it all so seamlessly. He had also been impressed by her strength, her courage, her fearlessness, and her wisdom. It took a lot of courage to deal with Gareth—and all the others—the way she had.

Ever since they had returned to King's Court, Thor had wanted nothing more than to be with her, to spend time alone. After the crypt, he thought perhaps he'd have his chance to find time alone with her, to take her away someplace special so he could, finally, propose. His mother's ring was burning in his pocket.

But Gwen had been detained by several advisors and counselors, all pulling her in different directions, needing her to make urgent decisions and pass judgment on various matters. He knew she would be detained for quite a while, and he wanted to give her time and space to handle her matters. In the meantime, he had matters of his own he wanted to tend to.

His sister. Alistair.

Ever since she had saved him on the battlefield and had brought him back to his right self, Thor had desperately wanted to see his sister. He needed to thank her, to know more about her, to find out everything.

Thor could still hardly believe he had a sister in this world. A *real* sister. The thought thrilled him. He could not explain it, but somehow he felt less alone in the world. He wanted to know everything about her, where she hailed from, whether she had ever met their mother, what powers she had, how she was different from him—and how she was the same.

Thor realized he partly wanted to know more about her in order to know more about himself. He still found himself a mystery, and he hoped that she might help solve it.

As Thor wound his way through the crowd of revelers, crossing King's Court as he searched for her, he recognized countless faces of fellow soldiers, men he respected, men he had fought with, and he braced himself, afraid they would all hate him, blame him for the time he'd spent fighting for Andronicus. To Thor's pleasant surprise, everywhere he went he was met, instead, with warm embraces, friendly smiles, with cries of love. People clapped him on the back everywhere he went, calling out his name. He was a hero.

Thor felt the need to apologize for his actions, but the people constantly reminded him of all the good he had done for the Ring, reminded him how he had killed more Empire with the Destiny Sword and with those dragons than any other soldier. He had even killed Andronicus. And even when he faced them in battle, he had never killed any members of the Western Kingdom, but only McClouds. They knew his momentary lapse under Andronicus' spell to be nothing more than a spell out of his control, and they did not blame him for it. On the contrary, they all viewed him as their greatest hero.

Thor spotted Godfrey in the crowd, with Akorth, Fulton and the royal healer, Illepra, with a large welt on his head. Thor went up to him, cringing, afraid the welt was his fault and that Godfrey would be furious with him, remembering the blow of the shield he had dealt him.

But instead, Godfrey smiled wide, threw out his arms and embraced Thor. Thor hugged him back, flooded with relief.

"Please accept my apology," Thor said. "I don't know what came over me."

"I'm not hurt," Godfrey said. "It is merely a lump on the head. Do not apologize, because I know very well what came over you: Andronicus' dark magic. You were not yourself, not the Thorgrin that I knew. Do not beat yourself up: it could have happened to any of us."

"On the contrary," Kendrick said, joining them and clasping Thor's shoulder, "do you not forget that it was *you* who risked his life to venture into the Empire to retrieve the Sword? That it was *you* who volunteered to face Andronicus alone and thus fell into ambush and capture? It was brave and noble of you. And you did it all for the Ring."

Kendrick hugged him and Thor hugged him back. Thor felt his heart warm, felt his waves of guilt starting to dissipate; he was overcome with relief, especially as he had thought of these two men as brothers, and especially as he was about to propose to Gwendolyn. Having her brothers' approval meant a lot. They would indeed be family, the only family he'd ever really had.

All of which made Thor remember the reason he had come here: to speak with his sister.

"Have you seen Alistair?" Thor asked.

"Last I saw," Kendrick said, "she was with Erec, on the far side of King's Court. Check the opposite side of the square."

Thor made his way to the other side of the courtyard, stopping along the way to greet various soldiers. Finally, he reached the far side and he stopped as he saw her there, standing with Erec, engrossed in conversation. Seeing her there was like seeing a part of himself. He suddenly felt nervous. Thor also felt guilty to interrupt them, and was about to turn around and go back, when he noticed Alistair had spotted him, and beckoned him to approach.

As Thor came up to them, Erec turned, too, and his face lit up with kindness. He embraced Thor, and Thor embraced him back, overcome with guilt as he recalled that the last time he had faced him it had been in battle.

"Forgive me, sire," Thor said to Erec, lowering his eyes. "I never meant to face you in battle. I would never mean to harm you. I was not myself."

Erec clasped Thor on the shoulder with one hand and looked into his eyes.

"I take no offense, young Thorgrinson. And a fine fighter you are—the finest I've ever faced. You sharpened my skills on that day."

Erec smiled down at him, and Thor could not help smiling back, relieved.

"I am glad to have you on our side," Erec concluded.

Thor noticed Alistair.

"I do not mean to interrupt," Thor said quickly, and prepared to retreat.

"No," Erec said, "brother and sister should have some time alone. It is *I* who will retreat."

Erec kissed Alistair's hand, turned, and hurried off into the crowd, clasping arms with several soldiers, who rushed forward to embrace him.

Thor was nervous as he turned and looked at his sister, laying eyes on her up close for the first time with a clear and present mind. She stared back at him, expressionless, and for a moment, he did not know what to say. She was stunningly beautiful, and her large blue eyes transfixed him. He could recognize some of his own facial features in hers—the jaw line, the nose, lips, forehead. It was almost like looking into a mirror, but at a female version of himself. Alistair, though, was much more beautiful, having all the fine, delicate features that he did not. As he examined her, it excited him to see that there was someone else in the world that resembled him.

"I don't know how to thank you," Thor said finally, after a long awkward silence, clearing his throat. "You brought me back."

"I only brought you back to yourself," she said. "I did nothing more."

As Thor heard her words, once again he felt a vibration course through him, one that put him at ease, that seemed so familiar, so comforting.

"You are a Druid, like myself?" Thor asked, hesitant.

Alistair nodded.

"We share the same blood," she said.

Thor felt happy, yet sorry for her at the same time. He understood the pain and mystery she must live under, to have Andronicus as a father and to have a mother they'd never met.

"Did you ever meet our father?" Thor asked her, hesitant, not wanting to upset her.

Alistair blinked several times, and Thor could see the idea pained her.

"No," she said, sadly. "Only on the battlefield, when I was with you."

It was strange, but Thor could almost feel her thoughts as she thought them; he almost knew what she was going to say before she said it. It was as if they were the same person.

"I live with the nightmare every day," she added, "of knowing that he is my father. I cannot understand it; nor can I reconcile it inside myself. How can I come from such a monster? Why would our mother choose him? It makes me sick to think of it. Are his traits somewhere inside me? Will they pass on to my children? I would give anything to have a different father; yet this is the father I was given. There must be some reason, some destiny I do not understand."

She sighed, and Thor could see the burden she lived under; it was the same one he shared, and it felt good, at least, to see he was not alone.

"At least now, thanks to you," she added, "he is dead. And I do thank you for it. It takes some of the pain away. So you see, my brother, I have as much to thank you for," she said, smiling.

Thor smiled back. His heart pounded as he braced himself to ask Alistair the next question, nervous to utter the words. Too much was at stake on her answer; he almost didn't speak.

"And our mother?" Thor finally mustered the courage to ask. "Have you met her?"

Alistair looked away, and breathed deep. She fell silent for so long, Thor was unsure if she would even respond.

Finally, she said: "I do not know if I've ever met her or only dreamt of her. My dreams are so vivid, I do not know if they are real, or if they are memories. I still dream of her all the time. She comes to me. She lives in a castle, perched high on the edge of a cliff, overlooking a great ocean. There is a long footbridge that curves and leads up to it. Light shines from the castle, a brilliant light, different colors in different dreams. I always see her, obscured by light. Sometimes she reaches out for me. I can never quite reach her."

She sighed.

"I have had this dream so long, I no longer know if it's real. My entire life I've seen her—yet I've never really seen her."

Thor breathed deep, overwhelmed to hear that someone else had the same experience, even the same dreams, as he.

"It is the same with me," he said.

She looked back at him, eyes wide in shock.

"Then you've never met her, either?" she asked in wonder.

Thor shook his head.

"I must," he said. "I'm determined to meet her. It is a journey I feel called to make. I feel there is some great mystery lurking at the edge of my consciousness, about who I am, who I am meant to be, that I will never fully understand until I meet her."

She gasped.

"I feel the same. Every day I wake up, I feel it, and yet, a part of me is afraid to. The timing is never right. Now is not the time to make the journey; now is the time for me to be at Erec's side. He is my husband-to-be, and we are finally united again, after all these wars."

"I understand," Thor said. "Nor do I want to leave Gwendolyn's side. Something is burning inside me, something greater than I can understand. It is more than just about meeting her: it is about meeting myself."

Alistair nodded.

"Whenever I use my powers," she said, "I feel it is her, coming through me. I feel connected to her. Though they are powers I do not even understand, and sometimes cannot control."

"Nor do I understand mine," Thor said.

"All my life, growing up, I had been afraid of it," Alistair said. "I assumed something was wrong with me, that I was some sort of freak. Others would look at me differently. I would have to leave, to move, to go from town to town. I had many foster families. Few of them were kind."

Alistair sighed.

"Finally, I just stopped using my powers. I suppressed them. It was only recently, when I met Erec, when I fell in love for the first time, that I felt comfortable to use them again. And then, again, once I met Gwendolyn. And then, for you."

Thor understood all of her words, all too well.

"Now I realize that they are nothing to be ashamed of," Alistair said. "They are part of who we are. They are a part of us."

Thor nodded, understanding.

"Do you know where she lives?" Thor asked.

Allison look back, then finally nodded.

"She left me something—" she began to say, but then was interrupted.

"Thorgrin! There you are!" came a jolly voice.

Thor turned to see Reece, standing there, smiling, clasping his shoulder. He embraced Thor, and Thor embraced him back.

Thor was thrilled to be reunited with his friend, but he also turned to Alistair, dying to hear what she was about to say.

But Alistair was backing away, preparing to leave.

"I'm sorry, I did not mean to interrupt," Reece said, looking back and forth between the two, realizing too late.

Alistair shook her head, leaving.

"We shall finish our conversation another time," she said. "I must return to Erec. Until next time, my brother," she said, turning and quickly hurrying off.

Thor was disappointed; he had been desperate to hear what she had to say about their mother, about where she lived, about what she had left her.

Reece was jubilant beside him, eager to talk, and Thor turned to him, overjoyed to see his friend, too.

"I have heard of your journeys, my friend," Thor said with admiration, "to the depths of the Canyon, to retrieve the Sword. I heard of the fine work you've done to save our kingdom. I would expect nothing less of you."

Reece shook his head humbly.

"And I have heard of yours," he said admiringly. Then his face darkened. "I'm sorry I could not be there for you. And I'm sorry to hear what happened to you. You have suffered greatly for all of us. I am thrilled you have returned to us. And I'm glad you are alive!"

They clasped forearms.

"And what of our other Legion members?" Thor asked.

"All alive," Reece answered proudly. "They have all returned with me, and are here."

Thor shook his head in admiration.

"You've done a fine job indeed, to descend to the bowels of hell and return alive."

Reece laughed, and clasped Thor on the shoulder.

"I have exciting news for you, and a question to ask you."

Thor studied his friend, curious; Reece's face was beaming and his smile was contagious. Thor had never seen him this happy, and he wondered what was going on.

"Anything for you," Thor said.

"Will you be my best man?" Reece asked.

Thor stared back, his eyebrows lifted in surprise.

"That's right," Reece added. "I intend to marry Selese."

"Has she said yes?" Thor asked.

"I'm going to ask her now. She does not know yet. But I wanted to tell you first," Reece said.

"I would be honored," Thor said, overjoyed for his friend. "I am so happy for you. You have made a wise choice. My answer is yes, on one condition: if you will be my best man, too?"

Reece looked back, confused.

Thor nodded.

"That's right. I'm asking you to be my brother-in-law. My *real* brother."

"Have you proposed to Gwendolyn?" Reece asked, excited.

"I am about to now."

Reece cried out in joy and embraced Thor.

"It was what I've always wanted," Reece said. "From the day I've met you. For you to be a *true* brother. Nothing makes me happier!"

Thor beamed.

"I am happy for you as well, my friend. Go to Selese. Don't keep her waiting. I wish you luck."

"And you, go to my sister. Perhaps we shall have a double wedding!"

Thor warmed at the thought.

"Perhaps we shall!" he said.

Reece turned and rushed off, and Thor turned and looked back up across the courtyard, inspired, searching for Gwen.

He spotted her amidst the crowd, finally emerging, a cheer greeting her.

The time had come to make her his wife.

CHAPTER SIXTEEN

Reece hurried across the courtyard, making his way past all the revelers, not stopping to celebrate with all of his friends. He was on a mission. He clutched his mother's ring in his palm and walked with single-minded intent, searching all the faces for Selese. His palms were sweaty despite the cold, and his throat was dry. Reece had been single-minded his entire life, quick to decide on everything and quick to follow his passions. He never liked to hesitate, on anything. He decided his best friends instantly, and he decided the girl he loved instantly, too—and he never looked back. Reece already felt he had waited too long, and he was determined not to let anything get between him and asking the love of his life to marry him.

Suddenly, his heart pounded as he considered what might happen: what if she said no? What would he do then? Would he be making a fool of himself? What if, despite saving him, she did not feel as strongly for him as he did her? Was he misreading the situation?

Reece marched on, determined, one way or another, to find out for himself.

After asking several people, Reece finally learned that Selese was with Illepra, the two of them on the far side of King's Court, still tending to the wounded, who had been filtering in throughout the day. The war had ravaged the Ring far and wide, and not everyone arrived back at King's Court at the same pace.

Reece passed through the huge, stone archway that led to the northern side of King's Court, a grass courtyard framed by crumbling stone walls, and as he did, he was shocked at the sight before him: in stark contrast to the revelers on the other side of the wall behind him, before him there were laid out hundreds of wounded. They were lined up in neat rows, moaning, being tended to by dozens of royal healers. It was a humbling sight; Reece was glad he was not among them.

Reece navigated his way in and out of the rows, scanning the faces of the healers, most on their knees, tending to the soldiers. He searched everywhere for Selese. This impromptu infirmary was vast, and Reece was beginning to give up hope—when finally, on the far corner of the courtyard, he spotted her, leaning over a soldier, placing a liquid on his tongue. Beside her was Illepra, tending to a soldier who had lost a leg.

Reece walked quickly to her, and as he did, he suddenly worried if this was the wrong time or place to propose. The atmosphere was so somber and grim, in stark contrast to the festivities in the adjacent courtyard. Selese, too, was hard at work, and he did not want to take her from her duties; she also appeared to be in a somber frame of mind.

Yet still, Reece could not stop himself. He had to be with her, and he was intent on finding out whether she wanted to be with him, too. He felt compelled to show her how much he loved her, to demonstrate to her as much loyalty as she had shown to him. After all, she had saved his life, and had risked her life to do it.

Reece's heart thumped in his chest as he approached her. He knew he could not waste another moment. He had always been taught that the only way to face your fears was to march right up to them—and asking Selese was more terrifying for him than facing a thousand warriors.

Reece approached her as she began to stand from her wounded, wiping her hands on her smock. She looked up and saw Reece approaching, and her eyes lit up with surprise and joy.

Reece came to embrace her, but she held up dirty palms.

"My Lord, I would hug you, but I am hardly dressed for the occasion," she said, smiling.

But Reece did not care; he stepped up and hugged her, and she hugged him back.

"You seem nervous," she said, examining him with a smile.

Reece stood there, staring at her, his heart pounding, unable to say anything. He was unable to smile or do anything, and he suddenly felt awkward. Was he ruining it?

She looked back at him with concern.

"Is everything all right?" she asked.

Reece could only nod, the words stuck in his throat.

Illepra now rose and turned, and she, too, stared at him with a puzzled look.

Reece looked all around, anywhere but back at Selese, and he saw all the wounded and sick, and he knew this was the wrong place to ask her. He impulsively reached down and took her hand.

"Would you come somewhere with me?" he asked.

"Now? Where?" she asked, baffled. "I must tend the wounded."

"There will always be more wounded," Reece replied, tugging her hand. "Come with me. Just for a few moments. Please."

Selese turned and looked at Illepra, who nodded back her approval.

Selese untied her bloody smock, brushed back her hair, and walked with Reece, linking arms, smiling, a bounce to her step as they strode away from the courtyard. Clearly, she was relieved to take a break from her somber duties.

They walked through an arched stone gate, leaving the perimeter of King's Court, and out into the countryside. They walked through a knee-high field of winter flowers, bright white, with large petals, a foot long, swaying in the wind and brushing up against their thighs. These winter flowers were dainty, light as a feather, and each time Selese reached down to touch one, they fell apart, their petals lifting up into the air, carried on the wind, and raining down all around them.

"Aren't you supposed to make a wish on these?" she asked, smiling, as they walked through the field of white, petals twirling all around them.

"My wish has already come true," Reece said, finally able to speak again.

"Has it?" she asked, smiling. "And what wish is that?"

Reece stopped and turned to her, deadly serious.

"That we would be together again."

Selese stopped and stared back at him, and her smile fell.

"You mock me, my lord," she said.

He squeezed her hands earnestly.

"I do not," he insisted, earnest. "I wish for nothing more."

Reece reached out, raised a hand to her cheek, and looked into her eyes with all the seriousness he could muster. He was more nervous than he had ever been.

"Selese, I love you," he said. "I have from the moment I laid eyes upon you, back in your village. From the moment I first heard your voice, I have thought of nothing else. In all my travels throughout the Empire, in all the people I've met and lands I've seen, I have thought of nothing but you. I owe you my life. But more than that, I owe you my heart."

Reece took a knee, held her hands, and looked up into her eyes as he smiled. His heart was pounding so strongly he felt he might have a heart attack.

She looked down, smiling, puzzled.

"Selese," he asked, his throat dry. "Will you marry me?"

Reece reached into his pocket and took out his mother's ring, shining even in the field of flowers.

Selese gasped.

She raised one hand to her mouth, and her eyes filled with tears. She rushed forward and embraced Reece, hugging him tight, her tears pouring down onto his neck.

"Yes," she whispered in his ear. "A thousand times, yes!"

They leaned back and kissed, and they held that kiss for as long as they could, white flowers raining down all around them, Reece not feeling the winter wind, as he finally had everything he ever wanted in life.

CHAPTER SEVENTEEN

Thorgrin made his way through the thick crowd of well-wishers surrounding Gwendolyn, hundreds of soldiers and subjects and nobles and lords and council members, all pressing on her, blocking her from all directions, all wanting to wish her well or to be heard about something. They all clearly looked to her as their queen now. As well they should, Thorgrin thought. Gwendolyn had led them through hard times, had demonstrated self-sacrifice and unwavering leadership, and had suffered travail in her own right, at her people's expense. She had stared suffering in the face, and had not crumpled in the face of adversity. She had led her people to victory and had come out the other side.

Thor recalled what a great king her father had been, and it was clear to him that Gwendolyn was an even greater ruler. He was proud of her, so proud, as he pushed his way through, finding it difficult to even get close to her in this throng. She was clearly loved.

Thor did not want to take her away from all this, but he had to. He could not wait a moment longer. Now was the time to ask her.

"Gwendolyn," he said, coming up beside her, Krohn at his heels.

She turned to him, and others parted ways as he stepped forward and stood beside her.

"Can I steal you away for a while?" he asked, smiling.

She smiled back. She leaned in and whispered in his ear: "I was hoping you would."

Thor's heart beat faster as he reached out, took her hand, and led the way through the thick crowd, their all parting ways for them, Krohn following. Gwen turned to her people, all watching, and said: "Go on, enjoy the festivities. I shall return in a while. Go on! Enjoy!"

There came a cheer from the crowd as the music started again, and the people turned back to themselves.

Thor took Gwen's hand and led her away, the two of them walking faster, both of them giddy, Krohn nipping at their heels, finally breaking free from all of their duties and responsibilities for a time. It was the first time Thor had managed to get time alone with her since landing in King's Court. Thor felt as if they were dating again—and he felt just as elated to be with her now as he did then. He could sense from her grip that she felt the same way, too.

They passed through the high stone gate leading out of King's Court, in disrepair yet still standing, and took the path heading west. This road, Thor noticed, once meticulously paved with stone and gravel, was now littered with holes and overgrown with weeds.

"Where are we going?" Gwen asked, excited.

They rounded a bend and Thor stopped and looked up to the cliffs before them, shining in the sun, and Gwen followed his gaze.

"The Kolvian Cliffs," she said. "But why?"

Thor held his tongue, wondering how much to say. He did not want to give it away. What he wanted to say was: *because it is the high ground, with the most beautiful view in the kingdom, overlooking King's Court. Because it is a quiet and romantic place where we have been together before. Because it is a place that means a lot in our lives. Because it is where I want to ask you the most important question of my life.*

But he could not see any of this. So instead, he said: "There is something up there I'd like to show you."

"*Show* me?" she asked with a laugh. "All the way up there? Is it another pet leopard?" she asked, as Krohn ran before them.

Thor smiled.

"No, not quite," he said.

Thor took her hand, and together they hiked up the cliffs; as they went, he noticed Gwen was more out of breath than usual, and that she stopped to rest more often than she had. He was growing concerned.

"Are you all right, my love?" he asked.

She nodded back to him.

"You keep grabbing your stomach," he observed.

Gwen blushed and looked away.

"I'm sorry. I'm just tired. And I have not eaten. I am fine. Let's continue."

They hiked up the rest of the cliff with renewed energy, until finally they reached the top of the highest peak. As they reached it, they turned and looked out.

Thor was in awe at the vista, and he could see that Gwendolyn was, too. He had seen it many times, and yet it never grew old: there, below them, was King's Court, glorious even in ruin, the afternoon mist embracing it like a shroud. Thousands and thousands of people celebrated, their distant cheers and music audible even from here. It was frustrating for Thor to see King's Court destroyed, yet it infused him with hope: it was both a vision of what had once been, and a vision of what could rise again.

"It's beautiful," Gwendolyn said. "Is this what you wanted to show me?"

She turned and looked all about her, searching the plateau, as if wondering if Thor had some surprise waiting for her.

Thor suddenly became nervous. His throat turned dry, and his heart pounded in his mouth. He reached up and patted the ring inside his coat, to make sure it was still there. It was.

Thor opened and closed his mouth several times, and he felt his knees grew weak. He was wracked with fear. He'd never felt this way in battle, not while facing an enemy. But now, here, facing Gwendolyn, he felt more nervous than he had ever been.

"Well, actually, it's not something I want to show you…but, well, um—"

Thor cut himself off, looking down and kicking the dirt, his heart pounding, having difficulty getting out the words, as his breathing shortened.

"It was—is—um…it was more a kind of, um, well…sort of something I um—"

Gwen laughed. It was a carefree laughter, a sound he hadn't heard from her in what felt like years, and while he was happy to see her so elated, it also made him blush.

"I haven't seen you this nervous since the first time we met," she said.

Thor took a deep breath, finally mustered the courage, and he looked Gwen directly in the eye. What if she said no to him? His whole world would collapse.

"Gwendolyn, I love you," he said, stepping forward and grabbing her hands.

She looked at him, baffled.

"I love you too," she replied. "Have we come all this way for you to tell me this?" she asked, a twinkle in her eye.

Thor shook his head.

"I *truly* love you," he said.

She stared at him, smiling.

"What has gotten into you?" she asked.

Thor shook his head again.

"Gwendolyn, that's not what I'm trying to say."

He cleared his throat, and took another deep breath, and she looked back at him in wonder.

"Are you sweating?" she asked.

Thor reached up and wiped his forehead with the back of his hand, and realized that he was sweating, despite the winter day. He cleared his throat again and faced her. It was now or never.

"Gwendolyn," he said, "you mean the world to me. I want to be with you for the rest of my life. All of my days. I have felt this way ever since the first day we met. I've never seemed to have the right moment to ask you. But now that moment has come. There is only question that means anything to me anymore."

Thor took a knee, reached into his shirt and pulled out his mother's ring. It was spectacular, huge, its precious jewels glowing, sparkling in the sun.

Gwen's eyes grew wide in wonder as they flooded with tears.

"Gwendolyn," Thor continued. "Will you marry me?"

Gwendolyn rushed forward, into Thor's arms, and she hugged him so tight, he could barely breathe. He stood and hugged her back, and she cried and cried, hot tears flooding his neck.

"Is that a no?" he said.

"Yes," she said in his ear. "Yes yes yes yes yes!"

Gwen leaned back and kissed him all over his face, and he kissed her back, again and again.

Finally, he smiled, looking down.

"You forgot to take the ring," he said.

Gwen laughed, and as she leaned back, he placed his mother's ring on her finger.

She looked at in awe.

"It fits perfectly," she said. "Where did you get this? I have seen royal jewels all my life, yet I have never seen anything like this."

"It was my mother's," Thor said. "It is meant for you. For you, and none other."

Gwen looked up at him, her eyes filled with tears, and they kissed. They held the kiss for as long as they could, and finally, they embraced, holding each other tight.

"Thorgrin, my love," she said softly, pulling back and looking at him. "There is something I wish to tell you, too."

She pulled back and looked into his eyes, and Thor looked at her and wondered what it could be.

"There was a reason it was hard for me to climb these cliffs," she said. "A reason that I have not been myself."

She reached out and held both his hands and smiled.

"Thorgrin: I'm with child."

Those words struck Thorgrin through the heart, coursed through his whole body, made him lose all sense of time and place. He was beyond elated. He felt as if he were part of something bigger than himself, something deeper in the universe. He felt his entire world spinning. He was overwhelmed with joy and gratitude.

"A child?" he asked.

She nodded, smiling.

He looked down at her stomach, and gently rested his palm on it. As he did, he felt an incredible energy racing through his entire body. He could feel the child spinning and moving, the slightest tremors in his palm. He felt a love and joy beyond what he ever thought capable of experiencing.

He embraced Gwendolyn, hugging her tightly, and she hugged him back.

"I love you," he whispered into her ear.

"I love you, too," she whispered back.

Thor draped an arm around her shoulder and pulled her tight, and the two of them turned and looked out at the vista, both suns sitting low in the horizon, King's Court awash in scarlet and violet twinkling in a thousand points of light. It felt to Thor like the Ring was being reborn, slowly coming back to life. All around them winter flowers bloomed, fields glowing white, and against the backdrop of the second setting sun, it was the most beautiful thing Thor had ever seen. It was an ideal moment, the perfect moment for his proposal, and he wanted to freeze it forever. It was magical. Just like his entire relationship with Gwendolyn.

As they looked out at the horizon, at the distant road to King's Court, Thor saw an endless caravan of humanity coming towards this city from all directions, some on foot, others leading horses, carts, cattle. They were all heading to the same place, all coming to celebrate the new Ring, all coming to celebrate hope.

"A stream of humanity," Thor observed. "People of all walks want to come back to King's Court, to celebrate. They all have faith in you."

"We will rebuild it," Gwen said. "Stone by stone. We shall make it as great a city as it ever was. And the centerpiece of all the celebrations will be our wedding. It will be the most magnificent wedding the Ring has ever witnessed. It shall be followed by our baby. Everything will be new again, and our people will rise from the ashes. We will do it together. Our love will build it."

They leaned in and kissed, and they held the kiss as the final light of the setting sun washed over them. Thor only wished he could hold the world this way forever.

SIX MOONS LATER

CHAPTER EIGHTEEN

Gwendolyn soared high in the air as she rode on the back of Ralibar, clutching for dear life, as she always did when she rode him, trying to predict his unpredictable temper. Ralibar dipped in and out of the clouds, dove up and down, snorting, sometimes even arching his back. He was the most strong-willed and temperamental creature she had ever met, and she could feel his emotions flaring within him.

Gwen was honored that Ralibar even let her ride him. She had discovered, moons ago, his fondness for her. Whenever Thorgrin went to ride Mycoples, Ralibar would become jealous and territorial, and would snort and shriek at Thor, trying to scare him away. Ralibar and Mycoples would stand off with each other, and it had been getting progressively worse—until one day, Gwendolyn had accompanied Thor to see him off, and they had all been shocked as Ralibar had turned to Gwendolyn, had lowered his head and, while first examining her suspiciously, had then leaned in and stroked her stomach with his face. Ralibar had purred softly, and for the first time ever, he had calmed.

Thor had watched in shock as Gwendolyn had reached up and stroked Ralibar's face, nervous as she felt his rough scales, ancient and a little bit moist. Ralibar had then shocked them all even more by lowering his head all the way to the ground, a gesture meant for Gwen to ride him.

Gwendolyn had mounted him nervously, not sure what to expect. It had been a wild and crazy ride, and she was uncertain whether he actually wanted her on or not. Yet, still, he had sought her out every day since and had gestured for her to keep riding him.

For a beast who was clearly endeared to Gwendolyn, Ralibar had a funny way of showing it. From the outside, it might even seem as if he hated her. He was a moody and tempestuous creature, perpetually in some sort of emotional storm, whether at himself, or humans, or other dragons. Gwen felt compassion for him: she got the feeling that he was a loner, a malcontent, yet she sensed that, beneath it all, Ralibar had a big heart, and that he might just be lonely. He flew erratically, and often acted as if he wanted Gwen off of him; yet when she tried to dismount, he threw a fit, and thus clearly wanted her to stay.

Despite all his craziness, Gwen had taken a liking to him; he had an odd way of getting under her skin. Over these last several months, Gwen had grown accustomed to his moods, and had learned to read his signs. The bond between them grew ever stronger, and it made Gwen feel happy in a way she had not expected. She even sensed Ralibar's moods starting to calm.

On this beautiful summer morning, in the picture-perfect weather, both suns shining, Gwen took her morning ride, as she always did. Nearby, Thorgrin rode Mycoples, the two of them lifting up into the air in the early morning sky, as they always did together, launching off from the top of King's Castle, their dragons intertwining as they flew. They had developed a morning ritual, and they followed it today: they circled the grounds of King's Court, then circled the towns and villages surrounding it, Gwen surveying her people, her kingdom, every single morning, to make sure all was in order.

Gwen loved this time together with Thor and with Ralibar and Mycoples, the most magical mornings of her life, watching the suns rise, watching the mists burn off the land below in all different colors. It also afforded her a bird's eye view of her kingdom, and more than once she had spotted some trouble down below that she would have not seen otherwise, which made her convene her council and set wrongs right. She had spotted fires, small villages dilapidated, people injured or struggling with their horses and carts, roads in disrepair…an endless number of small fixes to her kingdom. It allowed her to be an omnipresent queen. It also was reassuring for her people to look up and see her every morning, watching over them, setting wrongs right, riding on the back of a dragon. It enforced her image as a woman of power.

Gwen had never anticipated that she would fall so comfortably into the role of queen. But now that six moons had passed since the expulsion of the Empire and her peoples' return to King's Court, since she had begun the process of re-establishing her rule, she had found that being queen came naturally to her. It had been the most glorious six moons of her life. She had grown closer to Thor than she could ever imagine, the two of them finally having a chance to be together every day and night, sleeping in her former parents' chamber, in the castle, which she had painstakingly rebuilt.

Most glorious of all, she was now nine months pregnant, and her belly protruded more than she could ever imagine; she felt on the verge, any day, of giving birth. Her baby moved inside her all the time, and she felt his presence with her every moment, as if he were out there in the world with her right now.

She had not let it slow her down, however. Every day she had been focused on rebuilding, with Thor, her council, all the people she loved and trusted at her side, all working like an army to make King's Court as magical and resplendent as it had once been. Gwen was determined that King's Court become more than just a city: she wanted it to become a beacon of hope and optimism for all the survivors of the Ring. She wanted it to be a testament that they would all come back, even stronger than before.

To her amazement, she had succeeded. As Gwen looked down, circling the city, the summer wind in her hair, she was awestruck at how beautiful King's Court had become. It shone in the sun, completely rebuilt and bigger than before, sprawling now for miles in each direction, greatly expanded. It was a greater and more foreboding city than her father had ever dreamed of. She had managed to double in size everything her father had done, adding bigger ramparts, turrets, forts, moats, widening roads, thickening city walls…. King's Castle soared higher than ever, the Hall of Arms and the Hall of the Silver were rebuilt, and even the Legion grounds were back to what they once were. Thousands of her people had worked night and day to bring it back to life. Looking at it now, one could not tell it was ever destroyed.

The work went on, as it did every day, and even from up here there could be heard the perpetual sound of chisels and anvils and hammers ringing through the air. It was the sound of progress, and it was a part of daily life in King's Court now. As Gwen looked below, the sight amazed her anew each day, and she could hardly believe what she had accomplished. It made her feel that anything was possible. It made her realize that even if she reached the lowest and darkest times of her life, it was still possible to bounce back from anything—and make life even greater than it ever was.

As Gwen circled with Ralibar, she wondered what her father would think if he saw all this. Would he be proud? She had a feeling that he would. He had chosen her to rule, after all, and this would all be a testament to his choice. She wished more than anything that he was alive now to witness all this, yet she felt that he was watching with satisfaction.

Gwen directed Ralibar to dive down to the left, and Thor followed on Mycoples. She flew over the outer ring of King's Court, a new vast courtyard, replete with formal gardens and bubbling fountains, brand-new walls and arches. Gwen had it built of a shining white marble, mined from an ancient quarry, and it was, to Gwen's eyes, the most beautiful part of King's Court, this new courtyard which had never existed before. It was hard to imagine it now without it.

Even more exciting was the activity taking place down below, hundreds of workers scurrying about, working furiously to prepare for her wedding. They had been preparing for six moons, and the wedding had grown into a bigger and bigger affair. Scores of workers draped flowers of every color along the ancient stone walls, while others lined up thousands of chairs alongside a long red velvet aisle which was being rolled out. An altar was being constructed at the end of it, bedecked in flowers of every sort.

With the wedding just a half-moon away, people were already pouring in from all corners of the Ring, from both sides of the Highlands, from the Upper Isles—and even from countries outside the Ring, a steady string of dignitaries visiting from lands far away. They had sent delegations and had crossed the ocean, and Gwen had the Shield lowered long enough to let them cross the Canyon. Gwen looked out at the wide road leading to King's Court, and she saw, as she did every day, thousands of people heading for King's Court. They wore brightly colored robes of every color and fashion, from every corner of the world.

Today was the day of the summer festival, the first reaping of fruits, and they all poured in to celebrate. There would be festivals and revelries unlike any other, lasting for days, especially as they were also coming to celebrate the new capital of the Ring, and to attend her wedding.

Gwen felt butterflies at the thought. The wedding was nearly here, but a half-moon away. She felt her stomach flipping, and she hoped and prayed that the baby did not come before then. Over the last six moons, she and Thor had grown ever closer, and she could hardly wait to be married to him. She looked down and glanced at his mother's ring shining on her hand, as she always did, and felt an amazing energy radiating off of it.

Ever since Thor had killed Andronicus, he had been like a different person. He seemed as if he had found some sort of peace within himself, and he had settled into domestic life with Gwendolyn quite well. He had thrown himself into the rebuilding of King's Court, and of the Ring, and had trained every day with his fellow warriors, taking joy from their presence.

Ralibar suddenly jerked to the right and dove down unexpectedly, and Gwen held on tight as she felt her stomach plunging. She could sense by his movements that he was ravenous for his morning breakfast. She hugged his neck and leaned low as he turned for the forest, diving between the trees, scanning left and right for a meal.

"Ralibar, stop!" she commanded. "Not now!" she yelled, annoyed at his ravenous appetite.

But Ralibar, as usual, ignored her. He swerved in and out of the trees until he focused on a target, opened his great jaws, and snatched up a huge red deer.

Gwendolyn turned, hating to watch.

Ralibar lifted it in its jaws, then flew back up into the air, carrying the animal, protesting in its mouth, until he threw back his head and swallowed it.

Ralibar then set his sights back on the ground, and Gwen had a sinking feeling he was going to plummet again.

"Ralibar, NO!" she screamed.

He again ignored her. This time he set his sights on a lake, King's Lake, his favorite. He never missed an opportunity to skim it.

Ralibar dove low, Gwen clutching him, and as he neared it, he opened his mouth and breathed a wall of flame.

The flames singed the water, steam rising off it, and as the water bubbled and heated up, scores of fish suddenly leapt out of it, into the air, trying to escape from the boiling waters. As they leapt, Ralibar was there, waiting, jaws open. He swallowed entire schools of fish, flopping in his great jaws, some of them falling back into the water, as he gulped the rest down.

Mycoples flew beside them, but she did not bother eating. Perhaps because she was female, she did not seem to have Ralibar's appetite. Luckily, at least, Ralibar did not eat any humans.

A horn sounded in the distance, and Gwen was finally able to wrestle Ralibar away, and they all circled back around to see knights in armor holding lances and lining up on the far courtyard.

"The tournament begins!" Thor yelled to her. "I must not be late!"

Gwen nodded and they all flew back towards King's Court. The day's tournaments and festivities were beginning, and she knew that also meant that people would be lining up to petition her. It was time to begin the daily business of ruling her kingdom. As always, it came too soon.

They both flew over King's Court, the dragons flew together for a moment, and Thor reached out and took Gwen's hand, leaned over and kissed it. Then they forked, each going their own way, Thor to the fields and Gwen to her castle. It was time for the day to begin.

*

Thor, in full armor, charged on his horse, galloping at full speed, his lance held out before him and his face plate down as he charged for his opponent. Charging toward him was a warrior from a land he'd never heard of, from across the sea, wearing brown armor, a helmet with a long and pointed nose, a strange combination of mail and plate. His lance had strange markings, too, and as he aimed it for Thor's chest, his lance longer, Thor concentrated with all his might, focusing on how best to defeat his opponent. Thor tuned in, tried to sense the vibrations of the ground beneath him; he felt the slight tremors, and he slowed things down in his mind, until he felt the feelings of the horses, the weight of the riders, the angle of the lance. He sensed his opponent's intentions. From his appearance, he appeared to be aiming high—yet Thor's instinct told him he was going to aim low.

At the last moment, Thor adjusted accordingly, trusting his instincts, aiming his lance high, and dodging to the side. Thor's lance impacted his opponent's shoulder, knocking him back off his horse and sending him crashing to the ground in a great clang of metal.

There came a cheer from the crowd as his opponent rolled, bruised but unhurt.

Thor circled around, taking in the adulation from the huge crowd that lined up to watch the royal jousts, then jumped from his horse, made sure his opponent was okay, and extended a hand. The crowd cheered in approval as he did.

"I've never been defeated in battle," the knight said. "Much less by someone younger than myself, or with a shorter lance. Well-won!"

They clasped forearms and each led their horses by the reins to the side of the grounds, making room for the next joust.

Thor was beginning to feel his muscles stiffening; it had been hours of jousting, a growing crowd lined up far and wide to watch the highlight of the day's festivities. As Thor reached the side, Kendrick took his place, racing down the jousting lane and facing off against a knight whose armor came from another place Thor did not recognize.

The two charged, and Kendrick took out the soldier, to the cheers of the crowd. Thor cheered loudest of all.

Thor was elated to be here, on this day of the Summer Solstice, fighting with these great warriors, finally feeling as if he were one of them. For the first time, he no longer felt like an outsider.

Thor wanted to win on his own terms, as a regular warrior, with skills that matched others; he did not want to draw on his magical powers to influence his fight. So far, he had succeeded. While most of his friends had fallen, Thor had managed to make it to the final rounds of jousting, in the running with Kendrick, Erec, Conven, Elden, Reece, O'Connor, Brandt and Atme, along with several foreign knights. There were not many jousts left in the day.

A horn sounded and Thor watched a distant jousting lane and saw O'Connor charge against an opponent twice his size, from the southern province of the Ring; O'Connor missed his mark, and the opponent struck O'Connor in the gut, knocking him backwards off his horse. The crowd grunted and groaned as O'Connor hit the ground hard.

He lay there for a moment, and Thor worried if he was okay; but then O'Connor rose slowly to his feet and walked off. The crowd cheered for him. He was done with the tournament, but at least he was unhurt.

In the lane beside Thor, knights from distant lands charged each other. They met with a great battle cry, lances aimed high, and one screamed as a lance broke and a splinter pierced him through the throat. The crowd jeered, as it was a dirty move for the knight to strike so close to the throat, and dubiously legal.

The crowd groaned, horrified, as the knight fell off his horse, to the ground, writhing. Attendants rushed over to help him, to try to stop the bleeding, but within moments, he was dead.

A somber mood fell over the crowd as several attendants slowly pulled his body away. They all observed several moments of silence, Thor realizing once again just how dangerous these jousting games could be.

The soldier that had won, a massive fellow, twice as wide as the others, grabbed a new lance and turned and faced his next opponent. Thor's heart pounded to see that he faced Elden.

Elden charged fearlessly for him, and Thor prayed he did not meet the same fate his last opponent had.

They charged, their bulk shaking the ground, their armor groaning, Elden letting out a great battle scream as he held his lance before him. It seemed to Thor as if this knight were going to strike

Elden and win; yet at the last moment, Elden twisted to the side, aimed his lance at the knight's armpit, and managed a direct hit.

The knight fell from his horse, rolling on the ground, and the crowd cheered as Elden had won.

As Elden rode his victory lap, proudly, taking in the cheers of the crowd, his opponent, behind him, threw off his helmet, exposing a face filled with rage. The knight charged at the unassuming Elden, reached up, grabbed him from behind, and yanked him down off his horse.

The crowd groaned and jeered at the cowardly move, and Thor, enraged, rushed forward to Elden's aid, Reece, Conven, O'Connor and the other Legion at his side.

The knight jumped on top of Elden, raised a spear, and prepared to bring it down for Elden before he could react.

There came a snarling, and Krohn rushed forward, pouncing on the knight, knocking him down just before he could stab Elden.

The knight shook Krohn off, but it gave Elden time enough to roll around, reach back with his gauntlet and backhand the knight across the face.

There came a resounding crack as he broke the knight's jaw and knocked him out, unconscious, just as Thor and the others appeared.

Elden stood, to the cheers of the crowd, and attendants rushed forward and dragged the unconscious knight away.

Thor and the others clasped Elden on the back, relieved that he was OK, and a horn sounded as the fighting resumed.

Fight after fight, the jousting went on and on. Thor could hardly believe how many warriors partook in this day's festivities, representing all provinces of the Ring and dozens of countries from across the sea. The competition gave him a chance to test and hone his skills, and aside from one or two rotten apples, all the other knights fought with honor and respected the rules of the jousts.

The rounds continued, on and on. Elden eventually lost a joust, to a warrior twice his height, a knight who appeared to be invincible. But Kendrick took out that warrior the very next round.

As the second sun hung low in the sky, there eventually were but four warriors left in the competition: Thor, Kendrick, Erec, and a knight Thor did not know, a short stocky man, with black armor and menacing slits for eyes, who kept apart and who had not raised his visor once all day. Thor found himself facing him.

The two charged each other, Thor feeling all the eyes on him as the crowd roared in excitement. As they got closer, the sound of horses' hooves rumbling in Thor's ears, Thor prepared for impact—but something surprised him. His opponent raised his lance, and suddenly hurled it right at Thor.

Thor had not been expecting that. It sailed through the air, right for Thor's head. At the last second, Thor's reflexes kicked in, and he raised his shield just high enough to swat the lance away. At the same time Thor used his free hand to aim his own lance at the knight and strike him in the rib cage. The knight fell sideways from horse, tumbling down to the ground, and the crowd cheered.

Thor, breathing hard, shaken by how close he had come to losing, rode off to the side and turned and watched, as Kendrick and Erec, the last two aside from him, faced off with each other. He wondered which he would have to fight; neither would be easy.

The crowd thickened, as nearly everyone left in King's Court crowded in to watch these two great knights, leaders of the Silver, famed warriors, whose songs had been sung far and wide. They faced each other from far ends of the jousting lane, each with visors up, offering the other a salute of respect. Then they lowered their visors, raised their lances, their squires got out of the way, a horn sounded—and they charged.

The crowd was cheering as these two great warriors closed in on each other, their horses rumbling, raising up clouds of dust in the summer heat. Finally, they met in the middle with a clang, each knocking the other backwards.

The crowd groaned.

But neither of them fell off their horses, each of them good enough to be able to, somehow, hang on.

They each regained control, circled around, and, as the crowd cheered wildly, prepared to meet each other again. It was the first match of the day that had gone a second round.

Kendrick and Erec charged again, each ducking low, gaining incredible speed, holding their shining silver lances, the best the kingdom had, out before them. As they met, this time Erec raised his shield and blocked Kendrick's lance. Erec's shield was so strong that Kendrick's lance snapped in two on impact. Erec, in turn, used the opportunity to aim his lance beneath Kendrick's shield, striking him dead center in the chest and knocking him backwards off his horse.

The crowd cheered like wild as Erec circled around, jumped down from his horse, and gave Kendrick a hand up. They lifted their visors and Erec smiled down.

"Nicely fought," Erec said. "If your lance had not broken, you would have won."

Kendrick shook his head.

"You fought the better match," he conceded. "Next time."

Erec nodded and remounted his horse. Thor mounted his, realizing he'd be up against Erec.

Thor and Erec each circled around the entire perimeter of the jousting grounds, the final loop, as the crowd roared with a great cheer, chanting both Erec's and Thorgrin's names.

The two stopped at opposite ends of the jousting field, facing each other, and the crowd went wild. Thor felt nervous to face his old friend. He was determined to fight him on his own terms, and not to draw upon any of his powers. Thor wanted to see if he could win, as one man to another, one warrior to another.

They each lifted their faceplates in a gesture of respect, Thor facing off against his old mentor, a man he was once squire to. It was a funny feeling.

A horn sounded, and the two charged for each other. Thor focused with all his might and all his will, trying to drown out the screams of the crowd. He did not want to hurt Erec, and he tried to aim his lance for Erec's chest, where the armor was thickest. But as he tried to focus, Thor realized that Erec was different than all the other opponents he'd faced. He was faster, harder to pin down, and his custom-forged silver armor, with all of its interchanging plates, shined in the light like the scales on a fish. It made it even more difficult for Thor to concentrate.

The two met in the middle, and Thor braced himself, as he felt for the first time that day the impact of a lance on his chest. Yet at the same time, Thor felt his own lance impacting Erec's chest. The two of them hit each other at the same time and they each went flying backwards, off their horses.

The crowd groaned as each hit the ground at the same time. It was the first time of the day that had happened, and the rules of jousting demanded that if both fighters fell, then the fight must continue.

As Thor and Erec faced each other on foot, attendants ran out and handed each one a long mace with a studded wooden ball. They faced each other and charged.

The two of them fought hand-to-hand, slashing and blocking, maces clacking on armor. Thor knew that the rules demanded that whoever hit the ground first would lose—and he was determined not to lose.

But so was Erec.

Back and forth they fought, pushing each other forward and back; memories flooded back of Thor's real battle with Erec, when he fought for Andronicus. Thor felt overwhelmed with guilt; he lost focus, and as he did, for a moment Erec got the better of him. Erec landed several blows and Thor stumbled back, nearly falling, the crowd cheering as it seemed he was finished.

Thor shook his head and cleared his mind. He had to stay focused and forget about the past, to let go of his guilt. This was just a tournament now, not real life. If he won, he would not be hurting Erec.

Thor rallied and pushed Erec back—but then Erec rallied and pushed him back. The two of them went blow for blow, until Thor's arms grew tired, neither able to gain an advantage. They were well-matched. That alone made Thor proud, given that Erec was a veteran knight and Thor was years younger than he.

Erec brought his mace down in one great blow, and Thor turned his and blocked it. The maces locked, and Thor held it in place, his arm shaking against Erec's great strength. He felt that in moments he would give way. He did not want to lose, not in front of all these people. Especially not in front of Gwendolyn, whom he knew was watching with everyone else. Thor dropped to one knee, arms shaking, barely hanging in there.

Thor closed his eyes, and involuntarily summoned a power from some deep place inside. Without trying to, his magic, his true power, suddenly surfaced. He felt himself gushing with energy, a heat racing through his body.

Thor stood in one burst of energy, raised his mace, and pushed Erec's mace so that it went flying from his hand. Thor swung around in the same motion and struck Erec in the chest, and knocked him down, onto his back.

The crowd cheered like crazy, Thor the victor.

Thor lifted his visor, reached down, and gave Erec a hand up, feeling guilty.

The crowd came running in, all converging around him to embrace him.

"What happened to no magic?" Erec asked with a smile, goodheartedly.

"I'm sorry," Thor said. "I did not mean to."

Erec smiled wide, and Thor could see he was not upset.

"I'm proud of you," he said. "You are a great warrior."

The crowd closed in, hoisted Thor high up on their shoulders, and carried him off into the festivities. A chorus of horns sounded, and casks of ale and wine suddenly appeared, rolled out onto the fields by an army of attendants. The jousting fields instantly transformed into a field of festivity. More and more horns sounded, people drank and cheered, and it was clear the evening's festivities had begun.

*

Gwendolyn walked through the bustling crowd swarming in the rebuilt courtyard, thrilled to finally be out of King's Castle, done with her official duties of the day and out joining her people in the day's revelries. After all, it was the day of the Summer Solstice, and a day like this only came once a year. It also coincided this year with the celebration of the reconstruction of King's Court, and with the imminent celebration of her wedding. It would be a joyous year unlike any other—especially in the wake of such a year of darkness and gloom. Her people craved any occasion to rejoice, and they now had many of them.

Gwen took a deep breath on this beautiful summer day; she was determined to leave all the darkness behind her, and to rejoice with her people. The endless affairs of court could wait; she'd seen enough people already today. And now that the jousts were done and the horns had sounded, Gwendolyn was thrilled to finally have a chance to mingle with Thor.

Gwen was thrilled to see him so happy, and she had been so proud of him throughout the day, watching all of his jousts on pins and needles, cheering with the crowd, groaning when he was hit. She never doubted that he would win; he brought honor on himself, and on her, in everything he did. Even if he had lost, she would have loved him just the same.

Gwen held Thor's hand, and the two of them walked through the crowd to the cheers of thousands of well-wishers, as Thor led her through the parting masses and up the steep wooden steps towards the high platform overlooking the court. Thor led her halfway, and then stopped; as queen, Gwendolyn walked the final steps alone, and took the stage alone.

Thor stood below, in the front row, looking up and watching with thousands of others, Reece, Kendrick, Godfrey, Erec, Steffen,

Atme, Brandt, O'Connor, Elden, Conven, Aberthol and dozens of others at his side. The crowd grew silent as Aberthol slowly ascended the steps himself, leaning on his cane, seeming much older, each step an effort. In his other hand, he carried a long, tapered, unusual yellow sword, with a golden hilt.

Aberthol reached the stage and took his place beside Gwen, and the crowd grew silent. Thousands of people watched, transfixed, as Aberthol gingerly held out the long, yellow sword to Gwendolyn. She reached over, bowed her head, and took it from him carefully, grasping its golden hilt. It was the golden sword of summer, used once a year, every year, by kings, to initiate the Summer Solstice.

Gwen held the sword out before her and stood before a huge, round yellow fruit which hung from a rope before her. It dangled there, twice the size of a watermelon, bright yellow with white sparkling nubs, dazzling in the sun.

Aberthol turned and faced the crowd.

"The Summer Solstice is a precious day," he boomed out, his voice raspy but able to be heard in the rapt air. "A day of powerful omens. A day that portends the year to come. A day honored and celebrated by kings for thousands of years. As our ruler slashes this water fruit, it signifies the bounties of summer should be showered on us all throughout the year. It portends the blessing of a good harvest. And yet we also destroy the fruit, to signify that nothing lasts forever, and that our ultimate security comes from the almighty above."

Aberthol nodded and stepped aside.

Gwen examined the long, yellow sword, the one used by her father, and his father before him; it felt odd to be holding it. She remembered being a young girl and standing down there and watching each year, so anxious, hoping her father slashed the fruit just right, and that it was filled with water. She, like all people, wanted a good omen for the year to come.

Gwen took aim, her heart pounding, not wanting to miss, wanting to slash the fruit perfectly, as her father always did; he had always made it seem so effortless, showering all of his subjects with the bounty of the water fruit. She wanted this to be a good year and a good harvest, especially after all the darkness they had gone through.

Gwen breathed deep, raised the sword high, and brought it down with all her might, aiming for the center.

A perfect strike. She slashed the water fruit in half, and clear liquid gushed out of it in every direction, showering dozens of people in the crowd below.

There came a huge cheer, as horns sounded all up and down the courtyard, and people broke out into merriment. Musicians picked up their instruments, and the sound of trumpets and cymbals and horns and flutes and drums filled the air. Dancing broke out everywhere, strangers locking arms and spinning in jubilation.

The Summer Solstice had officially begun, and no time was wasted. Gwen looked down and saw tables already being rolled out everywhere, casks rolled up beside them, platters of meats and cheeses and fruits laid out as far as the eye could see. It would be a feast unlike any other.

Gwen looked up at the now-hollow fruit, swinging there, and as she examined it, she had a moment of dread: the inside of it, usually a bright yellow, was rotted to the core, black. She was the only one who could see it, from her angle, high up on the platform, and she quickly looked away. She did not want anyone else to see this, and she tried to push it from her mind, to pretend she never saw it. But it was, she knew, a terrible omen.

"Gwendolyn?"

Gwen looked over to see Thor standing there, smiling, hand outstretched; he had climbed the steps, and was waiting to help her back down.

Gwen put on a good face, and she forced herself to smile wide as she descended to the shouts and cheers of endless well-wishers, all of them embracing her, patting her on the back. Thor took her hand and she walked in a daze, filled with conflicting emotions, her stomach so large, as he led her past thousands of loyal and devoted subjects.

"They are enamored of you," Thor said. "They don't just admire you, they truly love you. Most unusual for a leader. You are like a mother to all of them, or a sister. You can see it in their eyes."

Gwendolyn looked around, and she saw that Thor was right. She felt all of their love, and it was the greatest feeling of her life. She had never thought she'd be capable of ruling a kingdom. She had always assumed that it was only something a man could do.

"I love them back," she replied.

Thor led her to a long feasting table in the midst of the courtyard, seated with all her family and council and dozens of nobles and lords and foreign dignitaries. Gwendolyn, ever the ruler, walked around the table, greeting each noble there, making a point to make everyone feel as welcome as possible.

Gwen spotted Kendrick and Sandara, Reece and Selese, seated beside Erec and Alistair, and she fell in beside them. Gwen had become so close to Thor's sister these last moons, she already felt like a sister to her, like the sister she'd never had. Gwen had also become equally close to Selese, her sister-in-law to be. She had always been close to Reece, and anyone he loved, she knew she would love, too. And she did love her, more than she ever expected, not out of fraternal obligation, but because she was discovering what an amazing person Selese was, and how devoted she was to her brother.

When Gwen had found out that she'd had the good fortune of being proposed to on the same day as Selese, she felt that it was meant to be, and had insisted that Selese and Reece share her joy, and be married together in a double wedding. Selese and Reece had been thrilled. The wedding preparations under way now were for all four of them, and in preparing and planning, Gwen had become as close to Selese as Alistair. In a way, it had been like she'd been given two sisters at once.

Gwen embraced her brothers, Kendrick and Reece, and looked about.

"Where's Godfrey?" she asked Reece, realizing one of her brothers was missing.

"Where else?" Illepra remarked, shaking her head in frustration. "Drinking and having fun," she added, and pointed across the courtyard.

Gwen turned and followed her gaze, and saw a stage being rolled to the center of the courtyard, Godfrey standing in its center, dressed in costume, Akorth and Fulton beside him, along with dozens of their tavern friends. A horn sounded, and the common folk began to gather about the stage.

"He's incorrigible," Illepra said. "I searched for him all morning, only to find him in one of the new taverns you ordered built. There are too many of them. King's Court has become a drinking haven!" she said, laughing.

"The people need a reason to celebrate, and a place to forget their woes," Gwen said, "as much as they need food and shelter."

Gwen sighed.

"One cannot keep the people back from the taverns," she added. "If you don't build them, they will drink anyway, in private. At least now they can come together, and we can regulate them."

"HEAR ALL AND ONE, COME TOGETHER!" Godfrey yelled out, as the stage was rolled out front and center.

Musicians quieted, the jugglers and fire-throwers stopped, and the crowd pressed in more closely, milling about the stage, an eager anticipation in the air, eager to see another play by Godfrey and his men.

"And what do you have for us this time?" O'Connor called out to Godfrey.

Godfrey stepped aside to reveal a tall, thin actor, dressed in a scarlet robe and hood, who stepped forward, threw back his hood and scowled at the crowd.

"I am Rafi! A man to be feared!" the actor hissed.

The crowd booed and jeered.

Godfrey stumbled forward, his belly out before him, crumpling his face, doing his best to act mean.

"And I am Andronicus!" Godfrey said. "The most feared of all commanders!"

The crowd booed.

"No—wait!" Godfrey called out, stopping, confusion on his face. "I forgot: I am dead! And no one fears the dead!"

Godfrey suddenly slumped down, collapsed on the stage and did not move, and the crowd shouted out with laughter and relief.

The actor playing Rafi stood over him and held out his hands:

"Rise, Andronicus! I command you!"

Godfrey suddenly jumped to his feet, and the crowd booed. But he then chased Rafi around the stage and caught him and strangled him, pretending to throttle him to death. The two of them wrestled on stage, and the crowd howled with laughter.

Finally, Godfrey pretended to kill him and rose, victorious, and the crowd cheered.

Another actor, lean and unshaved, stepped forward, frowning.

"And who are you?" Godfrey asked.

"I am Gareth, the former king!" the actor said.

The crowd booed. As Gwen heard his name, it sent a chill through her spine. She flashed back to killing him. She had no regrets—it was justice for her father. Yet still, the very thought of her former brother pained her. It was too fresh for her.

"And I, McCloud!" Akorth announced, rushing forward.

The crowd jeered, and threw tomatoes at him.

"You shall rule the Western Kingdom, and I shall rule the East!" McCloud said to Gareth.

They both reached out and clasped hands. But as they did, a woman stepped forward from the crowd, holding a long sword, and pretended to stab each of them through the chest. Each one sank to his knees, collapsing to the ground, dead.

The woman turned and faced the crowd, and raised her sword high.

"I am Gwendolyn, the greatest of all MacGil rulers!"

The crowd roared with approval, and Gwendolyn felt herself blush. She was overwhelmed with love for her people, but she also felt a deep sense of lingering sadness for all that transpired. Although six moons had passed, it all still felt like yesterday—and watching this farcical play somehow brought it all back.

"Excuse me," Gwen said to Thor.

She turned away from the stage, unable to watch anymore, and made her way back to the table. Thor followed on her heels, taking her hand, looking over at her with a concerned expression.

"Are you all right?" he asked.

She nodded, wiping back a tear, and forced a big smile.

"It's just the baby," she said.

Thor looked down at her huge belly, and he understood.

"You should not be on your feet too long anyway," he said.

He led her gently to her seat, and this time she sat. She needed to. She felt short of breath, especially on this hot day, and she took a long drink on her skin of water.

Thor sat beside her, and she soon felt better. They looked out, at the incredible bounty all around them, thousands of people eating in harmony, from all corners of the Ring, all corners of the Empire, here in the new King's Court. It was like a dream.

"Did you ever imagine it would be as glorious as this?" Thor asked.

She shook her head.

"I dreamed. And I hoped. But no—not like this. Seeing it…it's hard to believe."

"You have built a greater city than even your father had, even at his peak. It is now invincible. Finally, these people have found peace, thanks to you. You should be very proud."

Gwendolyn wanted to say: *Yes. You are right. Peace has come, and it will last forever.*

But she could not bring herself to utter the words. Deep down, something was gnawing at her, she was not sure what. She thought of the blackened fruit. She thought of Argon's prophecies. She knew she should feel safe, and yet somehow she did not feel entirely settled. Some part of her could not forget Argon's ominous words, that fateful choice she had made, back in the Netherworld, the sacrifice.

His prophecy. Argon's words rang in her head, like a stranger knocking at her door who would just not go away:

"It is when you feel most secure that you always have the most to fear."

CHAPTER NINETEEN

Thor held his torch high and walked beside Gwendolyn in the dark, a procession of thousands of torches winding its way through the summer night. The day's long festivities had finally morphed into night, and Gwendolyn led the huge procession out through the rear gate of King's Court and onto the wide path leading up King's Hill.

Thor was excited as he realized it was time for the annual Lighting of the Night, the mystical ceremony that occurred on every Summer Solstice. It was a time where the revelries could continue in a more subdued form, lasting throughout the warm summer night. It was a demarcation, a time that changed the nature of the holiday from revelry to a sacred time.

Gwendolyn marched slowly, somberly, as MacGil rulers had done for centuries on this night, lute players following far behind, playing a slow, mournful tune. It was their job to both entice and scare away the spirits that were rumored to dance on this night.

"I am hoping Argon will be there," Gwen said to Thor.

"I haven't seen him in moons," Thor said.

"Nor have I," Gwen said. "He has the strangest way of disappearing. You don't think he's left us forever, do you?"

Thor shrugged. With Argon, one never knew.

Thor took Gwen's hand as they walked, and he felt the energy coursing through her—not just hers, but also the baby's. Thor was so on-edge these days, waiting for the baby to come any day, preparing and getting nervous for the huge wedding, finally just days away. He was anxious for everything to go smoothly—the wedding, the birth. He wanted all of the endless waiting to be over already.

Gwen squeezed his hand, and he looked over at her.

"Tonight," she whispered, smiling. "When the last of this is done, we shall have more time together."

Thor smiled back. "There is nothing I wish for more."

High up, in the distance, there came two screeches—Mycoples and Ralibar—circling, letting their presence be known before they soared up and into the night. Thor took solace from their presence. They often flew off in the night, yet they always returned in the morning.

"When I see them," Gwen remarked, "I feel as if nothing bad can ever come to the Ring."

"As do I," Thor said. "With two dragons and the Shield restored, the Ring is finally impregnable."

They marched, thousands of people filing in behind them, all of them chanting a slow, somber tune designed to bring in the night. As they slowly ascended, the path taking them in broad circles, looping again and again, Thor looked up and saw the hill, rising gradually, hundreds of feet high. This hill was different than all the others, covered entirely with smooth grass, and paved with perfectly round circles etched into its sides. In between each circle was a small moat, filled with perfectly still, reflecting water. As they all slowly ascended the path, circling again and again, Thor watched all the torches reflecting in the water, a thousand points of reflected light lighting up the hill.

King's Hill was a magical and mystical place, Thor knew, a place only frequented once a year, despite its prominent position on the outskirts of King's Court. It was also, mysteriously, one of the few places unharmed in the war. As Thor walked, he could feel the power of this sacred place, the earth feeling alive, humming through his feet.

Thousands of revelers followed Gwendolyn as she took one step at a time, leading the way with her torch, towards the top.

"He's here," she said, looking up.

Thor looked up, and saw, with relief, that Argon was there, standing at the top, in white robes and hood, looking down, like a shepherd patiently awaiting his flock.

They were close to the very top, and Thor remained a few steps behind as Gwen continued on, taking her place a few steps below Argon on the highest plateau. She glanced back and saw her people all stood below, spread in circles on the paths all throughout King's Hill, and she waited patiently for Argon.

Argon finally closed his eyes and raised his palms out before him.

"The Night of Lights falls on the longest day of the year. Yet it also marks the beginning of days of darkness. Intermixed with light, there is always darkness—with joy, tragedy. Days are alive, contracting and expanding; people are not stagnant, either. Our universe is always in flux, and us along with it."

He took a deep breath.

"This a holy day, not just one for reveling. It is a day and night for reflection. Look at the waters before you. Look at your torchlight burning in them. Remember that light will fade. Remember from where you came. Your time here is but short, but a fleeting breath. We are all like a passing cloud, a summer breath, that is no more."

Argon lowered his head and stepped back, and Gwendolyn climbed the final few steps to the highest point on King's Hill. She stood there, beside Argon, and turned and faced the masses. As she did, everyone immediately took a knee and bowed their heads low.

Gwen reached out and raised her amber torch and slowly lowered it, touching it to the narrow strip of water at the top of the mount. As she did, the water mysteriously lit up in flames. Thor watched in wonder as the flames in the water spread, lighting the narrow moats of water all up and down King's Hill, rings of fire between the paths spaced out every twenty feet, lighting up the mount, and lighting up the night.

All the people settled in now that the waters were lit, taking spots beside the flames and getting comfortable for the night.

Gwendolyn came down, took Thor's hand, and together they found a spot in the grass, leaning against the hill, beside her brothers and close friends. Sitting nearby, beside the flames, were Kendrick and Sandara, Reece and Selese, Godfrey and Illepra, Erec and Alistair, Elden and Indra and Steffen and O'Connor. Krohn came up beside Thor and sat beside him, resting his head in his lap. Thor looked everywhere for Argon, but he was already gone.

The group sat staring out at the fires all around them, each holding a silver goblet of summer wine, as was the custom. They all waited as Gwendolyn raised her goblet first, as was the custom, took a sip, then reached out and splashed the rest on the fire. The flames mysteriously hissed and rose higher. The others all then raised their goblets, and drank. Thor took a long drink on his, and the strong, yellow summer wine went right to his head.

Thor leaned back beside Gwen, draped an arm around her, and placed his other hand on her belly. He felt a deep sense of content. His body was warm from the summer wind, from the flames, from the wine in his veins. He and Gwen lay back in the grass, as did the other couples in the quiet night, and they looked up at the night sky, filled with sparkling red stars. Thor felt there was no place he'd rather be. Everything felt so perfect in the world, and he hoped it would never change.

Nearby, Reece and Selese leaned back, kissing, sharing wine from a goblet, very much in love. Thor admired his friend's courage in proposing so soon, and he looked forward to their double wedding. Beside them were Elden and Indra, sitting up beside each other, each of them hardened warriors and neither of them expressive in their love for each other. Thor could tell they were in love, yet they were on the opposite spectrum on Reece and Selese in the way they showed it. The night was so quiet, punctuated only by the soft summer wind, and the sound of the flames. Yet the acoustics were odd up here, and the wind carried voices in the air, making Thor hear the others conversations, whether he wanted to or not.

"Now that the wars are over, I must visit my father," Elden said to her. "Assuming he still lives. It will be a long journey across the Ring to my home village." He looked at her cautiously. "If you'd like to journey with me?"

Indra stared, expressionless, staring into the flames. She almost appeared as if she were not interested in him—though Thor knew that she was. She just kept up her walls.

She shrugged.

"It's not like I have anything better to do," she said.

"Is that a yes?" he asked.

She shrugged again.

"Why not?" she said.

Elden reddened.

"Can't you just admit that you care for me?" he asked.

She turned to him, frowning.

"I am here with you because your group took me from the Empire. And I am certainly not going back to the Empire."

"Are you saying then you don't care for me?" he asked.

She shrugged and looked away.

"I'm here, aren't I?" she said.

They fell back into silence. That was the way it had always been between them, Indra determined to maintain her cold, masculine, indifferent front, refusing to show any affection for Elden. But Thor could see it in the way she stole glances at him when he wasn't looking, and he knew that she truly cared for him, much more so than she would ever admit—and perhaps, tragically, more so than Elden would ever know. Thor wondered what would ever become of the two of them?

"That is your third goblet of wine, is it not?" Illepra asked Godfrey, not far away, on the other side of Thor.

Godfrey smiled as he finished the rest of it in one large gulp.

"I wish it were the fourth," he said with a chuckle. Godfrey laughed and poured himself another.

Illepra frowned.

"You should not be drinking so much," she reprimanded. "Your injuries still need to heal."

"Heal?" he said. "That was six moons ago. I was healed within days."

"You need to stop drinking," she said. "It is time for you to leave it behind."

"What difference does it make to you?" he asked.

She reddened.

"I've saved your life twice now," she said. "What was the point, if you will just throw it away?"

"I never asked you to," Godfrey said.

She raised her hands to her hips.

"Since we returned to King's Court you had an opportunity to become someone new, to take part in the rebuilding. Instead, you spend all your time in the taverns, celebrating."

"Is there not much to celebrate?" he asked.

"Have you no better way to spend your time than to become a common drunkard?"

"Is there any better way to spend one's time?" he countered. "If there is, let me know. I haven't seen it."

She scowled.

"You promised me you would give up drink."

"And I did," he said sheepishly. "For a while."

Godfrey, amused with himself, broke out into fresh laughter.

But Illepra was unamused; she suddenly got up and stormed away, furious. Godfrey watched her go, a confused look on his face.

"I don't understand her at all," he said aloud.

"Go to her," Selese said.

"Why should I?"

"Are you that ignorant? Do you not see how much she loves you?"

Godfrey's face fell in wonder, then recognition, and then he turned bright red, and not from wine. For the first time, he seemed to really recognize it.

He looked down, and kicked the ground at his feet. But he did not move. Instead, he took another long sip of his wine.

Thor wanted to get away from all the voices, to give them all privacy, and so he took Gwendolyn's hand, stood, and the two of them began a leisurely stroll, walking along the edge of the fires. Thor sighed, wondering about the mysteries of love, of what brought two people close to each other. It all seemed inscrutable to him.

As they went, they came across Kendrick and Sandara, sitting on the outskirts of the group, in a darker corner of the hill. As they approached, Thor could hear them talking.

"But the Ring is your home now," Kendrick said to Sandara.

Sandara sat there, tall and proud, bearing the resemblance of the Empire, staring into the flames as she shook her head.

"My home is far from here. In a foreign land."

"In the occupied Empire. Would you rather be there?"

"Home is home," she replied.

"And what of us?" Kendrick asked. "Do you not care for us?"

She turned and looked at him, and stroked his cheek.

"I care more for us than I could say. That is the only reason I am still sitting here right now."

Thor took Gwendolyn's hands and they continued walking, further and further, until they came across Erec and Alistair, talking quietly amongst themselves.

"There appear to be many weddings in the air," Alistair said to Erec.

"And ours will come soon, my lady," Erec replied.

Alistair turned and looked at him, eyes widening.

"Really?" she asked, filled with hope.

He nodded back, earnest.

"I want us to marry in my homeland, in the Southern Isles. I want my father to meet you. And all of my people. I want you to have the reception you deserve. My father is King, and you will be a princess among my people. It shall be a grand wedding. One befitting of you. If you do not mind waiting?"

Alistair leaned in and hugged him tight, and he hugged her back, and they kissed.

"There are too many people here," Gwendolyn said. "I wish to be just with you. Come with me."

She reached out and took his hand, and she led him quietly, through the night, heading towards the royal castle.

CHAPTER TWENTY

Thorgrin walked slowly through his old village, bewildered. Here was the place he had grown up, and yet it seemed so foreign to him. The streets were empty, the doors to the houses all left open, as if it had all been abandoned in a rush.

He walked through it slowly, a harsh driving wind whipping his face, stirring up the dirt, and he had never felt so alone.

Thor turned the corner and saw his father's home, and he walked toward it with dread. It was the only home in the village with the door closed.

He reached it, turned the knob, and slowly pulled open the creaking wood door. His heart stopped.

Standing there, facing him, was not his father—but Andronicus.

Andronicus stepped out, smiling and sneering at the same time, his body half-decayed, and reached out a long bony hand for Thor's throat.

"My son," he said in his ancient, awful voice. "You may have killed me. But I can still haunt your dreams."

Thor reached up and swatted the bony hand away, slicing his wrists—and as he did, the landscape changed.

Thor looked down and saw that his wrist was bleeding, scratched not by his father's skeleton but by a thicket of thorns. Thor struggled to walk through the pile of thorns, higher than his head, scratching his arms every which way as he pushed through. He was entangled, and with each step he was in more pain, the thorns embedding more deeply into his skin.

Thor struggled with all his might, and finally broke through to the other side.

Before him lay a wasteland, sky the color of ash, the soil mud. On it lay thousands of corpses, the corpses of the Empire, of the McClouds, of every soldier Thor had ever met and killed in battle. There they all lay, moaning.

Rafi stood in the center, and raised an accusing finger at Thor.

"This blood is on your hands," he said, his voice horrifying, cutting right through Thor.

As one, all the corpses rose, turned to Thor, and charged.

Thor raised his hands and screamed.

"NO!"

Thor blinked, and found himself standing on a footbridge.

He looked down and saw the raging waters of the ocean below. He saw a single, small boat, bobbing wildly in the ocean, empty. He realized that he had been on that boat, sometime long ago, and now he had made it up here, on this narrow footbridge. Just one step to the right or the left, and he would plummet to his death.

Thor looked up, and saw that the footbridge stretched for miles in the sky, and ended at the top of a high cliff. At its edge there was perched a castle, overlooking the sky, the ocean. Light flooded in through the castle windows, a light so bright it hurt Thor's eyes to look.

On the footbridge, not far from him, stood a woman, wearing light blue robes, holding out a hand. He sensed instantly that it was his mother.

"My son," she said. "Your wars are done. The time has come to meet. For you to understand the depths of your powers. For you to know who you truly are."

Thor wanted desperately to take a step towards her, but he sensed something behind them, and he turned and saw standing, not far away from him, a boy, who looked like him. He was taller than Thor, with bright blonde hair, broad shoulders and a noble face. He had a strong jaw and a proud chin.

He looked up lovingly at Thor.

"Father," he said, reaching out a hand. "I need you."

Thor turned and looked back and forth between the two, torn, not knowing which to way to go.

Suddenly, the footbridge beneath him collapsed, and Thor felt himself plummeting, screaming, down to the raging waters of his death.

Thor woke screaming.

He sat up in bed in the darkness, breathing hard, and looked all around him. Gwen, awakened, sat up beside him, grabbing a candle from her bedside table, pulling it towards her and holding it up to Thor's face, examining him with concern.

"What happened?" she asked. "Are you okay?"

Gwen breathed heavily, and Thor could see it was burdensome for her to move in bed, being as pregnant as she was, and he felt badly for having wakened her. They lay in her parents' former chamber, now her chamber, in a huge four-poster bed piled with luxurious furs.

Krohn jumped up and came running over to Thor, licking him several times.

Thor jumped up from bed, threw on his robe, and hurried over to the small basin against the wall and splashed water on his face. He breathed deep, water dripping down his face, and looked out through the open-air arched window. Down below lay King's Court, perfectly silent and still, all the revelers gone home. The two moons hung low in the sky, one red, one violet, and they let in a soft light through the clouds.

Thor breathed deep, rubbing his face, trying to clear his mind. He had been having too many nightmares of late. He kept seeing the faces of all his opponents, reliving times from battles. It clung to him like a fog. He had also been having recurring visions of his son, and of his mother. He felt something ominous was on the horizon, but he did not know what.

Most of all, Thor was feeling an intense desire, growing stronger each day, to seek out his mother, to know who he truly was, to understand his destiny.

"Everything is okay," Thor said softly, his back to Gwendolyn.

He turned and walked over to her, and kissed her on the forehead.

"Go back to sleep," he added, taking her candle, returning it to her bedside table, blowing it out.

Gwen lay back, curling up beneath the covers.

"Come back to bed," she said.

"I will. Soon enough," Thor said.

He needed to get fresh air, to clear his mind, to shake off the demons of the night.

Thor walked across the room, Krohn following at his heels, and strode out of the chamber and into the castle hall, closing the door gently behind him.

It was brighter out here, several torches lit along the wall. The two soldiers standing at attention outside the door stiffened at his presence.

Thor turned and made his way down the twisting, ancient stone corridors, and finally up a narrow, spiral stone staircase, to the parapets. The roof was his place of refuge, a place he had come to escape the demons of the night.

Thor crossed the castle roof, Krohn at his heels, running his hand along the wide, smooth stones. He looked down at King's Court. It was beautiful, tranquil, shining beneath the moonlight, thousands of torches arranged neatly along the walls, everything built back perfectly. A few revelers slept on the castle grounds, too tired or drunk to make it back to their beds. King's Court was so safe now, they could sleep out in the open with no fears. The city grounds were strewn with the mess of the day's parties, hundreds of banquet tables still laden with leftover food, a mess that would have to wait to the next day to be cleaned up.

As Thor looked down, he marveled at all that Gwen had accomplished here. And he marveled at all the twists and turns life had taken for him. Growing up, he had never in a million years expected to find himself, an outsider, invited into King's Castle—much less living in it, standing atop it in the moonlight and surveying the court. As an outsider, he had just hoped and dreamed to maybe one day enter its gates. Now here he stood, at the very peak of it all. He was overjoyed, yet it was also so surreal. It was scary, in a way, being at the top of everything in life; a part of him feared there was nowhere left for him to go from here but down.

Thor felt so confused about life. Finally, he had everything he'd ever dreamed of. He had a wife-to-be whom he loved, and who loved him; he had a child on the way; he was respected by his peers, and loved by the people. And yet somehow, for some inexplicable reason, he still felt that something was missing from his life, and he did not know what. Was it not knowing his mother? Not knowing his destiny, his purpose? He felt he should be happy, and while on most levels he was, on some small level, he did not understand why he was not. What was it that he was missing? Was it just human nature to never feel entirely content, even once you had what you dreamed?

More than ever, Thor craved answers. He needed to see Argon.

Thor heard a great screech in the sky, and he looked up and saw Mycoples, circling high, making her presence known. She always knew when Thor was up here, and she always flew by to greet him.

"ARGON!" Thor called out to the night sky, leaning back and looking up at the stars. "WHERE ARE YOU!?"

Krohn whined, and Thor looked down, and then followed his gaze, and was shocked to see Argon standing there, dressed in a black cloak and hood, holding his staff, but a few feet away, staring at him calmly, expressionless, as if he had always been standing right here. His eyes shone with such intensity that Thor nearly had to look away.

"You needn't call so loudly," Argon said quietly.

Thor approached him, and the two stood side-by-side and turned and looked out at the city together.

"I've missed you, Argon," Thor said. "I have called for you many times. Where have you been?"

"I travel many worlds," Argon replied cryptically. "But I am always here with you, in your world, in some way."

"Then you know all that is happening," Thor said. "You know about my sister. My child. My son."

Argon nodded solemnly.

"But then why did you never tell me? You never told me any of this."

Argon smiled.

"It was not for me to tell," he replied. "I learned my lesson about interfering in human destiny. It is not something I intend to do again."

"What else are you not telling me?" Thor asked, wondering, desperate to know. He could not help but feel something ominous on the horizon, some great secret, something that had to do with him, and he sensed that Argon knew what it was.

Argon looked at Thor, then turned and looked back out at the city.

"There is much," he said finally, "that I would rather not know myself."

Thor felt a deepening sense of foreboding at his words.

"Am I going to die, Argon?" he asked flatly, desperate to know.

Argon waited a long time, so long that Thor worried that he might not ever answer him.

"We all die, Thorgrin," he finally answered. "Only a few of us truly live."

Thor breathed deep, wondering. He was overflowing with questions.

"My son," Thor said. "Will he be a great man?"

Argon nodded.

"Indeed," he replied. "A great warrior. Greater, even, than yourself. His fame will vastly outshine yours."

Thor burned with pride for his son, and his eyes swelled with tears. He was thrilled that Argon finally gave him a straight answer—yet he also sensed something was too good to be true.

"But for everything there comes a price," Argon said.

Thor's heart pounded as he considered this.

"And what is the price for my son?" Thor asked hesitantly.

"Fathers and sons are one. The bond is deeper than can be explained. One must sacrifice for the other, whether he chooses to or not. Sons bear the sins of their fathers—and fathers bear their sins yet to come."

Thor looked out at the city, worried. He sensed something dark on the horizon.

"I need to know when I will die," Thor insisted. "Will it be soon?"

Argon slowly shook his head.

"Your time has not yet arrived, young Thorgrin," Argon said. "Not today, anyway. There is still much left for you to achieve, greater things than even you can ever dream. Your training is not yet complete. You still have not mastered your powers. And you will need them, where you are going."

"Where am I going?" Thor asked, puzzled. "And what will I need them for? The Ring is at peace."

Argon turned and looked out, and slowly shook his head.

"Peace is merely an illusion, a blanket behind the always waiting flames of war."

Thor's heart beat faster.

"Where does the next danger lurk, Argon? Just tell me that. How can I prepare?"

Argon sighed.

"Danger lurks everywhere, Thorgrin. You can prepare only by learning to master yourself."

"My mother," Thor said. "I keep seeing her in my dreams."

"That is because she is summoning you. It is not a call you can ignore. Your destiny depends on it. The fate of your people depends on it."

"But how shall I find her?" Thor asked, looking out at the horizon, wondering. "I don't know how to—"

Thor turned to face Argon, but as he did, he was shocked to see that he was already gone.

"ARGON!" Thor called out, turning in every direction, looking about.

He stood there, looking, waiting, watching for hours, until even the first sun touched the sky—but no matter how long he looked, there came nothing in return but the howling of the wind.

CHAPTER TWENTY ONE

Gwendolyn sat on her throne in the rebuilt Council chamber, the early morning light of the first sun streaking in through the stained-glass windows, painting the room muted colors. She surveyed the vast number of people who filled the room in wonder. She could hardly believe how many people filled the chamber—advisors, council members, hangers-on, well-wishers, nobles, lords, attendants—and now, on a special day like today, petitioners, lining up outside the room, down the Hall, and outside the castle. It was an ancient tradition for rulers to hear petitions on the day after Summer Solstice, and Gwendolyn, regardless of how exhausted she was, would not let her people down.

Gwen was also taken aback by how resplendent this room now looked, since its reconstruction. Hardly six moons ago she had sat here, the room mostly rubble, freezing cold air gushing in through the open walls. Now it was a beautiful summer day, temperate breezes coming in through the open, arched stained-glass windows, and it was the finest hall in the two kingdoms. She had doubled the size of this famed hall, had doubled the size of the council table, and had built for them comfortable seats, so they could wait in dignity.

This hall was where she spent most of her days now. She wanted to be out there, walking the fields, carefree as she had been when she was a child—or spending her time with Thor, taking a stroll through her courtyards and gardens. But alas, the ruling of her kingdom required so many petty decisions and matters, hearing one person after the other. Many days she came in here, expecting to leave early, but before she knew it, the day grew long, and she left here after dark.

Today, she was determined for it to be different. After all, the Summer Solstice came but once a year, and today, the day that followed, was Departure Day; so many people would be departing on this day, embarking for somewhere in the kingdom. It was thought to bring good luck to depart the day after the Summer Solstice, and her people took it very seriously.

Nearby stood Thor, Reece, Kendrick, Godfrey, Erec, Aberthol, Steffen, Alistair and Selese, along with several close advisors, including all those who had once sat on her father's council. Gwen was tired from last night's festivities, and even more tired from the baby. The nurses had told her she was due any day, and she could feel it without being told. Her baby flipped like mad, and with each day, Gwen felt it harder to catch her breath. She sat there, first thing in the morning, already feeling like going to sleep, struggling to keep her eyes open.

She forced herself to focus. It was a big day, after all, one of the most important and auspicious days of the year, and her council chamber, already packed, was growing ever more crowded.

Gwen had been receiving foreign dignitaries and well-wishers since the sun rose, visitors from all corners of the Ring and of the Empire who had come for her wedding. A corner of the room was already piled high with wedding gifts for her, and gifts for her baby. Her wedding was still days away, and yet the gifts poured in: golden candlesticks, precious jewels, ancient rugs, delicacies of every sort.... There was already more than she could count, or ever use in a lifetime. She had been showered with great affection from the masses, and she was quickly becoming known as the people's Queen. Perhaps it was because she had suffered, and the people—all of whom had also suffered in their own way—related to her.

The masses absolutely loved her—as much as the nobles did—a rare thing in the kingdom. It was something that even her father had not enjoyed. His nobles had respected him, and the masses had feared and appreciated him. All had thought he was a fair king. But none had *loved* him. Her father had kept the people and the nobles at a distance; Gwendolyn kept her doors open and treated them like part of her family.

Having finished entertaining all of her foreign dignitaries, her external affairs were over for the morning, and it was time to turn to her internal affairs. Aberthol cleared his throat, banged his staff on the floor and stepped forward, beginning the proceedings. The room began to quiet.

"We begin with a report from the tax collector," Aberthol announced.

Earnan, her father's old tax councilor, stepped forward, bowed, and read from a scroll.

"Two thousand casks of wine," he announced, his voice dry. "One thousand casks of ale. Eight thousand chickens; six thousand hens. One thousand cows...."

He lowered the scroll and looked up, his face grim.

"The royal festivities and the queen's wedding, all hosted by us, represent a generosity of a magnitude never displayed before in the history of the two kingdoms. My lady, you are the most generous ruler that has ever sat on that throne. But these festivities are also cause for concern. We have nearly drained whatever was left of our royal treasury."

A grim silence blanketed the room, as all eyes turned to Gwendolyn.

"I am aware of the costs," she said. "And yet the people are happy. After all of their hardships, they needed a cause to rejoice. Every penny was well spent. Without a strong soul and spirit, there is no will."

"HEAR HEAR!" cried out the crowd in the hall, cheering in her defense.

"It may be so, my lady," he said, "but my responsibilities as treasurer are our reserves. They must be replenished. I propose that we raise a new tax on the people."

There came a boo throughout the crowd, until Aberthol slammed his cane several times and they quieted down.

Earnan cleared his throat and continued: "Rebuilding King's Court has cost us dearly, my lady. The people benefit. They must also help pay for it."

The entire room turned and looked at Gwen. She mulled it over, thinking carefully, until finally she reached a conclusion.

"I thank you for doing your duty," she said to Earnan, "and you do it well. I shall not tax my people, however. To solve the problem, you can take my own wealth."

Earnan's eyes widened in surprise.

"My lady?" he said.

"All of these gifts I have been given—all of these jewels and treasures—you may take for our treasury. Take it all. I would rather you take it from me than from the people."

Gwendolyn looked to Thorgrin.

"These wedding gifts are yours, too. This is assuming you agree?"

Thorgrin nodded back without hesitation.

"Of course, my lady," he replied. "These material things mean nothing to me."

Gwendolyn nodded to Earnan, satisfied.

"I believe it resolves the matter," she said.

Earnan bowed.

"It does. It is a most satisfactory conclusion, one I had not anticipated. The people are lucky to have you. I doubt any other ruler would have done the same."

The room erupted with a cheer of love and admiration.

"Whatever gifts you give away, we will give you more in the full again!" a commoner yelled from the crowd. There came another jubilant cheer.

Gwen was feeling tired, and she wondered how much longer today's meeting would go on. Her back was hurting her from the baby, and she squirmed, no longer able to sit comfortably on the throne.

Duwayne, her advisor on the masses, stepped forward.

"My lady, speaking of the needs of the people," he said, "our people have come to King's Court these last six moons and have helped us rebuild. Now that the work is done, they must return to their own villages. But they will be returning to homes and villages ravaged by war. Now it is our time to help *them* rebuild. We must allocate and distribute badly-needed resources for them: manpower, building materials, supplies, grain, gold. Now that King's Court has returned, the rest of the Ring must not be neglected."

Gwendolyn nodded, finding wisdom in his words.

"Agreed," she said. "I shall appoint one of my councilmen to oversee this. He will be given the duty of touring all the villages and towns of the Ring, and deciding which resources to allocate, on my behalf. Whatever my people need, they will get.

"Steffen!" Gwendolyn called out.

Steffen hurried over to her, bowing, looking at her with surprise.

"I appoint you as the new Lord of the Interior. You will speak with my voice and have all the power and resources of the royal treasury and royal forces in helping the Ring rebuild. You will travel town to town, you will meet all the townsfolk, and you will decide who will get what. Is this a responsibility that you will accept?"

All eyes in the packed hall turned to Steffen. He shifted and ran his palms on his thighs, clearly caught off guard, and uncomfortable being in the spotlight.

"My lady," he said, clearing his throat. "I am but a simple servant. I am not deserving of such rank and position. What you describe will be one of the greatest positions of power in your kingdom. Why should it be given to me? I am not deserving."

"That is precisely the reason why it will be given to you," Gwendolyn said. "Because you act with humility; because you are not puffed up with pride; because you are a loyal and devoted and trustworthy advisor; and because I trust you with my life. You also understand the common people, and you are a fine judge of character.

I trust you to speak with my own voice. The position is yours, and I ask you to accept."

Steffen bowed his head down low. As he raised his head, his eyes were watering.

"My lady, I accept with the greatest humility and gratitude. It is a position that I should hope to be able to live up to."

Gwen nodded

"Excellent. On this Departure Day, you will depart before the sun has set."

Gwen turned back to Aberthol, hoping there was no more left on the agenda for this morning; but he stepped forward and unrolled a long scroll, filled with items, and began to read from it. Gwendolyn sighed.

"Reports pour in, my lady, of forts throughout the Ring that were destroyed and need to be rebuilt, fortified. We also need to reinforce along the canyon bridges. The Silver and the Legion need to be strengthened, too, after all of their losses. They do not have the numbers that they did in your father's day."

Gwendolyn nodded.

"Kendrick and Erec," she announced, "you will be in charge of all matters relating to the Silver. I trust you to make us the fighting force that we were in our father's time."

"Yes, my lady," they both said.

"You will also be in charge of fortifying and securing all of the forts and crossings throughout the Ring. We need our military and our posts back to their prior strength. Replenish our Hall of Arms, and fill the Silver's barracks."

"Yes, my lady," they replied.

"Thorgrin," Gwen said, turning to him, "You will be in charge of rebuilding the Legion. Fill its ranks once again, make it the fighting force it once was, so that it will reflect upon the honor of all those boys who died serving our cause."

"Yes, my lady," Thor replied.

Aberthol held up another scroll, unraveled it and squinted. Then he began to read.

"Reports have arrived, my lady, from today's falcons, of trouble in the Upper Islands."

Gwen raised her eyebrow, wondering.

"What sort of trouble?" she asked.

"A dispatch from your regent, Srog. He reports of a discontent amongst its people." Aberthol squinted at the scroll as he skimmed it.

"He speaks of an instability amongst Tirus' sons, and it's spreading to the people. He warns of a possible revolt. He asks for reinforcements."

Gwendolyn leaned back in her throne and folded her hands across her chest. She had not expected this.

"And how do you interpret all of this?" she asked, turning to her councilmen. Gwen had learned from her father that it was always best to hear others' thoughts before expressing your own.

"Srog is a wise and capable leader," Erec said. "Silesia is a great city. If he's having difficulty ruling the Upper Isles, that does not bode well. I trust what he says."

"The other MacGils are a stubborn, hard-headed people," Kendrick volunteered. "Perhaps they cannot be tamed."

"You could free Tirus," Godfrey said. "That would appease them."

"Or you could abandon the Upper Isles altogether and consolidate your reign," Thor offered.

"Your father was never able to unite the island and the mainland in his lifetime," Aberthol said. "Nor his father before him."

"We must not let any rebellion flourish in the Upper Isles," Kendrick said, "or it could easily spread to the mainland. Perhaps we need to invade."

"I disagree, my lady," Reece said. "We need the Upper Isles. It is a strategic point in the Tartuvian Sea. And not all the Upper Islanders are rotten. There are many fine people among them, including our cousin Matus."

"True," Kendrick said. "We owe Matus our lives."

Gwendolyn sat back and considered it all carefully. She wondered what her father would have done. She knew he never trusted the Upper Islanders, his brother, his cousins; and yet, he never let them stray too far from his watch, either.

"I want to know more of what Srog has to say," Gwen said. "And I want another perspective on the island. Reece," she said, turning to him.

Reece stepped forward.

"You will depart for the Upper Isles today."

"*Me*, my lady?" he asked, shocked.

Gwendolyn nodded.

"You were always close to Matus. You are the same age, and he always trusted you, and you him. You will be my voice, my eyes and ears. Seek out Matus, seek out Srog. Tour the Upper Isles, listen to its people, and come back with a full report of exactly what is going on there. Based on your findings, I will decide whether to reinforce or depart."

Reece nodded, but he seemed hesitant. Gwen sensed the reason why.

"Do not worry of our double wedding," Gwendolyn said. "It is still a half moon away. You will be back in plenty of time. After all, I won't have it without you. Go then. Do not linger."

Reece looked much assured.

"Yes, my lady," he said, bowing.

Gwendolyn turned to Aberthol.

"Is there anything else?" she asked, exhausted. "If not, then I would like to get on with—"

Aberthol held up a hand.

"Just one more matter, my lady."

Gwen sighed. She was beginning to get a whole new respect for what her father had gone through.

"A dispatch from Bronson," Aberthol said. "He reports of unrest on the McCloud side of the Highlands."

Gwendolyn raised her eyebrows, looking at Aberthol with dread. Was nothing ever stable? Was that what it meant to be queen? To put out a never-ending stream of fires, perpetual unrest, discontent? Why could people not just stay happy and at peace?

"Unrest?" she asked.

Aberthol nodded, examining another scroll.

"He reports of his failed efforts to unite the two sides of the Ring. Six moons have passed, and they are resentful. They see the prosperity in the West, and yet they have seen none of it for themselves."

Kendrick was exasperated.

"Have they forgotten that their leader initially sided with Andronicus and helped to inflame this war?" he asked.

"If they hadn't spent all those moons before the war launching raids on our soil," Godfrey said, "then perhaps they'd have a greater share now of our prosperity."

"In their defense," Reece said, "they did join our side at the end."

"They are hardly being starved," Thor said. "Our men have given them plenty of our summer bounty and have helped them rebuild. All of them eat well."

"They may eat well," Aberthol said, "but they are not rich. There is a difference. They see what others have and they covet it. That has always been their nature. They see King's Court, shining, and they want their cities plated with gold."

Kendrick snorted.

"Well, then that is their problem, not ours."

"Wrong, my brother," Gwendolyn said. "Any problem, anywhere in the Ring, is *our* problem. Their discontent cannot go unnoticed. That is where momentum begins."

The room fell silent, and Aberthol sighed.

"It is the nature of the McClouds, my lady. They are a savage, crude people. They may not ever merge with the MacGils. You may have dispatched Bronson for a task he cannot fulfill."

"The rivalry between our two clans is ancient and strong," Erec said. "Thousands of years. We may not be able to smooth them over in six moons—even with an emissary like Bronson. Vendettas run deep. And the McClouds are not a forgiving people."

Gwendolyn leaned back and thought it all through carefully. Her stomach was hurting her again and she did not know how much more she could take for one morning.

"What you say may all be true," Gwen said, "yet that does not mean we should not try. We find ourselves in a unique moment in history: the tyrant McCloud king is dead; his son, Bronson, is loyal to us; their kingdom was destroyed, and we were, however briefly, united in the cause to oust the invaders. I see this as an opportunity to, once and for all, unite our two kingdoms."

"The problem with the McClouds," Kendrick said, "is that they are malcontents, and that they consider themselves in competition with us. They see King's Court, and they want the same. But they've never had a King's Court, and they never will. It is honor and nobility and refinement that build a King's Court, not a pile of stones. That is what they will never understand."

Gwendolyn sighed.

"Having a stable McCloud side of the Highlands is vital to our own interests," she said. "We do not want the threat of cattle raids over our head all the time. We want our people to live in peace. Which is how our father felt, and which is precisely why he had tried to forge an alliance with Luanda's marriage to a McCloud."

"Yet it did not succeed," Aberthol said. "We must learn from his mistakes."

"Nonetheless," Gwen said, "we must also learn from his efforts. I am not prepared to give up on peace so quickly. It may be harder, and messier—but it is longer-lasting, and it is the only path to our ultimate security. We must find a way to unite our two peoples. There is always a way. The question is how?"

She surveyed her men, and they all stood there, brows furrowed.

She settled on Godfrey, who stood there, bleary-eyed, unshaven, looking hung over.

"Godfrey," she said. "You have not spoken today. You always have some nugget of wisdom."

Godfrey looked up at her, caught off guard.

"Well," he said, flustered, running a hand through his unkempt hair, "I've always known one thing to bring men together," he, looking around warily. "And that is drink. Show me two men who hate each other, and I'll have them singing together over a pint of ale."

The room suddenly broke into laughter, and Godfrey looked around, unsure, then smiled self-consciously.

Gwendolyn smiled, as she looked him over. Her brother was kooky, and yet he held some primal wisdom. And he knew, better than anyone she knew, the heartbeat of the common man. Her father had taught her that sometimes the most complex solution came in the most obvious wisdom.

"You may be right," she said. "That may just be the solution. And I am going to appoint you to find out."

Godfrey's eyes opened wide, looking astonished.

"*Me*, my lady?" he asked.

Gwendolyn nodded, as the others in the room looked on, astonished.

"You are the perfect one. Travel across the Highlands. Seek out Bronson. Tell him I've received his dispatches. Then establish drinking halls. Help Bronson do what he cannot: bring these men together."

"My lady," he said, stammering, "I am not a leader. And I am no politician. You know this. Father knew this. He tried to hide me from court. And now you want to give me a position? Did you learn nothing from father? He knew, at least, that I was good for nothing here."

"Father did not see clearly in all matters," Gwen said. "I see much more in you. You have talents that other men do not, and you vastly underestimate yourself. You can bring together men of disparate backgrounds, better than any man I've seen. You lack the haughtiness inherent in most royalty. I trust you, and I need you to do this. Will you accept?"

Godfrey reluctantly nodded.

"For you, my sister," he said, "I would do anything."

Gwen nodded and took a deep breath, grateful the matter was settled. She could not bear to hear any more scrolls from Aberthol, so she pre-empted it as she saw him reaching for another, and rose from her throne, shaky.

The room immediately rose with her, and it was clear the session was over.

Thor came and took her hand, as Aberthol slammed his staff and the room broke up into relaxed conversation.

"Are you all right?" Thor asked her quietly; he must have seen how pale her face was.

Gwen breathed deep, grateful for Thor's support. She felt tired.

"I just need to lie down," she said.

*

Thorgrin stood outside the main gateway to King's Court, beneath the huge, arched stone entrance, holding his horse by the reins, as did all his friends, each getting ready to depart for their journey on Departure Day. Beside him, Reece checked and re-checked his saddle, brushing his horse, preparing for his trip to the Upper Islands; beside him, Elden prepared to venture off to search for his father, while O'Connor prepared to embark to see his sister. Conven prepared to go to his hometown and visit his wife—while nearby, Erec and Kendrick prepared to set off to do the work of the Silver. Even Godfrey was gearing up for his journey to McCloud territory. They all were heading in a different direction, all hoping to catch the good luck of embarking on Departure Day.

Thor clasped forearms with Reece.

"I will miss you, old friend," Thor said.

"And I you," Reece said. "I'll be back before the second moon rises, in time for our joint wedding. You need not worry."

"The Upper Isles are not far," Thor said. "But they are fraught with danger. Watch your back."

"Don't worry, I'll be going with him," came a voice.

They both turned to see Krog standing nearby, smiling as he prepared his horse, stuffing a short sword into an extra scabbard.

"You are?" Reece asked, surprised.

Krog nodded back, standing there with a stern expression.

"But why?" Reece asked. "I thought you don't even like me."

"I don't," Krog said emphatically. "It's something to do. And like I said, I owe you for saving my life back there. I need to pay it off."

Reece shook his head.

"I don't want anyone tagging along out of some sense of obligation," Reece said. "You can join me if you want—but not because you feel indebted to me."

"I will come for any reason I wish," Krog said defiantly, then turned and stormed off, preparing his horse.

Reece and Thor exchanged a curious glance, and Reece shook his head.

"I swear, I'll never figure him out," Reece said.

"Keep your eyes open," Thor repeated. "Those MacGils may be cousins, but don't trust any of them."

"Do not worry, my friend," he replied. "They don't want a war on their hands they cannot win. They would never dare harm a member of the royal family. And if they do, well," Reece grinned, "I've got weapons at my side, and I'm only too happy to defend myself."

Thor smiled back.

"I know, friend. I've fought many battles with you at my back. I wish you were staying here to help me pick and train the Legion."

"I suspect you will manage just fine on your own," Reece said. "In fact, by the time I return, I suspect the Legion will already be brimming with new faces."

Thor smiled.

"We shall see."

"Reece, may I have a minute?" came a female voice.

Reece turned and saw, standing behind him, Selese. She looked upset.

"I don't want you to leave," she added, her voice grave.

"But I am hardly leaving," Reece said. "It is just a few days' voyage."

Thor turned away to give them privacy, and as he went he still heard their hushed voices, carried on the wind.

"Our wedding is but a half-moon away," Selese added.

"I am aware of that, I assure you," he replied. "I did not volunteer this mission."

"I do not want you to go," she said, her voice trembling. "I'm normally not like this, but I have a bad feeling about it. Just stay here. Help us prepare for the wedding. Gwen can send someone else."

Reece shook his head.

"I would never turn down a request from my sister. It goes against my honor. Besides, it's Departure Day," he said. "It is an auspicious day to embark."

She shrugged.

"Not for all," she said. "My father embarked once on Departure Day. He never returned."

Reece saw a tear on her cheek, and he stepped forward and stroked her face with the back of his hand.

"I am touched, my love, for how much you care for me," Reece said. "And I promise you I shall return."

"I love your sister," Selese said, still looking down, not meeting his eyes. "After all, we're being married together. She has become as close to me as a sister. And yet, in this case, I wished she would have chosen someone else to go."

"The kingdom she rules is vast, and there are not many people she can trust—not like a brother," Reece said. "Enough of this gloomy talk. It is all for naught, I assure you. I shall be back in but a few days, and we shall be together forever."

Reece leaned in and kissed her, and she stepped forward and hugged him tightly, clinging to him.

Thor mounted his horse and from this vantage point, he looked around at all his brothers, all of them mounting their horses. It was odd to see all these men in one place who, in but moments, would be scattered across the kingdom. Soon, Godfrey would be on the other side of the Highlands; Kendrick and Erec would be far off securing forts and bridges; Conven, O'Connor and Elden would be returning to their villages, each seeking out their own family members; Steffen would be far away, tending to distribution in the small villages. And Thor himself would be many days' ride from King's Court, scouring the towns for new recruits for the Legion.

The festivities were over, the Summer Solstice already behind them, as if it had never happened. They were now getting down to the hard work of running and restoring the kingdom. Thor knew that soon enough, they would all be reunited again. Yet he could not help but wonder how much each of them would be changed when they returned.

A distant horn sounded, Thor kicked his horse, along with the others, and they all charged off, away from King's Court, each forking in their own direction on the dusty road. Thor knew he should be filled with joy, with optimism; yet for some reason, a part of him could not help but feel as if he might not see all of these men again.

CHAPTER TWENTY TWO

Bronson marched out of the tall, vertical gates of Highlandia, flanked by the McCloud generals, his father's former men, along with dozens of attendants, and he sighed, in an irritable mood. He was annoyed that he was being led to the sight of yet another dispute, yet another cattle raid, yet another headache in his impossible effort to unite the McClouds and the MacGils. He was seriously starting to wonder whether it was even possible to bring peace between the two perpetually warring clans.

It darkened his mood even more to be led here by his father's former general, Koovia. Over the last six moons, McCloud had come to distrust Koovia; it was starting to dawn on him that Koovia was not the ingratiating general that he had at first made himself to be. Koovia had initially pretended to be all too eager to help unite the two sides of the Highlands; yet the more Bronson got to know him, the more he observed him increasingly trying to undermine his efforts, to keep the two clans apart from each other. Koovia was, deep down, wary of the MacGils—as he had been during his father's time—and increasingly uncontrollable.

Working with Koovia was a necessary evil, given that all the McCloud soldiers loved him, and that he somehow retained a hypnotic fix on his men. Bronson had pondered imprisoning him, more than once, but refrained for the negative consequences that would come. As it was, Bronson was on shaky ground here, trying to control these people, trying to control the MacGils on the other side of the Highlands, and trying to get them all to live in harmony. It had been six moons of hell.

Bronson had forgotten how stubborn his people were, how hard-headed, how prone to violence and aggression. Having spent some time on the MacGil side, Bronson was realizing more and more the stark differences between the two clans. The last several hundred years had really bred two different peoples. Bronson felt that he himself acted more like a MacGil, and he felt more of a sympathy with the MacGils. Coming back to his people now actually embarrassed him, seeing how crude they were, how prone to go to war against people who meant them no harm.

When Bronson had first arrived, the McClouds had been grateful to all the MacGils for liberating them from the grip of Andronicus and of the Empire. They had been grateful for Bronson's presence here, for his help in rebuilding. They had even expressed a desire and enthusiasm to unite the two kingdoms.

But the more time Bronson spent here, the more he felt it was a front, that his people were not actually interested in uniting, that they wanted to stay apart, and that they distrusted the MacGils deeply. The MacGils seemed more open to trusting the McClouds, despite a long history of being attacked unprovoked; yet every day since Bronson's arrival, some McClouds had undermined the effort in yet another raid or dispute.

McCloud followed Koovia, wondering where he was leading him today.

They hiked along a low ridge as they emerged from the castle, blooms of summer all around them, the Highlands covered in tall, colored grasses. Bronson looked down on both sides of the ridge and as far as he could see were bright flowers, covering both slopes of the Highlands. The sight was quite a dramatic change from winter, where the Highlands were nothing but snow and ice. Standing up here, Bronson felt a cool breeze, always cooler this high up.

Still, it was a picture-perfect summer day, clouds gathering lightly in the sky under the rays of the first and second suns. From up here, looking down, Bronson felt as if he were atop the world, looking down on the two kingdoms, these two kingdoms he still hoped to make one, and he wondered, with a land like this, how anything could possibly be wrong in the world.

As they rounded a bend, McCloud heard the bickering carrying on the wind, and he saw two angry parties before him, dozens of MacGils on one side, and dozens of McClouds on the other, angrily arguing with each other, as a flock of sheep milled about them. Bronson sensed their anger even from here, and he knew he would be walking into a firestorm. He sighed, bracing himself.

"This is where it happened," Koovia explained, as they approached.

They neared, and Koovia screamed for silence. Slowly, the warring clans quieted and all eyes turned to Bronson.

"What happened this time?" Bronson asked, already impatient.

"It is very simple what happened," said one of the McClouds, an old man, faced lined with stubble, missing teeth, standing protectively over his sheep. "These MacGils came up here and raided our sheep and tried to bring them back over the Highlands. We caught them before they went. You must imprison them now, if you are the strong ruler you claim to be."

There came a cheer from the McCloud side. Bronson turned and looked at the MacGils; they stood there patiently, meekly, a younger bunch with intelligent eyes, awaiting their turn. As he looked beyond them, Bronson saw the beautiful summer countryside, and wished he could be anywhere but here. With all this bounty, all this beauty, all around them, what did these men have to fight about?

"And your side of the story?" he asked the MacGils. "Did you come up here and steal these cattle?"

"We did, my Lord," the MacGils answered plainly.

Bronson stared back in surprise, not expecting that answer.

"Then you admit your crime?"

"No, my lord," they replied.

Now Bronson was confused.

"How is theft not a crime?"

"You cannot steal what is yours, my lord," they replied. "Those cattle were ours to begin with. We just stole them back."

"Stole them back?" Bronson asked. His stomach was burning.

The MacGils nodded.

"The McClouds raided our cattle last week. We came and took them back. See those markings?"

They bent over, grabbed a sheep, turned its leg, and showed a brand on it.

"The mark of the MacGils. Plain for anyone to see."

Bronson stared, and saw the marking, and realized they were indeed correct.

He turned and faced the McClouds, now annoyed with them for stealing—and for lying.

"And what have you to say for yourselves?" he asked.

The elder McCloud shrugged.

"I found them wandering the hills."

"Wandering the hills on the MacGil side," the MacGils retorted. "That doesn't make them yours."

The old men shrugged.

"You let them loose, then they are not yours anymore."

"They were not loose! They were grazing! Sheep graze. That is what they do!"

The old man shouted and cursed at them, and the MacGils started to curse them back. A cacophony of noise arose, men cursing each other, sheep bleating.

Bronson rubbed his forehead, his headache worsening. The day had hardly begun, and there was yet a long day ahead. Why could these men not get along? Was his cause here hopeless?

He had to admit, even though they were his native people, the McClouds were the instigators. In every case he had seen, they were always the ones at fault. It was as if a part of them just did not want peace.

Bronson stepped forward, and there came a lull in the squabbling as all eyes turned to him.

"If these are his sheep, then these are his sheep," Bronson finally said to the McClouds. "It does not matter where you found them. He took back what was his."

He turned to the MacGils.

"Take them and go," he said. "I am sorry for your trouble."

The MacGils nodded, satisfied, and corralled their sheep and began to lead them down to their side of the mountain.

"You can't just let them go!" the old man yelled out to Koovia. "Stop them! Our new King is too weak to support us! Use the might of your army! Unless you are too weak, too!"

Bronson bristled at the old man's words, and he could see Koovia bristling, too, and thinking it all over himself. He could see that Koovia wanted to go after those sheep.

But Koovia instead turned and shoved the old man, and he stumbled back. He grabbed the hilt of his sword.

"Say another word old man, and we will see who is weak!"

Koovia stepped forward in a rage, and the old man backed away.

Slowly, the McClouds turned and stormed down the hill.

Koovia, still scowling, turned and faced Bronson.

"You don't know your people," he said. "You are not a King in their eyes, or regent, or whatever it is that Gwendolyn has named you. To them, you are weak. A puppet. The McClouds are used to taking what they want by force. That is their way. You will never change them. So stop wasting your time here, and go back to Gwendolyn."

Bronson frowned, fed up.

"You are my general," Bronson said. "You answer to me. I don't answer to you. I speak with the authority of Gwendolyn. Both sides of the kingdom will be united. And you will do your part by allowing the MacGil soldiers to patrol with you."

Koovia reeled back in surprise.

"What do you mean?"

Bronson scowled; he could tell by Koovia's face that he was lying.

"I have heard the reports," Bronson said. "For many moons you have told me you were allowing the MacGils to patrol with our men—yet the other day I was told MacGils came to your camp and you shut them out. Are the reports not true?"

Koovia seemed flustered.

"The MacGils are not our people," he said, defensive. "What does it matter to you? You are not one of them. You were raised here. Your father would be ashamed of you."

Bronson darkened.

"I know where I was raised. I am your leader. You answer to me. And I say that our men will train together."

Koovia shook his head slowly, looking Bronson up and down.

"You may be leader for now, but you won't be for long. Our people responded to your father because he used force. Brutal force. That is what our people need. You will not employ it—and to our people, that makes you weak. And the weak always fall."

Koovia turned his back and marched away, his men falling in behind him. Bronson stood there and watched them go, back down the hill, his headache increasing.

He could not help but wonder what on earth he was doing here.

*

Luanda paced in her castle chamber, the room alight with torches, impatient as night fell, waiting for Bronson's return. He'd been gone all day, yet again, on matters related to the unification. It was, she knew, an exercise in futility, and it just made her mad at her sister. Gwendolyn had always been so naïve. What had she been thinking? That the two clans would really unite?

If she had just asked her, then Luanda would have told her at once that it would never work. The McClouds, she knew from experience, were savages. If Luanda was queen, she would have simply sealed up the Highlands, created a great wall, doubled the patrols and let the savages rot here. She would protect the Western kingdom of the Ring, and let be what may be on the Eastern side.

But Gwendolyn, always the idealist, had to let her little fantasies play out—and even worse, she had to assign Bronson to try to enforce it. Each day was getting worse in this awful place, and Luanda knew that nothing good could come of it.

It was not Luanda's problem. Exiled here, to the other side of the Highlands, she might as well have been sentenced to prison—or to death instead. Being stuck here, having to live with these savages, in this empty castle, with nothing to do all day but wait for Bronson to return home, was the worst possible punishment Gwen could have given her.

At first, of course, Luanda had been grateful her life had been spared. But now, six moons later, her gratitude had turned to resentment. The more time passed, the more she was feeling like her old self, feeling a growing restlessness. She was sorely disappointed; she had been sure that at some point Gwendolyn would have granted her mercy and relented and let her back into her homeland, into King's Court. She could not believe that she was still stuck here, banished, that she had been shut out of all the wedding preparation and festivities going on across the Highlands. That she had been left to rot here all alone. It was almost too much to bear. Her sister, she felt, should have exhibited more mercy.

Luanda fumed for many moons, as her hair slowly grew back, spending many days crying. Until one day, finally, a plan had come to her, a way out of her misery, a way to gain back control. It dawned on her, as clear as day: if she had a child, that child could not be banished from King's Court. Luanda was a young, healthy woman, and she could bear children. Royal children. After all, she was the firstborn of King MacGil, and her child would carry the bloodline. Gwendolyn might have won this generation, but Luanda realized that things could change with the next. She was determined, and she would stop at nothing, would do everything in her power, to make sure that her offspring ousted her sister's. She would find a way to put them on the throne, and regain power.

The idea had hardened in Luanda's mind over these past moons, and she had made Bronson sleep with her, every day and every night. Each day she had awakened expecting to be able to report the good news that she was pregnant.

And yet here she was, fuming, six moons later, and still no baby. It had been a failure, like everything else in her life. It was not working, for whatever reason. It might not *ever* work, she realized. She had awakened so hopeful every day, but now, she was losing hope. Their marriage seemed doomed; all of her plans seemed doomed. Even this, her backup plan, was falling apart.

The door opened and Luanda spun, caught off guard, as Bronson stormed in, ignoring her. Bronson marched across the room, lost in thought, clearly fixated by his day's business.

Luanda had no time for his brooding; she came up behind him, grabbed his shoulders, and began to pull off his clothes. Maybe this time would be different.

"What are you doing?" he asked.

"I've been waiting for you all day," she said, slipping out of her robe, standing there naked.

Bronson barely noticed her, though, as he crossed the chamber and went to his desk, leafing through a pile of scrolls.

"You've been gone all day," she said. "Now it's time for us."

She came up behind him and stroked his arms and shoulders. She could feel the tension in them.

Finally, he turned around.

"Please, Luanda, not now. I've had a terrible day."

"So have I," she said, irritated, losing patience. "Do you think you're the only one who is unhappy here? I must sit here all day and wait for you. I have no one and nothing here. I want a baby. I *need* a baby."

Bronson examined her, seeming confused.

She pulled him towards her, threw him down to the bed and jumped on top of him.

"Luanda, this is not the time. I'm not ready—"

Luanda ignored him. She did not care what Bronson wanted any more.

But to Luanda's shock, Bronson pushed her off the bed.

Luanda stood there, humiliated, in a rage. She was furious at Bronson. At her sister. At herself. At her life.

"I said not now!" Bronson said.

"Who cares if it's now or later?" she yelled back. "It's not working!"

Bronson sat on the edge of the bed, looking dejected.

"My sister will give birth any day," Luanda added. "And I will have nothing to show."

"It is not a competition," he said calmly. "And we have all the time in the world. Calm yourself."

"No, we don't!" she screamed. "And you are wrong: the entire world is a competition."

"I am sorry," he said. "Let us not fight."

Luanda stood there, breathing hard, fuming.

"Sorry is not good enough," she said.

Luanda threw on her robe, marched past Bronson and stormed out of the room. She would find a way to get out of this place and to regain power—no matter what she had to do.

CHAPTER TWENTY THREE

Srog stood at the top of the highest peak of the Upper Isles, peering down through the rain and mist at the Bay of Crabs. He looked closely at the long jetties of boulders that stretched into the sea, squinting into the fog and blinding rain. He was dripping wet, doused by the rain, his clothes and hair wet, as he stood there beside his generals.

Srog had learned to ignore the rain ever since moving here. It was part of life on the Upper Isles: each day the sky was overcast, blanketed by rolling clouds, the wind ever-present, and the climate much cooler, even in summer. There was always either the threat of rain, or the presence of it. No day was dry. The Upper Isles, he had learned, deserved their reputation as a gloomy, miserable place, the weather fitting its reputation—and the people matching the temperament of the weather.

These past six moons Srog had come to know these Upper Islanders; they were a wily people, and could never be fully trusted. His six moons of ruling here had met with nothing but frustration, the people here clearly determined to thwart his rule at every turn, to sabotage his efforts. They were a rebellious folk, and they were intent on breaking off the yoke of the new queen Gwendolyn.

"There, my Lord," the general cried out to be heard over the wind. "Do you see it?"

Srog peered into the mist and saw bobbing there, in the rough ocean, the remnant of one of the queen's ships, tossing in the waves, smashing into the rocks. The waves crashed all around the boat, and the ship smashed again and again into the rocks. The ship, empty of men, spun in each direction. Srog could hear the splintering of wood even from here as it was smashed to pieces against the rocks.

"The anchor was cut early this morning," the general continued. "By the time our men detected it, it was too late. They could not salvage it in time, my Lord."

"You are certain it was cut?" Srog asked.

The general reached out and held in his hand a severed piece of rope.

"A clean cut, my Lord," he explained. "No rock did this. It was a man's dagger. Sabotage."

Srog examined the rope, and realized he was correct.

Srog sighed, weary from this place. He had spent most his life in Silesia, a grand, civilized city, where the people were honest and noble. He had ruled it well, uniting upper and lower Silesia, achieving what no Lord had ever managed to do. Silesia was a palace next to this dump, and Silesians were nothing like these Upper Islanders. After all his time here, Srog was slowly settling into the conclusion that the Upper Islanders enjoyed their subversion; they thrived on it. More and more, he sensed that they were a people who could not be ruled.

Each time Srog found an Upper Islander he could trust, that person, too, betrayed him. He was now at the point where he trusted no one.

"Increase patrols at the ships," Srog said. "I want a soldier on duty at the moorings, all through the day and night. Understood?"

"Yes, sir," the general said. He turned and hurried down the ridge, ordering his men, who all burst into action.

Srog looked down and surveyed the dozens of queen's ships anchored at the wide sandy beach, and prayed that none of them met the same fate. This was the second ship this month that had been destroyed by sabotage, and he was determined not to lose another one.

Srog turned and hurried through the awful weather, followed by his advisors, jogging back to the warmth of the castle. It was hardly a castle—more like a fort, built square and low to the ground, with no artistic imagination or aesthetic appeal. It was utilitarian, uninspired and cold, much like the people of this place.

Srog hurried through the doors, opened for him, and rushed inside. The door slammed behind them, and he finally found quiet from the raging wind and rain. He stood there, his body dripping from the rain, and took off his outer shirt, as he was accustomed to by now, hanging it on a hook. He marched through the fort, running his hands through his wet hair, guards stiffening to attention as he went.

Srog passed through various corridors and finally entered the great hall, small compared to the castles he was used to. A square room with low ceilings, it had a large fireplace along one wall, with table and chairs positioned close to it. The Upper Islanders always stayed close to a fire, needing warmth and heat to dry off from the weather, and now there were several dozen men seated around the table.

Srog took a seat at the center of the table, close to the fireplace, and ran his wet hand through his hair and over his clothes several times, doing his best to dry it off. Several mangy dogs moved out of his way as he came close. They sat nearby, repositioning themselves, and looked up at him, waiting for food.

Srog threw them a piece of meat from the table, then reached over, grabbed a goblet of wine, and drank the whole thing, wanting to make this place go away. He rubbed his head in his hands. This island gave him a massive headache. A second ship sabotaged by these people. What was wrong with them? Why did their resentments and petty rivalries run so deep? Srog was beginning to feel that Gwendolyn had made a mistake to try to unite the Upper Isles with the mainland. He was feeling more and more that she should abandon the whole place, and let it fall prey to its own destiny, as her father had before her.

Srog looked up and saw seated across from him Tirus' three sons, Karus, Falus and Matus. Around the rest of the table sat several dozen more warriors and noblemen of the Upper Isles, all loyal to Tirus, all deep into their drink and food, as torches were lit all around them. They were all settling in for the night.

Up here, they celebrated the Summer Solstice a day late, and this meager, somber meal was this Isle's version of celebration. Srog shuddered, and not just from the wet and the cold. He missed King's Court; he missed Silesia, and he pined to be back on the mainland. He could not help but feel his time here was futility.

Srog wished he could understand these Upper Islanders, but try as he did, he could not. They claimed that the source of their upset stemmed from Tirus' imprisonment; yet after six moons of observing them, Srog did not believe that was all of it. He felt that, even if Tirus were set free, these people would still find some cause for subversion.

"And what reports today, my lord?" Matus asked, sitting beside him. Srog had learned that Matus was the only Upper Islander he could trust.

"Another ship sabotaged," Srog answered grimly. "Lost to the rocks. Gwendolyn will not be happy."

Srog looked down at the scroll before him, finished penning his letter for Gwendolyn, and handed it to a waiting attendant.

"Send this off with the next falcon," Srog ordered.

"Yes, my Lord," the attendant said, hurrying off.

Srog wondered if the attendant truly would follow out his order, or if the missive would, as so many others, get lost mysteriously.

"Sabotage is a strong word," Falus said darkly.

The other soldiers around the table slowly quieted, all turning and looking Srog's way.

Srog stared back at Falus, Tirus' eldest son. He resembled Tirus exactly. He stared back, defiant.

"The queen's ships are meant for smoother waters," Karus added. "Perhaps the tides snapped the ropes."

Srog shook his head, annoyed.

"No tides did this," he said, "and the queen's ships can traverse waters stronger than these. It was the work of men."

"Perhaps it was the work of one of your men?" Falus asked. "Perhaps you have a traitor amongst you?"

Srog was exhausted by Karus' and Falus' subtle reasoning, both staring back at him with the same dark, defiant eyes of their father.

"And perhaps some great sea monster with perfectly square teeth jumped up and ate the rope," Srog answered sarcastically.

Some of the warriors about the table snickered, and Falus and Karus reddened and grimaced back.

"You mock us," Falus said, threateningly.

"Your people are sabotaging our ships," Srog said, his voice rising. "And I want to know why."

The room grew tense.

"Perhaps they are unhappy that your queen has imprisoned our leader like a common criminal," came a voice from the end of the table.

Srog looked over to see that it was one of the nobles; a muted grunt of approval arose among the table's other nobles.

"Your leader," Srog countered, "was a traitor to the Ring. He joined the Empire against us. Gwendolyn's sentence was lenient. He deserved hanging."

"He was a traitor to *your* Ring," said another noble. "Not ours."

The other nobles grunted in agreement.

Srog stared back, his anger rising.

"Just because you live on these isles, it doesn't make you separate from us. You are still protected by our armies."

"We do fine in these Upper Isles without your help," one said.

"Perhaps our people just don't want you here," said another. "Perhaps they don't like the look of the Queen's ships filling our shores."

"No one likes to be occupied," said another.

"You are not occupied. You are free. Your men come to our shores, and we come to yours. We protect you from foreign enemies, and our ships come to you filled with supplies for your countrymen, supplies you dearly need."

"We do not need protecting," said another noble. "Nor do we need your supplies. If you MacGils would stay on your mainland, we would have no problems."

"Oh?" Srog countered, "Then why did you MacGils invade us unprovoked and try to take the mainland for yourselves?"

The nobles reddened, unable to respond. They looked at each other, then slowly, sourly, one of them got up, scraping his chair back along the stone, standing and facing his men.

"My meat has soured," he said.

He turned and walked from the room, slamming the door behind him.

A thick, tense silence followed.

Slowly, one at a time, the other nobles rose and walked from the room.

Now Srog sat with just three men at the table—Tirus' three sons, Falus, Karus and Matus. Srog looked about, and felt more on edge ever.

"Just release our father," Falus said to him quietly. "Then our men will let your ships be."

"Your father tried to kill our queen," Srog said. "And he betrayed us twice. He cannot be released."

"Then as long as he's in his cell, do not expect our people to tolerate you," Karus said.

The two brothers stood and began to walk out. They stopped and turned to Matus.

"You're not joining us?" Falus asked, surprised.

Matus sat there defiantly.

"My place is here. At this table. The queen's table."

Falus and Karus shook their heads in disgust, then turned and stormed out.

Srog sat there, at the mostly empty table, feeling hollowed out.

"My Lord, I apologize for them," Matus said. "Gwendolyn was more than kind to spare my father's life."

"I do not understand your people," Srog said. "For the life of me, I do not understand them. What does it take to rule them well? I ruled a great city, far greater than this. But with these people, I cannot rule them."

"Because mine are a people not meant to be ruled," Matus said. "They are defiant by nature—even to my father. That was the secret my father knew. Do not try to rule them; the less you try, the more they may come around. Then again, they might not. They are stubborn people, with little to lose. That is the reason they live here—they do not want anything to do with the mainland. They are wrong in almost everything they do, but they might be right about one thing: you might do yourself and Gwendolyn a greater service to bring your assets elsewhere."

Srog shook his head.

"Gwendolyn needs the Upper Isles. She needs a unified Ring. All the MacGils are of one family, sharing blood. This division, it makes no sense."

"Sometimes geography creates a great divide amongst a people over time. This family has grown apart."

An attendant came by and placed a new goblet of wine before Srog, and he picked it up.

"You are the only one I can completely trust here," Srog said, appreciative. "How is it that you are unlike the rest of your people?"

"I despise my father," Matus said. "I despise everything he stands for. He has no principles, no honor. I admired Gwendolyn's father, my uncle, King MacGil, greatly. I always admired all of the MacGils of the mainland. They live by their honor, no matter what it takes. That is the life I've always wanted."

"Well, you have lived it yourself," Srog said approvingly.

Srog raised the goblet to his lips, prepared to drink, when suddenly, Matus leapt forward and swung around, and knocked the goblet from his hand. It went flying, landing on the floor, echoing as it rolled across the stone.

Srog stared back at him, shocked, not understanding.

Matus crossed the room, picked up the goblet, and held it up for Srog to see.

Srog came closer, and noticed a black lining at the bottom of it.

Matus reached down, ran his finger along it, held it up, and rubbed his fingers together. As he did, a fine black dust drifted down to the ground.

"Blackroot," he said. "One sip, and you're dead."

Srog stood there, frozen, looking at it in horror, his blood running cold.

"How did you know?" he asked in a whisper.

"The color of your wine," Matus answered. "It seemed too dark to me."

As Srog stood there, frozen in horror, not knowing what to say, Matus looked both ways, then leaned in close.

"Trust no one. *No one.*"

CHAPTER TWENTY FOUR

Romulus stood at the helm of his new ship, hands on his hips, huge, rolling waves sending the ship rising and falling, smashing into the foam, as he watched the coastline of the Empire's capital come into view. Behind him sailed his fleet, thousands of Empire ships, all returning home from their defeat. Romulus peered into the horizon, as the mist began to lift, and spotted the host of soldiers waiting to greet him on shore, as he suspected he would. His stomach tightened, as he prepared for the confrontation to come.

Ragon, clearly, had received word of his return, and assembled all his men. The number two general beneath Romulus, Ragon had surely heard, by now, of Andronicus' death, of Romulus' assassination of the former council, and of Romulus' seizing position as Supreme Commander. If Romulus had been victorious, Ragon would be awaiting him with parades and accolades—he would have no choice.

But because Romulus was returning in disgrace, Ragon was waiting to greet him in a very different way. Ragon, Romulus knew, was waiting to imprison him, to make it clear to all the armies that Romulus was stripped of power, and that Ragon was the new Supreme Commander. Romulus knew how he thought, because Romulus would do the same thing in his shoes.

But Romulus did not plan on ceding power so easily. His men, he knew, would be watching their exchange closely to see which commander would come out victorious. Romulus had not fought his entire life to capitulate, and no matter how many soldiers he faced, it was time to rule with an iron fist. He gripped the hilt of his sword until his knuckles turned white, preparing.

Romulus' ship soon touched shore, and as it did, he waited patiently, as his men lowered the long plank from their ship down to the beach. They lined it, standing at attention, and he walked between them, taking all the time in the world. His men followed behind him, and he made a show of appearing calm and confident for all the world to see.

Tens of thousands of Empire soldiers, lined up in neat formations, awaited him below, all behind Ragon. Romulus knew that his men could not win the battle; there were too many of them, the entire main body of the Empire army, awaiting. He would have to win another way.

Romulus strutted proudly onto the shore, heading right for Ragon, unafraid.

Ragon stood there, tall, muscular, his broad face covered in scars, and scowled back, flanked by his soldiers. Romulus walked right up to him and stopped, and in the thick silence, the two of them faced off, each determined.

"Romulus, of the first battalion of the Eastern Province of the Empire," Ragon boomed, loud enough to be heard by his men, "You are hereby set to be imprisoned and executed for crimes against the Empire."

All of the men, on both sides, stood there, unmoving, the air thick with tension. Ragon, wasting no time, turned and nodded to his men, and several of his soldiers took a step forward to arrest Romulus.

At the same time, without needing to be told, several of Romulus' men stepped forward to protect him.

The soldiers froze on both sides, facing off, hands on their hilts, and awaiting commands.

"Any resistance is futile," Ragon said. "You have tens of thousands of men—but I have *hundreds* of thousands, and the backing of every country in the Empire. Submit now and die a quick and easy death. Prolong this, and your men will be killed, and you tortured."

Romulus stared back, silent, expressionless, carefully thinking through his next move.

"If I surrender," Romulus said, "you will promise my men safe passage?"

Ragon nodded.

"You have my word."

"Then I will surrender on one condition," Romulus said. "If you yourself are the one to arrest me. Give me, at least, that honor."

Ragon nodded, seeming relieved.

"Fair enough."

Ragon took the iron shackles from his guard, and stepped forward towards Romulus.

"Turn around and place your hands behind your back," he commanded.

Romulus turned slowly, his heart pounding, as Ragon approached. Romulus listened carefully, focusing on the fine sound of the shackles, the sound that came as he raised it and brought it down toward his wrist. He was waiting, waiting, for just the right moment.

Romulus felt the cold metal of the shackles touch his wrist, and the time was right. He spun around in an instant, and in the process, elbowed Ragon across the face, shattering his cheek bone. In the same motion, he snatched the shackles from his hand, stood over him, and swung them down with all his might, breaking Ragon's nose.

The two armies still faced off, each unsure how to react; it all happened so quickly. Romulus took advantage of the hesitation: he wasted no time as he reached down, grabbed Ragon by the back of the head, drew his dagger, and held it tightly to Ragon's throat.

Ragon, gushing blood, could barely breathe as Romulus dug the blade against his throat.

"Tell them that you cede to me as Supreme Commander," Romulus growled.

"Never," Ragon murmured.

Romulus pushed the blade harder against his throat, until blood started to trickle. Ragon gurgled, but said nothing.

Romulus shifted the point of the blade to Ragon's eye, and as soon as he began to apply pressure, Ragon screamed out.

"I CEDE TO ROMULUS!" he screamed.

Romulus nodded, satisfied.

"Very good," he said.

Romulus, in one quick motion, sliced Ragon's throat, and Ragon slumped to the ground, dead.

Romulus stood there, staring back at the thousands of Empire soldiers. They all faced him, unsure, and Romulus knew this was the moment of truth. With their leader dead, would they defer to him?

As Romulus stood there in the silence, waiting, watching, it feeling like an eternity, finally, the rows and rows of Empire soldiers all dropped to a knee, the air filled with the sound of tens of thousands of suits of armor clanking, as they all lowered their heads and bowed to him.

Romulus drew his sword and raised it high above his head, breathing in deep, taking in the moment, the entire strength of the Empire bowing to him, now, finally, under his command.

"ROMULUS!" they all chanted as one.

"ROMULUS!"

CHAPTER TWENTY FIVE

Thor charged on his horse, galloping down the main road that led from King's Court, heading south, oddly enough, in the direction of his home town. Krohn ran at his horse's heels, as he had been for hours, the two of them embarking together on this quest.

It was time to rebuild the Legion, time for a new Selection, and as he rode, Thor felt a surreal quality to his mission: instead of being on the receiving end, instead of being the one to stand in his village and wait hopefully for the Silver to appear, now it was he, Thor, who was doing the choosing. The roles had reversed. It was such an honor, he could scarcely believe it.

Thor also felt a tremendous responsibility on his shoulders: rebuilding the Legion was a sacred task in his eyes. He had to fill the shoes of the dead boys who had given their lives defending the Ring; he had to choose the next generation of the very best warriors. It was not something he took lightly, and he knew that he must make his choices very carefully.

Throughout his entire childhood, Thor had spent days peering over the horizon, dreaming of the great warriors that might one day pass through this town, his humble little village, of being picked and chosen. And now here he was, the one who was traveling the countryside, riding through all the towns. It was an honor beyond what he could ever imagine. It did not even feel real to him.

Thor rode and rode, until he and his horse—and Krohn—were all breathing hard, and finally he rounded a bend and in the distance, a small village came into view. He decided to make for it; he knew they could all use a break, and this village would be as good a place as any to begin the Selection.

As he approached, Thor dimly recognized the place from the large, crooked tree at its entrance, a farming village a half day's ride north of his home town. It was a place he had traveled a few times growing up, joining his brothers as they traded for wool and weapons. He hadn't set foot here in years, but he remembered it to be a provincial town, much like the place he had grown up in, and he did not remember the people as being especially friendly. If he recalled correctly, it had seemed to be populated back then with vulgar types, striking hard bargains, and seeming just as happy not to have visitors as to have them.

It had been many years, though, and Thor knew his memory might be distorted, and he wanted to give this village another chance. After all, it was a farming village, and there might be some good recruits here.

As Thor charged for the town, raising dust as he approached, he could already see all the boys lining up, at attention, waiting nervously. He could see the parents behind them, even more nervous. Thor pondered how much had changed since he himself had waited for the Selection. Back then, the Silver had arrived in chariots, in a huge entourage of soldiers; now, it was just he, Thor, alone. These were lean times, and until the Legion and the Silver were rebuilt, it would take time to rebuild everything. Thor had been offered an entourage of soldiers to accompany him—but he had denied it. He felt he did not need anyone to accompany him; he felt that if he could not defend himself, alone, on these highways, then he was not worthy of the task.

Thor pulled into the dusty town, clouds of dust settling around him on the hot summer day, and he pulled his horse to a stop in the center of town. He sat there, looking down at the potential recruits, dozens of boys, lined up, most dressed in rags, looking nervous. He marveled that he must have looked much like these boys had, when he was on the other side of it.

Thor dismounted and slowly walked down the center of the village, Krohn at his side, going from boy to boy, looking each one over carefully. Some seemed scared; some proud; others lethargic, indifferent; and others still over-eager. He could see the same look in their eyes that he once wore: most wanted out of this place desperately. They wanted a better life, to travel to King's Court, to train with the Legion, to achieve fame and renown, to see the Ring and the lands beyond. Thor could easily tell which of these boys had been placed here by their parents, which were not fighters. He could tell by the way they held their bodies, by a certain hardness or gleam in their eye.

As Thor reached the end of the line, he saw several older boys who were a head taller than the others, with broad shoulders. One of them glared at Thor, looking him up and down reproachfully. Thor could hardly believe his insolence: he would have never done that to a member of the Silver.

"They sent *you* to choose *us*?" the boy asked Thor derisively. He was a large, farming boy, twice the size of Thor, and a few years older.

"How old are you?" the boy added, stepping out of the line and staring at Thor, hands on his hips.

"He looks younger than us all," said the boy beside him, equally derisive. "Who are you to pick us? Maybe we should pick you."

The other boys chimed in with laughter, and Thor reddened.

"To insult a member of the Legion is to insult the queen herself," Thor said firmly, calmly, walking towards the boy. Thor knew he had to face this conflict head-on; he could not tolerate such a public insult.

"Then I insult the queen," the boy sneered back. "If she is sending *you* out for the Selection, then the Selection must really be hurting."

"Are you a fool?" one of the boys hissed to the insolent boy. "Do you not know to whom you speak? That is Thorgrinson. The most famed warrior of the Ring."

The large boy squinted his eyes at Thor skeptically.

"Thorgrinson?" he repeated. "I should think not. Thorgrinson is a great warrior, twice the size of any man. The wielder of the Destiny Sword. This boy here is but a boy, another common boy sent on a Queen's errand."

The boy stepped forward towards Thor threateningly.

"You tell the Queen to send us a *real* man to choose us, or else to come here for us herself," he said. He then stepped forward and raised his hands towards Thor's chest, as if preparing to shove him backwards.

But this boy did not realize whom he was provoking. Thor was now a hardened warrior, having been through life and death, in the Ring and in the Empire, and as a warrior, he was highly attuned to any and all potential enemy movements. As the boy came close and raised his hands, Thor was already in motion.

Thor stepped aside, grabbed the boy's wrist, twisted it behind his back until the boy screamed out in pain, then he shoved the boy hard, and sent him stumbling to the ground, landing face-first.

The other boys watched in shock; they weren't laughing now. They stood there, silent.

Thor turned his back and walked down to the opposite end of the line, looking over the other boys. He heard a sudden snarl, and he turned and saw Krohn, snarling at Thor's attacker, who was rising from the ground and preparing to charge Thor from behind.

But the boy looked down, saw Krohn, and thought better of it.

Thor turned and faced them.

"You are not joining the Legion," Thor said to the boy and to his friends. "None of you."

The other boys looked at each other, suddenly upset.

"But you *have* to pick us!" one said. "Our parents will give us a beating!"

"We are twice the size of any boy here!" cried another. "You can't turn us down. You need us!"

Thor turned, sneered, and walked right up to them.

"I don't need any of you," he said. "And size does not matter. Honor does. And respect. That is what builds a warrior. Both of which you lack."

Thor turned his back on them and began to walk away and as he did, he heard a scream. The largest one broke free from them the line and charged Thor's back, swinging his fist for the back of Thor's head.

Thor, though, sensed it coming with his lightning-fast reflexes; he swung around, backhanded him with his gauntlet, connecting with the boy's jaw and sending him spinning down to the ground.

Another boy rushed for Thor, but before he could come close, Krohn charged, leapt onto him and sank his fangs into the boy's face. The boy shrieked, trying to get Krohn off, as Krohn thrashed left and right.

"I YIELD!" the boy screamed, frantic.

"Krohn!" Thor commanded.

Krohn let go, and the boy lay there, bloody, moaning.

Thor glanced at the other boys one last time, and they looked like a sorry lot. This village was, after all, exactly as he remembered, and he felt he had wasted his time to come here.

Thor turned to leave, when one boy stepped out from the line at the far end.

"SIR!" the boy called, standing proudly at attention. "Thorgrinson, please forgive me for speaking. But we have heard far and wide of your reputation. You are a great warrior. I wish to be a warrior, too. I *yearn* to be one. Please, allow me to join the Legion. It is all I have ever dreamed of. I promise I shall be loyal and serve the Legion with everything I have."

Thor looked the boy over doubtfully. He was young, and skinny, and he looked somewhat frail. Yet he also had something in his eyes, a hollowed-out look, a look of desperation. Thor could see that he really wanted it, more so than any of the others. There was a hunger in his eyes that made Thor overlook his size, that made him think twice.

"You don't seem the fighter," Thor said. "What can you do?"

"I can throw a spear as good as any man," the boy said.

Thor went to his horse, drew a short spear from the saddle, and handed it to the boy.

"Show me," Thor said.

The boy looked down in awe at the weapon's fine quality, its gold and silver shaft, feeling its weight. Thor could see that he was impressed. This was no easy spear to wield; if the boy could throw this, he was indeed as good as he claimed.

"That tree there," Thor said, pointing to a large, crooked tree about thirty yards off. "Let's see if you can hit it."

"How about the one beyond it?" the boy asked.

Thor looked out and saw, a good thirty yards past that tree, a small, narrow tree. Thor looked back at the boy in surprise.

"I know of no Legion or even Silver who could hit that tree from here," Thor said. "You are a dreamer. And I have no time to waste for dreamers."

Thor turned to head back for his horse, but he heard a cry, and turned to see the boy take several steps forward, raise the spear, and hurl it.

The spear soared through the air, past the first tree, and on to the second. Thor watched in awe as the spear lodged into the center of the skinny tree, shaking it so that its small apples fell to the ground.

Thor looked back at the boy, in shock. It was the most masterful throw he had ever seen.

"What is your name, boy?" he demanded.

"Archibald," the boy said proudly, earnest.

"Where did you learn to throw like that?"

"Many long days in the open plains, tending cattle, with nothing else to do. I swear to you, sir, joining the Legion is all I've ever wanted from life. Please. Allow me to join your ranks."

Thor nodded, satisfied.

"Okay, Archibald," he said. "Make your way to King's Court. Seek out the training ground for the Legion. I will meet you back there in a few days' time. You will be given a chance to try out."

Archibald beamed, and clasped Thor's hand.

"Thank you. Thank you so much!" he said, clasping both Thor's hands.

Thor mounted his horse, Krohn following, and kicked, preparing for the next town. Despite the rocky start, he felt encouraged. Perhaps this Selection would not be a waste of time after all.

*

Thor rode and rode, until the second sun began to set, making his way ever south, on the lookout for the next village. Finally, as the second sun hung sat as a red ball on the horizon, Thor reached a crossroads atop a small hill and stopped. His horse, and Krohn, needed a break.

Thor sat there, all of them breathing hard, and looked down at the vista of rolling hills before him. The road forked, and if he took it to the right, he knew, it would ironically lead him to his home village, just a few miles around the bend. To the left, the road forked east and south, toward other villages.

Thor sat there and thought for a moment. How ironic it would be to return to his old village, to see his former peers, to be the one to decide if they would join the Legion. He knew there were good boys back there, and he knew that's where he should go. That's where his duties demanded he be.

Yet somehow, deep down, he just couldn't bring himself to return there. He had vowed never to lay eyes on his hometown again. Surely, his father was still there, his disparaging, sour father, and he didn't want to see him. Surely most of those boys were still there, too, the ones who had been so scornful of him growing up, who had viewed him, and treated him, as a cattle-herder's son. He had never been taken seriously by any of them.

Thor did not want to see them. He did not want to go back and have his petty revenge. He did not want to go back at all. He just wanted to wipe that village from his memory, even if it meant shirking his duty.

Thor finally kicked his horse and turned away from the road that led to his village, forking instead, to parts unknown.

*

Hours passed as Thor rode through wooded, unfamiliar territory, searching for a new village, venturing deeper into a part of the Ring he had never been. Night began to fall, the second sun disappearing below the horizon, and it was getting darker. Thick clouds gathered around him, soon the sky turned black, and thunder clapped overhead, as rain began to pour.

Thor was getting soaked, as were Krohn and his horse, and he knew they couldn't continue on like this; they'd have to find shelter for the night. He peered into the thick woods on either side of the narrow road, and he decided to turn off and seek shelter beneath a canopy of trees.

The forest was wet and dank, thick with trees, and Thor dismounted, not wanting his horse to get hurt in the darkness. He walked alongside it, tripping on gnarled roots, Krohn beside him, as they all ventured deeper and deeper into the dark forest.

Thor wiped rainwater from his eyes, wiped the hair from his face, trying to see where he was going. There was no sign of shelter anywhere, and the rain poured through the trees.

Finally, up ahead, Thor spotted a cave, a huge rock emerging from the earth, black inside. As the rain poured down harder, he led the others to it.

They entered, Thor relieved to finally be dry, quieter in here, the only sound that of the rain pouring outside. Krohn shook his hair and the horse neighed, both of them clearly happy to be out from the wet as well.

Thor walked to the end of the cave, on guard, making sure they were not sharing it with anyone, then finally stopped about twenty feet in, satisfied. It was a shallow cave, but dry, and large enough for them to take shelter from the storm.

Thor set to work making a fire, salvaging the dry branches he found on the floor of the cave, and soon it was roaring, the twigs crackling. Thor remembered the pieces of dried meat in his saddle, and he fed the horse, then Krohn, then himself.

Thor sat before the flames, rubbing his hands, trying to dry off, and Krohn came up beside him and lay his head in his lap, while the horse stood by the cave's entrance, lowering his head and chewing the grass. Thor chewed his dried meat, warming himself on the surprisingly cool summer night. He felt sleepy from the long day, and soon, his eyes were closing on him.

"Thorgrin," came a voice.

Thor opened his eyes to see Argon standing over him, looking down at him in the cave. Argon stood there, eyes opened wide, shining, holding his staff, dressed in his robe and cloak. Thor was shocked to see him here. He looked over and saw Krohn sleeping, beside the embers of the dying fire, and he wondered if it were all real.

"Thorgrin," Argon repeated.

"What are you doing here?" Thor asked.

"You have come to me," Argon said. "You sought me out. In this cave."

Thor furrowed his brows, confused.

"I thought I was lost," he said. "I thought I made a wrong turn. I did not mean to come here."

Argon shook his head.

"There are no wrong turns," he said. "You are exactly where you are supposed to be."

"But where am I?" Thor asked.

"Follow me and see."

Argon turned, and Thor rose to his feet and followed him as he walked outside the cave. Thor still did not know if he was awake or asleep.

Outside, the rain had stopped. All was silent. The forest was eerie, dim, not dark and not light, as if it were twilight, or the time before dawn. It felt as if the entire world were still asleep.

Argon continued walking, and Thor struggled to keep up with him through the forest trail. He was beginning to get concerned about finding his way back to the cave.

"Where are we going, Argon?" Thor asked.

"To complete your training," Argon replied.

"I thought my training was complete," Thor said.

"Only one stage of it," Argon said. "It is no longer about what you need to learn. Now it is about what you need to do."

"To do?" Thor asked, puzzled.

"This journey, this road, your town, the storm—it's all come for a reason. You've come here for a reason. The time has come for you to tap into a part of yourself you have not yet reached."

They finally broke free from the woods, and before them lay a vista of rolling hills.

Thor followed Argon to the top of a small hill. He stopped, and Thor stopped beside him.

"Your problem, Thorgrin," Argon said, standing beside him, looking out, eyes aglow, "is that you do not realize how powerful you are. You never have. You still don't trust it. You still don't trust who you are. You are so reliant upon human weapons and training, upon swords and spears and shields.... But you have all the power you need, right inside you. And yet you are afraid of it."

Thor looked down, reddening, realizing Argon was right.

"I am," Thor admitted.

"Why?"

"I feel that to use my powers would not be fighting fairly," Thor said. "I feel that I need to prove myself on the same terms as everyone else. I guess I still feel that my powers are…something to be ashamed of."

Argon shook his head.

"That is where you are wrong. What is different about you is precisely what you should be most proud of."

Argon closed his eyes, breathed deeply, raised both arms, and waited. Thor heard a trickling noise, then felt a raindrop, and looked up to the sky and watched it begin to pour.

He looked back at Argon, amazed.

"Can you feel it, Thorgrin? Can you feel the water pouring down on us? Permeating everything? Feel it in your skin and hair and eyes. Breathe it in."

Thor closed his eyes and held out his palms, and felt the drops hitting them. He tried to focus, tried to become one with the rain.

"Now stop it," Argon commanded. "Stop all of it. Stop this rain."

Thor gasped, unsure of himself.

"I can't do that," Thor said.

"You can," Argon said. "Rain is just water, and water is simply the universe. It is us. Now do it. Raise your hands and stop it."

Thor closed his eyes tighter, concentrating, and raised his arms. As he did, he felt his palms tingling, and he began to feel the energy of the rain in the air. It was intense. Heavy. Limitless.

Thor slowly pushed his palms higher and higher, taking on the energy, and as he did, the rain began to slow. Then it stopped, the water hovering in the air. Then, Thor reversed it, shooting it back up to the sky.

The sound of the rain stopped, and Thor opened his eyes, amazed, to see the land dry all around him.

"I did that?" he asked, surprised.

"Yes," Argon replied. "You and you alone."

Argon turned his back, and held his arms up to the sky.

"There is more you can do, Thorgrin," he said. "Do you see the night? Do you see the darkness? It is but a veil. Lift that veil. Allow it to be day."

Thor stood there, flabbergasted.

"Me?" he asked. "Turn night into day?"

"Night is but the absence of light. Let there be light. You are advanced enough now."

Thor gulped and closed his eyes. It was hard to imagine himself with that sort of power, but nonetheless, he held out his arms and raised his palms to the sky.

"Feel the fibers of night," Argon said. "Feel the threads of blackness. They are but illusion. The whole world is but illusion. This, the sky we live under, the sky we breathe every day, it is not a sky of man—it is a sky of magic, a sky of wonder. It is a sky of spells."

Thor tried to follow the instruction, tried to feel the blackness. He felt a tremendous heaviness weighing on the tips of his fingers.

"Now, Thorgrin," Argon added, "transcend the illusion."

Thor felt his fingertips burning, nearly on fire, and he closed his hands and bunched his fists. He squeezed his fists as hard as he could, and felt a heat searing his entire body. He leaned back his head and screamed.

When he opened his eyes, Thor was awestruck. There, before him, it was daylight. Night was gone.

"All of nature is under your control," Argon said, turning to him, as Thor stared out in wonder. "The fox and the mouse, the eagle and the owl. There, up high, on that branch. Do you see that owl? It, too, is under your control. Command it. Leave your limited world behind, and see the world through its eyes."

Thor looked up at the huge, black owl, a magnificent creature, and he closed his eyes and focused, concentrating. Thor opened the owl's eyes, and its eyes were his own. He saw the world through its eyes. It was incredible.

Thor turned the owl's neck, and it looked out in every direction, at the limitless landscape. He saw beyond the forest, above the tips of the trees. In the distance, he saw a road.

"Excellent," Argon said, beside him. "Now see where that road takes you."

Thor kept his eyes closed, seeing the world through the eyes of the owl, and silently commanded the owl to lift off. He could feel the great owl flapping its wings above him, and soon it soared through the air, flying along the tops of the trees. Thor watched the landscape through its eyes, looking down through the trees, following the road that led through the forest.

The road twisted and turned, and soon it led him to a familiar place. Thor was surprised to see his hometown below.

Standing there, alone in its center, was a woman he was shocked to recognize.

His mother.

She stood there and looked up the sky, as if looking for him, and held up her arms.

"Thorgrin!" she called.

"Mother!" he called back.

Thor opened his eyes with a start, jolted out of the vision, and looked over to Argon.

"My mother," he said, breathing hard. "Is she there? In my village? How can it be?"

"She waits for you," Argon said. "It is time to meet her. Your very life depends on it. The final clue you need lies there. In your hometown."

Thor turned and looked out at the road before him, wondering.

"But how can it—" he began to ask Argon.

But as Thor turned, he saw no one. Argon was gone.

"ARGON!" he screamed out.

There came no reply save for the sound of a lone owl, screeching high up in the air.

CHAPTER TWENTY SIX

Selese walked slowly down the aisle on her wedding day, and she knew something was not quite right. All the chairs were empty on either side of the aisle; she looked over and saw, instead, rows of thorn bushes, black and ominous. She looked down and saw that mice scurried beneath her feet, and that the aisle, instead of being lined with flowers, was lined with mud. She was terrified.

As she reached the end of the aisle, Selese looked up and saw Reece standing there, at the altar, waiting for her. But as she approached, desperate to get close to him, she noticed a huge spider web between them, and she found herself walking face-first into it. It wrapped all over her face and body, sticking to her. She flailed, hysterical, trying to peel it away. She finally managed to tear it off, but as she did, she noticed she was tearing off her wedding dress instead, leaving her in rags.

Selese stepped onto the altar, shaking from fear, and looked across at Reece.

He stood there, staring back blankly, expressionless.

"I wish we could marry," he said. "But I love someone else."

Selese gaped, not understanding—then suddenly, there appeared a woman next to Reece, a beautiful girl, Reece's age, who reached up and wrapped one arm around his, turned him and led him away.

The two of them walked back down the aisle, and Selese just stood there, horrified, and watched them go.

Selese felt the ground tremble beneath her, and looked down and watched in disbelief as a hole opened in the earth. The hole grew greater and greater, and before she could get out of the way, she found herself falling, into the blackness.

She shrieked, flailing, raising her hands for someone, anyone, to save her. But no one did.

Selese woke screaming.

She sat straight up in bed, sweating despite the cool summer night. She looked all about her, trying to understand where she was, what had happened.

It was a dream. It had seemed so real—too real. She sat there, gasping. She reached up and rubbed her face and hair, trying to feel for the spider web. But there was none—nothing but her cool, clammy skin.

Selese surveyed her surroundings and saw she was still in the safety of the Queen's castle, in the luxurious room given to her by the queen, and lying on a pile of furs. A slight breeze stirred through the window, it was a perfect summer night, and absolutely nothing in the world was wrong.

She got up, crossed the room, and splashed water on her face. She breathed deeply, rubbing her eyes again and again, trying to understand.

How could she have had such a dream? She had never had nightmares in her life. Why now? And why had it been so vivid?

Selese walked over to the open-air window and stood there, looking out at the night. Beneath the faint light of the second moon, there was King's Court, in all its splendor. She could see her wedding preparations, perfect below, everything in order for her double wedding with Gwendolyn. Even at night everything was so beautiful, the flowers glowing beneath the moonlight. The wedding was still a half-moon away, and yet all was ready. Selese was in awe at the spectacle it would be.

Selese was so honored to be getting married together with Gwendolyn, so grateful for the kindness that her future sister-in-law had shared with her. She also felt overwhelmed with a surge of love for Reece. She did not need any of this lavishness; all she wanted was to be with Reece.

But as Selese stared down below, all she could see was her dream. That horrible aisle; the thorns; the web; falling through the earth; the other woman. Could any of it be true? Was it just a horrible dream—or was it some sort of omen?

Selese stared out at the clouds racing beneath the moon, and she wanted to tell herself it was all just fancies of the night. Perhaps it was just the stress of preparing for the wedding.

But deep down, Selese could not help but fear it was something more. She could not help but feel that Reece, out there somewhere, was in terrible danger.

And as she looked down at the beauty of all those wedding preparations, she could not help feeling, with a deep sense of dread, that their wedding would never come to be.

CHAPTER TWENTY SEVEN

Reece grabbed hold of the thick, knotted rope, leaned over the edge of the ship, and threw up yet again, as the ship tossed and turned on the rolling seas, as it had been ever since he left the mainland. He grabbed hold of the thick knotted rope and did his best to straighten himself. He leaned back and wiped his mouth, grateful that they were close.

Despite the summer month, Reece shivered. It was unforgiving here in the Upper Isles, much colder than it had been on the mainland; the currents, too, were more turbulent, and the cool ocean spray hung in the wind, keeping him wet. It had been an awful journey, sailing into a driving wind, the boat carried high, then low, on the sea the entire way, causing nearly all its passengers to throw up.

Reece did not know how they had made it this far, in this raging ocean, in this desolate place. It had not been a long journey, and yet it felt like years. There was something about the climate here, the endless, monotonous grey, that just put him in a foul mood. The damp cold had sunk into his bones, and he could not wait to set foot on shore and get himself beside a roaring fire.

Beside Reece stood Krog, also grabbing the railing, but not throwing up as the others. On the contrary, he smiled down at Reece.

"Looks like one of us has a stronger stomach than the other," Krog mocked, grinning wide.

Reece caught his breath, wiping his mouth. Krog's mockery made it all worse.

"I hate you," Reece said.

Krog smiled wider.

"Why have you joined me on this journey?" Reece asked. "To help me? Or to torture me?"

Krog grinned, patting Reece on the shoulder.

"Maybe a little bit of both," Krog replied.

Reece shook his head, overcome with yet another wave of nausea. He was not in the mood for Krog.

"I never should have saved your life," Reece said.

"You're right," Krog replied. "That was your first mistake. Now you're stuck with me. Loyalty dies hard."

"You call this loyalty?" Reece asked. "You have a funny way of showing it."

Krog shrugged and turned away.

The ship jerked, and Reece looked up and watched as they narrowly avoided a long stretch of rocks, then finally touched shore, the ship landing on the sand with a jolt. All hands rushed forward and dropped the anchor beside Gwendolyn's fleet, then hurried to lower the planks and secure the sails.

Horns sounded up and down Gwendolyn's fleet of ships, their unique pattern heralding the arrival of a member of the royal family, and on the shore below Reece could see, lined up, dozens of Gwen's soldiers, ready to greet him in a show of respect. Reece noticed that Tirus' people were conspicuously absent from welcoming him.

Standing before all the men, Reece spotted Matus, Tirus' eldest, his cousin, the one person here he had remembered most fondly from his youth. He hurried forward, shielding his eyes from the mist and helping the others secure the planks, clearly excited for Reece's arrival.

Reece's men lowered the plank and Reece hurried down it, Krog and the others following; the wind picked up and sheets of rain poured down as Reece reached the shore.

Matus hurried forward and Reece embraced him, clasping forearms.

"Welcome, my Lord," Matus said.

"I am not a lord," Reece said, "I am merely a member of the royal family, as are you, cousin. Thank you for greeting me."

Matus smiled.

"I would have it no other way. Srog asked me to apologize on his behalf—he was detained by an urgent matter at court and asked me to give you a tour first, then bring you to the castle—if you don't mind my company."

Now it was Reece's turn to smile.

"I would have it no other way," he said. "I wish to tour the isle first anyway."

The two of them turned and set off, Reece walking side-by-side with Matus, all of their men falling in behind them.

They walked for hours, covering all the landscapes of the Upper Isles, the sun finally breaking through the clouds as Matus filled him in on everything. The two of them talked like brothers, and it all came back to Reece, how close they had been as children, how well they had always gotten along. They were each the youngest of their siblings, and each the same age, and each knew what it meant to grow up in an ambitious royal family.

They caught up on their childhoods, on all the affairs of the MacGil families, and as Reece passed through various towns and villages, some childhood memories came back to him in flashes. He remembered playing in certain places, waiting for his father outside certain forts. He remembered, even back then, it being a cold, hard place, a climate he did not wish to return to.

As he went, Reece took in all the stares of all the locals, observed as much as he could, and noticed they were not all that friendly. He sensed some tension in the air.

"It is quite different being here now than it was when we were young," Reece said. "When I was a child, there was harmony upon our arrival, a great respect and fanfare shown my father. Now, I observe a certain coldness in your people."

Matus shook his head apologetically.

"I apologize for them," he said. "You indeed have a keen eye. Our people are still upset about Tirus. They are humiliated about the failed invasion of the Ring. They are malcontents. That is their nature. They are an obstinate people. I come from here, and yet I still don't completely understand them. Then again, I've never felt much like one of them."

"No," Reece said, appreciating Matus' honesty, "you have always been more like one of us. Sometimes I think you were born to the wrong side of the royal family."

Matus roared with laughter.

"I think so, too."

They walked and walked and Krog followed, several feet behind, closer than the rest of the entourage, and Matus glanced back and gave Reece a curious glance.

"Who is your friend?" Matus asked.

Reece grimaced.

"He's not my friend," he said.

"You got that right," Krog chimed in.

"I told you to wait for me at the ship," Reece said to Krog, exasperated.

But Krog ignored him, continued to follow, one hand resting on his sword hilt and looking all about, as if on the lookout for danger.

"I intend to protect you," Krog said.

"I don't need protection," Reece said, annoyed.

"I intend to repay my debt," Krog said. "And I don't trust these Upper Islanders."

Matus raised an eyebrow.

"Is your friend always this suspicious?" Matus asked, glancing back over his shoulder.

Reece shrugged, annoyed but resigned to the fact that Krog was uncontrollable.

"He's not my friend," Reece repeated.

They continued on their hike, and finally crested a small hill. From here, down below, Reece spotted, not far away, a small lake in the hills. He noticed a woman, carrying an empty bucket, kneel beside the lake and begin to fill it up.

Reece watched her, curious. There was something about her which seemed familiar, but he could not figure out what.

Reece took several steps closer, examining her profile, wondering how he knew her.

Then, she suddenly raised the bucket, turned and faced him. She was shocked to see him, and she froze.

She stood there, and as her eyes locked on Reece's, the bucket slipped from her hands, splashing at her feet. She did not even bother to look down at it.

Reece could not have moved if someone pushed him. His heart pounded in his chest as he stared into those eyes, losing all sense of time and place. They were hypnotic. They were eyes he knew, eyes that had been embedded into his consciousness. They were eyes he had, for many years, dreamt of.

Standing there, hardly a few feet away, Reece was shocked to realize, was his cousin. Stara. The love of his childhood. The girl he would stay awake for, late at night, dreaming of. The girl he had never forgotten. The girl he had secretly hoped to marry most of his life.

There she stood, and now, she had grown into the most beautiful woman he had ever seen.

As Reece stared into her crystal blue eyes, however much he tried, he could not summon thoughts of Selese. All thoughts of the woman he was about to marry flew from his head. He could not help it. Reece was hypnotized by Stara.

And as she stared back, unmoving, her eyes perfectly still, crystal-clear, like the lake behind her, Reece could see that she was as equally hypnotized by him. Their love, the strongest thing Reece had ever felt in his life, so strong it pained him, had never died. It had never even faltered.

Reece forced himself to turn his thoughts to Selese, to their wedding. But standing here, before Stara, rooted to this place, all free thought was impossible. He was in the grip of something greater than himself, something he did not understand. As he stood there, he knew that fate had interceded, and that his life, and the lives of everyone around him, whether he liked it or not, were about to change forever.

CHAPTER TWENTY EIGHT

Bronson sat in the feasting hall of his fathers, in the old McCloud castle, seated at the head of the long table, Luanda beside him. Seated up and down the table, on either side, were McClouds and MacGils, grizzled warriors all of them, each sticking to their side of the table, none, despite Bronson's efforts, intermingling with the others. Bronson surveyed it all, and his head hurt. Nothing was going as he had planned.

Bronson, in an act of desperation, had summoned all of these warriors together for a feast, to try to bring them closer to one another, to hash out any differences. He had chosen representatives from feuding clans on both sides of the Highlands, and he had thrown a lavish feast in their honor, replete with music, wine and delicious food. And yet, thus far, the night had not been going well. They each stuck to their side of the table, talking to their own clansmen, and ignoring the others. They were both so stubborn, like two kids refusing to look at each other. It had made for an awkward feast at best, and Bronson was beginning to wonder if he had made a mistake to even attempt this.

This feast had followed hours of festivities, a miniature festival which Bronson had ordered to celebrate a wedding of a MacGil clansman to a McCloud bride. It was originally supposed to be a quiet, simple wedding, in a humble village on the MacGil side of the Highlands; but when Bronson heard of it, he insisted that the wedding be a huge, public affair. This was exactly what he needed, and he personally paid for the expenses of it, thinking this would be the perfect event to help bring the two warring sides together. This young couple was truly in love, and Bronson hoped that maybe their love and goodwill would spread to the people.

The day's wedding, though, had been an awkward affair, with both clansmen staying on their sides, and the disapproving families of the groom and bride not even intermingling.

It had spilled over to the feasting hall, and Bronson had figured that the mood would be more relaxed at night, after the wedding, after all the dancing, once the men relaxed with drink and a good meal.

And yet here they all were, late into the night, the McCloud bride the only McCloud on the MacGil side of the room. Bronson had tried many times throughout the night to break the ice, but nothing seemed to work.

"You had better do something," Luanda whispered into his ear.

He turned and looked at her. She leaned in close, staring at him intently.

"This feast of yours is a failure. It is not bringing goodwill between them. And if this does not, nothing will. You must bring them together somehow. I do not like what I see."

"And what is that?" Bronson asked.

"A war erupting between them both."

Bronson turned and looked out at the room, and felt the tension in the air, and on some level, he knew she was right. Luanda had a talent for always seeing things for what they were.

"A toast!" Bronson yelled out, standing and slamming his mug on the table until the room quieted.

Bronson knew the time had come to take decisive action, to be a great leader. He had to set the tone for harmony between the two clans.

"A toast to two great families!" he boomed. "To two great clans, coming together in peace. It is amazing how love can unite us all. Let us all follow this couple's great example and come together, from both sides of the Highlands, to create one nation, one Ring, in harmony with each other."

The bride and groom raised their mugs, as did several on the MacGil side; yet no one on the McCloud side bothered to. Bronson realized that the MacGils were more open to peace than the McClouds. It was hardly surprising: having grown up amongst the McClouds, he knew them to be obstinate.

"I have a better idea!" yelled Koovia, standing amidst the McCloud clansmen, slamming his mug on the table, his voice booming, commanding attention. He looked drunk, his face red with scorn, and Bronson did not like what he saw.

The room quieted, as all eyes fell on him.

"I suggest that our new leader, Bronson, prove himself to be a leader—instead of being a puppet of the MacGil girl!"

The McClouds cheered, as Bronson's face reddened. Before he could reply, Koovia continued:

"A true leader of the McCloud kingdom would assert his royal privileges on a wedding night!" Koovia boomed.

The McCloud warriors screamed and cheered, banging their mugs on the table, whipped up into a drunken frenzy.

"Of what does he speak?" Luanda asked Bronson, confused, as the room erupted into a clamor.

But Bronson was fuming, too busy to address her.

"You do not mean what you say!" Bronson yelled back to Koovia.

"Of course I do!" Koovia boomed. "Your father took the privilege, many times. Any true McCloud king must—that is, if you *are* a king."

There came another great cheer from the McClouds, as they slammed their mugs.

"What is it that he speaks of?" a MacGil warrior finally called out, confused.

"I speak of the deflowering of the bride on her wedding night!" Koovia boomed defiantly, back to the MacGils.

All the MacGils on their side of the table suddenly stood in an uproar, angrily muttering towards the McClouds.

Bronson detected motion out of the corner of his eye, and he looked up and saw several McCloud soldiers circling around the outskirts of the room and barring all the exits.

Bronson felt a pit in his stomach as he realized he had been setup. This was all a trap, schemed by Koovia.

"You have tricked us with your feast!" the MacGil warrior screamed accusingly to Bronson.

Bronson wanted to call out that he knew nothing of this, but before he could reply, Koovia interceded.

"You are completely surrounded!" Koovia yelled to the MacGils. "There is no way out. Hand over the bride. It is time for our king to have his way with her. And if he won't—we will!"

The McClouds all cheered, driven to a drunken furor, while the MacGils all drew their swords. The McClouds drew theirs, too.

As they stood there, facing off, Koovia walked around the table, right up to Bronson, several of his men following, while Bronson stood and faced him.

"Take the bride, and you will be our leader," Koovia said to Bronson. "If not, you will face death yourself by my own hand, and I shall be the new McCloud king."

The McCloud soldiers cheered.

Bronson stared back at Koovia. He had been cornered in, outmaneuvered. He should have known better. His people always viewed kindness as weakness. They were even more primitive than he had realized.

"You can take the kingship from me if you like," Bronson replied calmly, "but you will not touch the bride. You will have to kill me first."

Koovia scowled.

"As I thought," he said. "A pathetic leader to the last."

Bronson drew his sword and blocked Koovia's path to the bride.

Koovia drew his sword, and the tension thickened, as the two prepared to face off.

Suddenly, Luanda stepped forward, between them, and calmly reached out a hand and laid it gently on Koovia's sword.

"Bronson speaks out of line," she said. "Of course he will perform his kingly duties."

Koovia looked back, caught off guard.

"You are a great and strong man," Luanda added. "Lower your sword, and I will be sure Bronson does as you say. Blood need not be shed here tonight."

Koovia looked at her, then slowly relaxed his hand, as he lowered his sword just a bit. He looked her up and down and grinned.

"You are a nice piece yourself," Koovia said. "After Bronson has her, I might just take you."

She smiled back at him.

"I would love that, my Lord," Luanda said. She stepped forward and whispered in his ear. "It has been a long time since I have slept with a real lord."

Koovia grinned wide and Luanda leaned back and met his smile. He relaxed his hand, and as soon as he did, Luanda burst into action.

Luanda quickly extracted a hidden dagger from her waist, spun around, and in one lightning fast motion, stabbed Koovia in the throat.

His eyes bulged open as blood gushed down over his chest and he raised his hands to the blade.

But it was too late. He collapsed to his knees, then slumped forward, face-first, dead.

The entire room stared in shock.

A moment later, both sides charged each other with a great battle cry, each aiming to kill the other.

As Bronson stood there, in the middle of it all, he knew, without a doubt, that the next war of the Ring had begun.

CHAPTER TWENTY NINE

Thorgrin felt something licking his face, and he opened his eyes to see Krohn standing over him. He woke slowly, disoriented, and sat up, wondering where he was. He spotted his horse, still standing near the entrance to the cave, and he remembered coming here, through the forest, at night and in pouring rain. Now sunshine streamed in through the cave, birds chirped, the world was dry, and Thor sat up, disoriented, wondering if any of it had ever happened.

Had his encounter with Argon been real? A dream? Or somewhere in between?

Thor stood and rubbed his eyes, and tried to distinguish what was a dream from what was real. He looked all around, searching for Argon, but he was nowhere to be found. He felt a heat coursing through his body, felt stronger than he ever had. Had they truly had a training session? Thor felt as if they had.

Above all, Thor felt as if a message had been conveyed to him, and he felt it ringing in his ears. His mother. The final clue to finding her awaited him in his hometown. Was it true?

Thor walked to the edge of the cave and took a few steps out and looked at the forest. Water dripped from branches in the early morning sun, and the forest was alive with the sounds of animals and insects awakening for the day. He looked out at the early morning sunlight, the rays streaking in through the leaves, and his dream hung on him like a mist. He knew, with burning clarity, exactly what he needed to do; he needed to go back to his hometown. He needed to see for himself if the final clue was there. The way to find his mother.

Thor mounted his horse, kicked it, and, Krohn at his heels, charged through the forest. He intuitively knew the path this time, the exact way to leave this forest, the path that would lead to his hometown. He closed his eyes as he rode and recalled seeing the forest from the owl's eyes, seeing the entire landscape, and no longer did he feel lost. He looked at the nature all around him, heard the noises of the animals, and he felt one with them; he felt stronger, omnipotent, as if he could go anywhere in the world and not get lost.

Thor soon reached the edge of the forest and looked out and saw the road before them, winding, leading over hills and valleys, to the crossroads he knew would take them to his village. He recognized the mountains in the distance, the lonely road he had taken his entire childhood to leave his village.

Thor looked at it with a sense of apprehension. A part of him really did not want to return to his hometown. He knew that when he arrived, there would be all those boys, and his father, waiting to greet him, patronizing and condescending. He could already feel the stares of the village folk, of all the boys he had grown up with. They wouldn't see him for who he was now; they would still see him as the boy they once knew, a shepherd's youngest boy, someone not to be taken seriously.

But Thor kicked his horse, determined. This was not about them. It was about his greater mission. He would put up with them all for a chance to find his mother.

Thor charged down the road, towards the village. He braced himself as he rounded a bend, slowed his horse, and finally entered through the town, the small, sleepy farming village he remembered, without even a proper wall around it, or a gate to mark its entrance. Growing up, he had thought this was the greatest place in the world. But now, having been to so many places, seen so many things, this town seemed small and pathetic. It was just another poor village, with nothing special. It was a place for people who had not made it elsewhere, who had settled for this poor and forgotten region of the Ring.

Thor turned and rode down the main street of his village, bracing himself, expecting to find it bustling, as it usually was, with all of the faces he recognized. But what he saw surprised him: the streets were not as he expected, filled with people, animals, children—instead, they were completely empty. Desolate. His village had been abandoned.

Thor could not understand the sight before him. It was a typical, sunny morning, and it made no sense for these streets to be empty. As he looked more closely, he was surprised to see that many of the buildings were destroyed, reduced to piles of rubble. He looked down and could see residues of tracks in the streets, signs of a great army passing through here. He looked at the stone cottages, and saw stains of blood on some of them.

With his professional soldier's eye, Thor knew right away what had happened here: the Empire. Their army had invaded this region of the Ring, and clearly they had passed through this poor village; the people here were unfortunate enough to be caught in his way, and this place had been decimated. Everything Thor had once known was gone—as if it had never been.

Thor dismounted and walked somberly through the streets, feeling awful as he walked past shells of structures he barely recognized. It was slowly dawning on him that everyone who had once lived here had either fled or was now dead.

It was an eerie feeling. This place he had known most his life as home, was abandoned. The oddest thing about it was that Thor had had no desire to return here and would have been glad never to lay eyes on this place again; and yet now that he saw it like this, he felt regret. Seeing it like this made Thor feel, strangely enough, as if he had no home left in the world, no trace of his origins at all.

Where was his true home in the world? Thor wondered. It should be a simple question to answer, and yet the more Thor lived, the more he was beginning to realize that that was the most difficult question of all.

Thor heard the rattle of a pot, and he turned and braced himself, on guard, to see a small cottage, still standing, one wall destroyed. The door was ajar, and Thor's hand fell to the hilt of his sword, wondering if there was a wounded soldier inside, or perhaps a scavenger.

As he watched the entrance, an old, heavyset woman came out, carry her pot, wobbling, dressed in rags. She carried her pot, overflowing with water, over to a pile of wood. She had just set it down when she looked up to see Thor.

She jumped back, startled.

"Who are you?" she asked. "No one has come through here since the war."

Thor dimly recognized her; she was one of the old women perpetually hunched before their cottages, cooking.

"My name is Thorgrin," he said. "I mean you no harm. I used to live here. I was raised here."

She squinted up at him.

"I know you," she said. "You are the youngest of the brothers," she added derisively. "The shepherd's boy."

Thor reddened. He hated that people still thought of him this way, that no matter how much honor he achieved, it would never be any different.

"Well, don't expect to find anyone here," she added, scowling, setting to her fire. "I'm just about the only one left."

Thor suddenly had a thought.

"In my father still here?"

Thor felt a lump in his throat at the idea of seeing him again. He hoped he would not have to. And yet at the same time, he hoped he was not dead. As much as he hated the man, for some reason, the thought bothered him.

The woman shrugged.

"Check for yourself," she said, then ignored him, turning back to her stew.

Thor turned and continued to walk through the village, now a ghost town, Krohn at his heels. He meandered through the streets, until finally he reached his former home.

He turned the corner and expected to see it standing there, as it always had, and he was shocked to see it was a pile of rubble. There was nothing left. No house. He had expected to see his father, standing there, scowling back, waiting for him. But he was not there, either.

Thor walked slowly over to the pile of rubble, Krohn at his heels, whining, as if he could sense Thor's sadness. Thor did not know why he was sad. He had hated this place; and yet still, for some reason, it bothered him.

Thor walked over to the pile of rocks and kicked them with his toe, rummaging, searching for something, he did not know what. Some clue, maybe. Some idea. Whatever it was that had led him back to this place. Maybe this had all been a mistake? Maybe he had been a fool to follow his intuition? Maybe this had all been wishful thinking? Perhaps there was no clue after all that could lead him to his mother?

After several minutes, Thor finished kicking over the rocks. He sighed, preparing to turn around and leave. This had all been a mistake. There was nothing left for him here. Just ghosts of what had once been.

As Thor turned and began to walk back, suddenly Krohn whined. Thor turned and spotted Krohn in the distance, on the far side of the yard, near the small structure where Thor had lived, away from the rest of the family. Krohn was whining, looking back and rummaging through rocks, as if urging Thor to come look.

Thor hurried over, knelt beside Krohn, and looked, wondering.

"What is it, boy?" Thor asked, stroking his head. "What do you see?"

Krohn whined as he pawed at a large rock, and Thor reached down and pulled back the heavy stone. He found more stones, and he kept extracting them until finally he saw something. Something was flashing, catching the sun.

Thor reached down, into the crevice in the rocks, and pulled it out. He held up something small, brushed off the dirt, and glanced at it in wonder. As he brushed off all the dirt he saw that it was shiny, yellow, round. He looked closer and finally realized it was a gold locket.

There was fine lettering on it, and Thor saw it was carved in inscriptions, in a language he could not understand. Thor ran his fingers along the edge of it, and he came across something, like a clasp. He pushed it, and the locket popped open.

To Thor's surprise, he saw an inscription in gold on one side, and a golden arrow, swirling, on the other. It moved every time he turned it. It came to a rest, and kept pointing in one direction. Every time he moved, the arrow adjusted.

Thor rubbed off the dirt and read the inscription, this in a language he knew. As he read the words, his heart stopped.

For my son. Thorgrin. Follow the arrow. And it will lead you to me.

Heart racing, Thor stood and turned and held up the locket, and he found the arrow pointing in a particular direction. He looked out at the sky, the horizon, and he knew this arrow would lead him to the Land of the Druids.

As Thor grasped it, he felt a tremendous coursing through his palm, through his entire body. He knew that it was real, that all of this was real, and he felt certain that the time had come to find his mother. The time had come to find out the truth about who he really was, who he was meant to be.

Thor looked out at the sky, and resolved that as soon as his child was born, as soon as the wedding was over, he would leave.

Thor looked out at the horizon, and felt his mother was closer than ever.

"Be patient, mother," he said. "I am coming for you."

CHAPTER THIRTY

Gwendolyn stood on the upper parapets of her castle, looking down at King's Court, admiring all the wedding preparations, admiring how magnificent the rebuilt city looked. Now that everyone had left for Departure Day, Gwen had needed to take a break herself, had needed some time alone up here. It was a beautiful day, the sun was shining, a warm summer breeze swayed the branches of the fruit trees, and Gwen leaned back and breathed in the fresh air.

There came a screech, and Gwen looked up and saw Ralibar, soaring high above, intertwining with Mycoples, the two of them making broad circles around King's Court. Gwen smiled, thinking of her morning ride on Ralibar, recalling how gentle he had been today. The two were becoming closer, as if he sensed how pregnant she was, and was flying with extra care. She felt reassured to see him circling, as if being watched over, protected.

Gwen looked out at the horizon and knew that Thor was out there somewhere and would be returning soon, and that, finally, they had nothing left to fear. Everything was perfect now, and yet for some reason, she did not feel at ease. She did not know why, but she could not help but feel as if something dark was on the horizon, was coming for them all. Was it real? Or was it just her own mind playing tricks on her? Her mind spun with so many small matters related to ruling her kingdom, it was hard for her to think clearly.

"The affairs of state," came a voice, "can weigh on you like a rock."

Gwendolyn turned around, thrilled to recognize that voice, and saw Argon, standing there, holding his staff, wearing his cloak and hood, his eyes shining right through her. He walked up beside her, his staff clicking on the stone as he went, and stood beside her, looking out with her over her kingdom.

"I'm glad you're here," she said, turning and looking out beside him. "I have been ill-at-ease as of late. And I don't know why."

"But don't you?" he asked cryptically.

She turned and looked at him, wondering.

"Am I wrong?" she asked. "Tell me honestly: is something terrible about to happen? Is our peace about to be shattered?"

Argon turned and stared at her for so long, the intensity of his eyes nearly made her turn away. Finally, he uttered one word which sent a chill through her:

"Yes."

Gwendolyn's heart pounded at his words, and she felt her blood run cold. She stared back, feeling a slow panic creep over her.

"What is it?" she asked, her voice trembling. "What will happen?"

Slowly, Argon shook his head.

"I have learned my lesson of interfering in human matters."

He turned back out, surveying her kingdom.

"Please," she pleaded. "Just tell me enough, enough to prepare. To do whatever I have to in order to protect my people."

Argon sighed.

"You are much like your father," he said. "You don't even know how much. He always wanted to be the greatest ruler he could be; but sometimes, fate gets in the way."

He turned and stared at her, and for the first time, she saw compassion in his eyes.

"Not all kingdoms are meant to last," he said. "And not all rulers. You have done a marvelous job, greater than any MacGil before you. You have wrested control from a doom that was supposed to happen, and you have done so with courage and honor. Your father looks down on you now and smiles at you."

Gwen felt a flush of warmth at his words.

"Yet some things," he continued, "are beyond your control. We are all at the mercy of a greater destiny that courses through the universe. The Ring has its own fate, as a person has a fate."

Gwen gulped, desperate to know more.

"What danger could affect us now?" she asked. "The Shield is restored. The Empire is gone. Andronicus is dead. McCloud is dead. We have two dragons here. What can harm us? What more can I do?"

Slowly, Argon shook his head.

"Hiding amidst the most glorious flowers, are the most poisonous snakes; behind the most brilliant sunshine are the darkest clouds, the fiercest storms, waiting to gather. Do not look at the sun; look at the clouds behind it, the clouds you do not yet see. Know for certain that they are there. Prepare. Do it now. It is up to you, and no one else. You are the shepherd that leads the flock, and the flock knows not what comes."

Gwendolyn shuddered, Argon confirming what she felt herself. Something horrible was on the horizon, and it was up to her, and her alone, to take action, to prepare. But what?

Gwen turned to ask Argon more, but before she could open her mouth, he was already gone. She stared at the clouds, at the sky, at the horizon, wondering. The day seemed so perfect. What lurked beyond?

*

Gwendolyn sat in the reconstructed House of Scholars, before a long, ancient wooden table completely covered in books and scrolls and maps, studying them all intently. This was the only place in the kingdom Gwen came for solace, for peace and quiet; these ancient, dusty books always setting her at ease, connecting her to her childhood. Indeed, Gwen had devoted a great deal of her time these last six moons to personally overseeing the reconstruction of this building that had meant so much to her, to Aberthol, and to her father. She had insisted on its being restored to be as beautiful as it had been, and yet even grander, big enough to hold even more volumes. Most of their precious volumes had been burned, or stolen by the Empire; but deep in the lower levels, Aberthol had wisely hidden stores of books that remained untouched. Andronicus, savage that he was, had not realized how deep beneath the earth the House of Scholars had been built—precisely for times like this, times of war—and luckily, some of the most precious items had been saved.

It was these volumes that Gwendolyn pored over now. There were others besides, as Gwendolyn had made it her mission to have her men scour the Ring to find any precious volumes that might be scattered. They had returned with loaded wagons full of volumes which she had paid for personally, and soon she had rebuilt the House of Scholars to a library greater than it had ever been. She loved this new house even more, and she was amazed that she had pulled it off, never truly thinking it could be rebuilt from the ashes when she had first seen it in that sorry state. It was the thing she was most proud of since the reconstruction had begun.

Gwen had been tucked away here all day, ever since her fateful meeting with Argon, scrutinizing book after book, scroll after scroll, reading up on what all her ancestors had done in times of trouble, times of invasion. She wondered how all of them prepared, in times of peace, for a looming disaster. Gwen might not be able to control what was to come, but the one thing she could control was her scholarship, and it always gave her comfort and a sense of control to read during times of crisis.

As Gwen read about ancient refuges and escapes, she realized that the one thing she had not planned for in the reconstruction of King's Court was an escape route. After all, King's Court was the most fortified city of the Ring—what need could there possibly be for escape? And where could they possibly escape to that was more fortified?

And yet Argon's words rang in her head, and she felt a need to prepare. She felt that if she were to be a good leader, then she should have a backup contingency. Some sort of escape plan. What would they do if King's Court were overrun? It was painful to even consider, as they had just rebuilt it—yet she felt a need to have a plan in place. What if somehow the Ring were destroyed again? What if somehow the Shield were lowered, or destroyed? Then what? She could not leave her people exposed to slaughter. Not on her watch.

Gwendolyn read for hours and hours about the sacks of all the great cities of the Ring throughout the centuries. She read the history, once again, of all the MacGils, of her father's father, and his father's father. She felt more connected than ever to her ancestors, as she read anew about their trials and tribulation, all the hardships of all the kings before her. She found herself getting lost in their history. She was amazed to see that others experienced what she was going through, had the same woes and challenges of ruling a kingdom that she had, even so many centuries ago. In some ways, nothing ever changed.

Yet, despite everything she read, she found no reference anywhere to any escape contingency. The closest reference she found was an obscure footnote from a tale of six centuries ago: an ancient sorcerer had managed to bring down the Shield for a time, and the creatures of the Wilds had crossed the canyon and overrun the Ring. The second MacGil king, realizing he was unable to fight them all, took his people—a much smaller amount than they had now—loaded them on ships, and evacuated them all to the Upper Isles. When the Shield was restored and the creatures left, he moved them back to the mainland of the Ring, saving them all and killing the creatures that remained.

Gwen, intrigued, examined the dusty, ancient maps, illustrating pictures of the routes they had taken. Crude arrows showed the way they had traveled to board the ships, then the routes to the Upper Isles. She studied the diagrams, and thought it all through carefully. It had been a primitive plan for a primitive time, a time when the Ring was much smaller. And yet it had worked.

The more Gwen thought about it, the more she realized that there was great wisdom in that plan—wisdom that could be applied today. In the event of a disaster, couldn't she do the same as her ancestors had? Couldn't she evacuate her people to the Upper Isles? They might not be able to return to the Ring, as her ancestors had. But they could at least wait out the invasion, or the disaster, at least live there long enough to decide what to do. They would be safe, at least, from a mass invasion: after all, the Upper Isles were an impossible place to attack, with their jagged shores in every direction, funneling all enemies to narrow choke points. A million attacking men were as good as one hundred. The Empire could send tens of thousands of ships, but they still would only be able to attack with a few at a time. And the nasty weather and currents helped defend the Isles even more.

Gwen's eyes were tired from reading, and yet she sat upright as she considered it all, feeling a jolt of excitement. The more she considered it, the more she warmed to the idea. Perhaps a retreat to the Upper Isles was the perfect plan in the case of a disaster.

Gwen closed the book, rubbed her eyes, and leaned back and sighed. Was she getting carried away? Lost in catastrophic thoughts? After all, it was a beautiful, sunny summer day outside, and her wedding, the day of her dreams, was but a half-moon away. They were not being attacked or invaded, and they were stronger than her ancestors had ever been. She knew she should leave all this dark thinking behind and go out there and enjoy the day. She was too prone to catastrophic thoughts; she always had been.

As Gwen stood and prepared to leave, she accidentally knocked over a large, heavy book, and as she did, a smaller book, previously hidden, fell out from it, onto the floor, in a small cloud of dust. It was a tiny, scarlet, leather-bound book, and as Gwen picked it up with curiosity, she turned the pages and found them brittle. This curious volume was so old, its pages had turned brown with age.

As Gwen glanced at the ancient language it was penned in, she was surprised to see what it was: *Sodarius' Book of Prophecies.* She had heard of it her whole life, but was never even certain if it truly existed. She'd heard rumors of it, but no one she had ever met had ever actually laid hands on it. It was supposed to contain the most fantastical predictions for the future of the Ring, some of which were accurate, and some of which never came to pass.

Gwen's hands trembled with excitement as she realized what she was holding. She turned the pages quickly, combing through, until she came to the prophecies that addressed her time and place. She stopped, her breathing shallow, as she came upon her own name.

The seventh and final ruler of the MacGils will be the greatest. She will lead her people through their greatest victory. Yet she will also lead them through their greatest downfall. Gwendolyn will be her name.

Gwen stopped, hands shaking, hardly able to believe what she was reading. She hesitantly turned the page:

Gwendolyn will lead her people to—

Gwen looked down and saw with dismay that some of the pages were burnt, cut off mid-sentence. The remainder of the book only showed snippets of phrases, all of them cut off, broken mid-sentence. She turned pages frantically, desperate to know what will happen. She scanned, looking for anything, and she could not believe it when she stumbled upon Thorgrin's name:

Her husband Thorgrin will die, too, and his death will come when—

Gwen turned the pages, anxious to see the exact predictions, her hand shaking. She felt sick to her stomach as she read the dates. It couldn't be.

Gwen took the book and threw it across room, smashing it against the wall, and she burst into tears.

She told herself it was all nonsense, the writings of a hack from centuries ago. Yet despite herself, Gwen could not help but feel it to all be true.

"My lady?" came a frantic voice.

Gwendolyn spun to see Aberthol's concerned face at the doorway, peeking into the room.

"I'm sorry," Gwen said, "I didn't mean to throw the book—"

Aberthol shook his head.

"That is not why I have come," he said. "I have just received urgent news. Terrible news, I'm afraid. My lady, you must go at once. Your mother is dying."

Gwendolyn felt a jolt at his words.

She jumped up from the table and ran from the room, past Aberthol. She felt an awful pain in her stomach as took the stone steps three at a time, and continued running down the hall.

She burst out the front door, into the fresh air, wiping tears away, trying to push away morbid thoughts. She ran through the fields, heading for her mother's castle, desperate to get there fast enough.

Her mother dying. *How?* she wondered. She had been meaning to spend more time with her. Every day she meant to, but she had been so busy with affairs of court.

Gwendolyn ran and ran, not wanting to miss her mother's final breath, pushing herself harder and faster.

Suddenly, a horrific pain ripped through her stomach. Gwen collapsed in the middle of the fields, all alone, screaming. She lay there, looking up at the sky, as her stomach hurt her more than she could say. She could hardly breathe, as she felt supreme cramps rushing over her in waves, one after the other. The baby flipped like crazy, the pains so intense she could not move.

Gwen leaned back and shrieked to the heavens, lying there, alone, utterly alone, experiencing an agony beyond what she could describe. She wanted someone to come to her. But she knew no one would, not out here. It would have to happen here, in this place, with no help. She was flooded with panic as she wondered if the baby would survive. If she would survive.

But nothing could stop it now. Gwen leaned back and shrieked and shrieked, until her cries were met, high up, by the cries of a bird, high in the sky.

Her baby was coming.

NOW AVAILABLE!

A SEA OF SHIELDS
Book #10 in the Sorcerer's Ring

"A breathtaking new epic fantasy series. Morgan Rice does it again! This magical sorcery saga reminds me of the best of J.K. Rowling, George R.R. Martin, Rick Riordan, Christopher Paolini and J.R.R. Tolkien. I couldn't put it down!"
--Allegra Skye, Bestselling author of SAVED

In A SEA OF SHIELDS (BOOK #10 IN THE SORCERER'S RING), Gwendolyn gives birth to her and Thorgrin's child, amidst powerful omens. With a son born to them, Gwendolyn and Thorgrin's lives are changed forever, as is the destiny of the Ring.

Thor has no choice to but to embark to find his mother, to leave his wife and child and venture away from his homeland on a perilous quest that will have the very future of the Ring at stake. Before Thor embarks, he unites with Gwendolyn in the greatest wedding in the history of the MacGils, he must first help rebuild the Legion, he deepens his training with Argon, and he is given the honor he has always dreamed of when he is inducted into the Silver and becomes a Knight.

Gwendolyn is reeling from the birth of her son, the departure of her husband, and the death of her mother. All of the Ring gathers for the royal funeral, which brings together the estranged sisters, Luanda and Gwendolyn, in one final confrontation that will have dire implications. Argon's prophecies ring in her head, and Gwendolyn feels a looming danger to the Ring, and furthers her plans to rescue all of her people in the case of a catastrophe.

Erec receives news of his father's illness, and is summoned back home, to the Southern Isles; Alistair joins him on the journey, as their wedding plans are put in motion. Kendrick seeks out his long-lost mother, and is shocked at who he finds. Elden and O'Connor return to their home towns to find things are not what they expect, while Conven falls deeper into mourning and towards the dark side. Steffen unexpectedly finds love, while Sandara surprises Kendrick by leaving the Ring, back for her homeland in the Empire.

Reece, despite himself, falls in love with his cousin, and when Tirus' sons find out, they set in motion a great treachery. Matus and Srog try to keep order in the Upper Isles, but a tragedy of misunderstanding ensues when Selese discovers the affair, right before her wedding, and a war threatens to erupt in the Upper Isles due to Reece's inflamed passions. The McCloud side of the Highlands are equally unstable, with a civil war on the verge of breaking out due to Bronson's shaky rule and Luanda's ruthless actions.

With the Ring on the verge of civil war, Romulus, in the Empire, discovers a new form of magic which may just destroy the Shield for good. He forges a deal with the dark side and, emboldened with a power that not even Argon can stop, Romulus embarks with a sure way to destroy the Ring.

With its sophisticated world-building and characterization, A SEA OF SHIELDS is an epic tale of friends and lovers, of rivals and suitors, of knights and dragons, of intrigues and political machinations, of coming of age, of broken hearts, of deception, ambition and betrayal. It is a tale of honor and courage, of fate and destiny, of sorcery. It is a fantasy that brings us into a world we will never forget, and which will appeal to all ages and genders.

About Morgan Rice

Morgan is author of the #1 Bestselling THE SORCERER'S RING, a new epic fantasy series, currently comprising eleven books and counting, which has been translated into five languages. The newest title, A REIGN OF STEEL (#11) is now available!

Morgan Rice is also author of the #1 Bestselling series THE VAMPIRE JOURNALS, comprising ten books (and counting), which has been translated into six languages. Book #1 in the series, TURNED, is now available as a FREE download!

Morgan is also author of the #1 Bestselling ARENA ONE and ARENA TWO, the first two books in THE SURVIVAL TRILOGY, a post-apocalyptic action thriller set in the future.

Among Morgan's many influences are Suzanne Collins, Anne Rice and Stephenie Meyer, along with classics like Shakespeare and the Bible. Morgan lives in New York City.

Please visit www.morganricebooks.com to get exclusive news, get a free book, contact Morgan, and find links to stay in touch with Morgan via Facebook, Twitter, Goodreads, the blog, and a whole bunch of other places. Morgan loves to hear from you, so don't be shy and check back often!